Andre entered.

I was caught sitting on his bed clutching his pillow. The envelope stood halfway out of his bag. He almost rounded the footboard until I crawled onto my knees on his bed.

He stopped.

"Are they done?" I asked, holding his gaze. I flexed my toe, pushing the envelope into his bag.

"They're finishing." He stepped to the edge of the mattress. Even as he towered over me, my hips half the size of his, I felt powerful. His stare hung on me like he was helpless in the pull of my movement.

Like he was at my mercy.

"I didn't mean to wind up on your bed."

His fingertips touched my hips. "But you are."

"What would you have done if I wasn't here?"

"I would have been in a lot of pain, and a lot of trouble. Then again, I might have had the information I'm missing had you shared the contents of the letter with me."

"What letter?" I asked, my touch trailing up his back, mimicking what he did to me. "The one you tried to slip out from underneath my shirt? I don't have it anymore. Maybe you should ask your *Ispolniteli* friends if they have it."

"I'm going to need the letter, Karolina." His tenor shifted; the pragmatic face he wore when he was calculating his next move dominated him.

The outer suite door closed.

"I should go," I said. I was almost at the door when he appeared at my side.

Praise for M.R. Noble:

"In between bouts of fighting and the intensity of paranormal, dark fantasy, there are moments of comedy that make this series opener a real page-turner."

~ *Booklist.*

Dark Eyes: White Lies

by

M. R. Noble

The Dark Eyes Series

Dark Eyes: White Lies

Cover Art by *Kristian Norris*

The Wild Rose Press, Inc.
PO Box 708
Adams Basin, NY 14410-0708
Visit us at www.thewildrosepress.com

Publishing History
First Edition, 2023
Trade Paperback ISBN 978-1-5092-4710-3
Digital ISBN 978-1-5092-4711-0

The Dark Eyes Series
Published in the United States of America

Dedication

This book is dedicated to lovers.

Be it mother, father, lover, or friend, fight for the joy of love, as it is memories of joy that get one through the painful patches in life and back into the bliss.

Acknowledgments

First and foremost, a heartful thank you to the sensitivity reader for the indigenous content of this book—a woman who is very dear to my heart, and a proud member of the Oibwas/Chippewas of Georgina Island.

Thank you to my agent Marisa Corvisiero, who will always accept a six-o-clock in the morning hello over coffee from one of her overly friendly Canadian authors.

Thank you to my editor at the Wild Rose Press, Melanie Billings, who has believed in my work since my first query.

A *merci* and cheers to Kirsten Koza and Kimmy Beach, my elders in the craft, who encouraged me as a baby writer to find my footing and grow. May I keep growing and be ever inspired by such talent.

Hugs and thanks to everyone who has reviewed this book and provided support along the way, the Writers' Community of York Region (WCYR) included. If pain is the ink in the pen, then encouragement is the quill from which the creativity of one's emotions can flow.

Arigatō to my sensei. Perseverance, perseverance, perseverance.

Lastly, thank you to readers of The Dark Eyes Series. Thank you for believing in Karo and staying by her side throughout her journey. Here we go again. Buckle up.

Chapter One

My high heels scuffed the concrete as I fought to keep my eyes open. *Bloody House of Commons dress code*. If I wasn't still an intern, I could get away with jeans and flats like the other pencil pushers. They'd sacrificed making the climb into important parliament positions for comfort. If I didn't have to be in the ninetieth percentile to keep the ruse of earning my position, I would have done the same.

Three more hours remained of the day. If I could get through them, I was going home to medicate and fall into bed. Another night of broken sleep plagued with dreams I didn't want would kill me. Yet, tomorrow the sun would rise, and I'd still be here to ghost through another day.

My intern hours bled past my contract time.

Now I was late for class.

I climbed the stairs to the auditorium of my advanced-psychology class. When I reached for the door handle, I shook the coffee I hadn't known I had spilled off my hand, staining the Remembrance Day poster plastered to the door. The hinges squeaked like they were hooked up to a microphone, and all my classmates turned when I entered. I slid into the nearest empty seat.

The professor introduced the concept of impression memories when I got my laptop open. I started to take notes but zoned out from sleep deprivation. My screen blurred. Why was I having these dreams? Having nightmares of Kazimir torturing me could be expected. Being disturbed by the images of my father's massacre of the Fire Charmed people also seemed reasonable. What was not reasonable were my dreams of Andre. Was my internal monologue trying to process our last bitter encounter? Or was I dreading the day I would see him again? As my newly assigned spy partner, and with the receipt of my encoded orders from Russia, it was only a matter of days now. Three, to be exact.

In my mind, I could see his face. My dream replayed in my head. We're sitting on the deck of the boat in the Black Sea. His skin is aglow with the colors of the rising sun. I want to reach out to him. To tell him he will be okay, that we'll be okay, together. I want to make his pain go away. I straddle him and push him onto his back.

The professor's microphone crackles.

"The spectrum of human emotion is vast," she said. "We're going to look at why people connect and how a simple interaction can resonate within the human psyche. These impression memories form a connection on an emotional level within the brain, and for some, it's a connection which can last for years."

I raised my hand.

She nodded at me.

"Why?" I ask. "Why do those connections form? I mean, it seems unreasonable a single moment can generate a connection with so much power?"

"It has to do with bonding," she replied. "We see something in the other person which reminds us of a family member or a close friend. Sometimes, we subconsciously see a piece of ourselves in the other person. Maybe a characteristic we wish we had the courage to indulge, or a past trauma which is similar to what we ourselves have endured."

I push my laptop aside. "That's fine. But again, how can a single blip in time create such an impact? I mean, who's to say that one moment is going to stick with you?"

"It revolves around your emotion for the person in the moment and why the interaction resonates with you."

"But that makes no sense!" I instantly dropped my voice, but it was too late. The man beside me gave me a look that said, by his standards, I belonged in a first-year class.

"If you have further questions, we can take this discussion into after-class hours," she said and then moved on with her lecture.

"It's not logical," I whispered to myself, but it didn't rewrite the lecture slides I took notes on for the next hour.

I didn't stay behind to speak with the professor.

I left ten minutes early and headed back to my condo. As I walked, I ran an inventory of my objective for tonight's break-and enter scheme at the House of Commons. My ID badge gave me access to half the building, but the currency of secrets wasn't exchanged where a student could overhear. My pending mission was coded *Bunny Ears*. One could assume I was to overhear a conversation or message. I needed the names of all the House of Commons personnel, and I needed to know where their access was granted. If I assumed my shitty eighties' answering machine would provide those details, and I was wrong, I would blow my first mission. Miruna's survival depended on my success.

I turned the corner one block away from my building. My footsteps picked up a bizarre echo, then were drowned out by a gust of wind barreling down the street. The air suctioned from the high-rises. My ears popped. I ducked down an empty alleyway to escape. Ever since Bronwyn's first attack months ago, wind was no longer just wind. I pulled up my vampiric senses and braced for an icy assault.

The gust flew by, carrying a cloud of frosty dead leaves with it.

I relaxed. Then, I disbanded the fire magic I called into my palms on instinct. I took a step and heard a crunch beneath my heels. In front of my feet was *Karolina* spelled in leaves on the concrete, their tips frozen by the bitter cold of winter approaching.

I whirled around.

My vision took in the details of the alley, to the glasses of the man watching TV on the thirteenth story of the condo across the street. I listened for the quiet beating of hearts in the immediate vicinity, none close enough to have spelled the leaves before me. I knelt and hovered a hand near my name. There was no faint tingle of Charmed magic present. This was new magic.

I rose and slipped back onto the street, noting the heartbeats which passed by me. The biting wind kept the streets of Ottawa thinned out. It wasn't a city built to encourage walking. Another black-window-tinted car rolled by. Ottawa was a parliament town; whether dignitaries were residents or visiting, no one wanted their daily routine observed.

Facial recognition technology changed the city

climate. My friends and I had a conversation regarding the advancement in class, one which our teacher couldn't resist participating in. He stated on record the University does not recognize the technology's existence, but then said when video cameras became popular in the nineteen-seventies, the urban planning of Ottawa changed drastically. He thought it was due to the anticipation of facial recognition. Conspiracy theorists made the most interesting professors. How would he react to a vampire spy, let alone vampirism?

I walked into my condo lobby. As I headed to the elevator, the gum-smacking receptionist flagged me down.

"A hot guy was here," she said. "He asked me about you."

"Did he tell you his name?"

"No, he just said you guys were friends, and he'd try to catch you later."

My stomach clenched. She knew Roman's name from how often he visited, but it could be another one of my friends from school. I still had time. I stepped into the elevator and pressed my button.

"Oh, penthouse. Do you live with your parents?"

I turned to the man next to me.

"I guess that's a no."

He had over a foot of height on me. A long face the color of light, milky coffee. His hair was raven black. He showed me his teeth as he laughed at my sudden muteness.

"A lady wouldn't disclose," I said, still recovering from the pleasant surprise of his good looks. "We're so vulnerable these days. All the home invasions you see on TV."

"I see," he said. "Forgive me, but I have the distinct feeling you might be a bit more than just a lady."

Amusement took hold. "You might be right. I'm not a lady at all."

"Oh, really." He played along. "What are you then?"

"I'm the best of the good bad girls."

The elevator dinged, and I saw it was my floor. I was busy talking and didn't notice he hadn't pushed a button.

"I seem to have missed my stop," he said and held his arm in the doors for me to take my time. "Do you know what floor the sky lounge is? My company has rented the room for a conference."

"The very top." I lingered by the door. "What's your company name?"

"Anishinaabe Water Protection Inc."

"Well, have a nice day…"

"Ben."

I stepped backward through the closing doors.

Charming. Too charming. I was over my condo threshold and through the veil of magic that guarded my door within seconds.

"Hey, Karo." Ina, my roommate, said as she typed on her laptop at the kitchen counter.

A slight push on my heels, and I was zooming through our living room.

Ina's coffee splashed onto her cookies as I grazed her barstool. "What's the issue this time? Are you going to type a paper at warp speed?"

I was already out onto my master bedroom balcony and wouldn't chance speaking out here. It was a risk to scale the railing up to the next terrace. My neighbor could be home, or worse, I could be seen, but I couldn't afford to assume Ben was harmless. I'd been wrong before.

I climbed onto the balcony above. The wind licked my knuckles as I gripped the frosty metal railing. I didn't look down. I tuned my vampiric hearing into focus.

A large group inside chattered.

An object banged against a table, and the ruckus subsided.

"Fellow council members, we want to acknowledge the honor our elders give us by attending this meeting today."

So, Ben was not only charming but also the chair of this meeting. I quit my eavesdropping at the end of their meeting agenda. Ben was a bleeding heart for the environment and was saving the world one freshwater lake at a time. I was glad to know people like him still existed. While I was out sucking blood and betraying my country, he was protecting its resources.

I practically slithered back onto my balcony and hauled my paranoid ass inside. I pulled the cork from a half-filled bottle of merlot on the counter and filled a glass to the brim. Red wine sloshed onto the glossy hardwood as I sat down on the couch, the spilled droplets reminding me of Romania. I wiped the spots up with my sock while I lit a candle with my palm.

"This is the third time this week," Ina said.

"I'm a spilly talker."

Her mug clinked on the marble island. "You weren't speaking, and not the spill, the wine."

"Negative coping strategies."

Ina rapped her fingers on the counter. "You know what *wouldn't* be a negative coping strategy?" She twirled around on her barstool to face me. "A girls' night."

"I can't tonight. Vampire business." I didn't want to look at her and see the disappointment on her face.

"The same business which had you running through our apartment?"

"That was a bite from the paranoia bug."

She raised an eyebrow.

"A cute guy flirted with me in the elevator."

Ina grunted. "Naturally, he was out to get you and was part of the underground?"

"Yeah."

"Yeah, he was? Or, yeah, you're losing your shit?"

"The only thing he's guilty of is flirting with women who are bad for him." I took a swig of wine. "I think he has a taste for it."

"Poor him."

"Yes, he should flirt with good girls, ones that work for a preservationist corporation."

"You mean ones who won't rip his heart out and eat it like a raw steak."

I snapped my head to her.

She laughed. "Listen, Karo, you have to compartmentalize. It's the only way to survive." She clutched her gold bracelet. It was the gift her mother gave her when Ina finally joined her family in Canada after she paid for their immigration. Life at the Grand Hotel was hard for Ina. I had witnessed all the vampires pawing at her. Loukin believed in the kinder treatment of humans, what he thought was a semblance of equality, but it hadn't stopped vampires from treating

Ina like prey. Even though Loukin had ethical blood banks, I had witnessed Ina attempt to fight off a vampire in the hallway.

Yet, she survived in the underground.

She even flourished.

She'd been the personal assistant to Loukin himself, and she'd helped me navigate the social scene of the underground. I'd bartered for Ina's release and immigration to Canada as a condition of my blackmail. She lived with me for free as my thanks for her friendship, at least until her immigration process was complete. Loukin still kept her on the payroll. He said he was happy *I'd made a friend*, and she could help me learn more about the world I was now dealing secrets within.

But the less I told Ina of my plans, the safer she'd be.

My goal was to take out Uncle Loukin and the hypocrisy of the world he built. Which would start with finding out what he needed to know and bleeding him misinformation.

"I'm learning from you, Ina," I said. "I'll get better at it." I downed the rest of my glass.

"You better."

"Yeah, I better, because I'm breaking into the Restricted Data Center of the House of Commons tonight."

"Whatever you are doing, do not give your identity away. There are other countries' spies at play in the city. There always are."

I snorted. "At this point, I could care less about an altercation."

"There are things out there, Karo, which could kill

a vampire, let alone a half-breed. It wouldn't matter how many elements of the Charm you have if you give yourself away to the competing spies around parliament."

I stared at a black fleck on the wall. When Ina didn't have faith in me staying alive, I knew things were bad.

"Maybe I'll surprise you."

Ina got off her chair and took my empty glass. She found my gaze. "Maybe not."

Chapter Two

I sat cross-legged on my bed and wiggled my toes. Focused solely on my feet, I summoned the Earth Charm.

A tingle tickled my big toes and flashed up my legs. My body hummed. I opened my eyes and saw a luminescent gold aura blanketing my skin. I smiled. My earth magic used to be unreliable as my least accomplished study, but a few months of battling for my life brought me up to par.

This spell had to be done well.

Ina's skepticism in my survival scared me shitless, and my fear was motivation. I wondered what species the competing spies might be. How could they kill me so easily? I could use my Earth Charm as a disguise, but the spell must be executed as efficiently as possible. I couldn't break concentration.

The heat vent blew hot air against my skin. I used the sensation to map out the details of my face. My magic flowed into my head, following my train of thought. The outer parts of my skull hummed like they were expanding.

My cellphone blared with its personalized ringtone for Roman, the song we'd played on repeat the summer before I started university.

I counted down from thirty in my head, desperate to hold onto the sensation I'd just achieved. In the ensuing silence, I imagined a larger nose. I pictured it growing. My cheekbones became less pronounced. In my mind, I watched them sink into my skin. My lips withered, looking shoestring thin.

I open my eyes and walk to my dresser. The golden glow dissipated as I looked into my mirror. My face was a punch to the gut. The goal was to tinker with each individual facial feature, and, together, I'd wind up with a foreign face.

Instead, I looked inbred.

But my next attempt may only worsen my disguise.

The clock read *3:00 AM*. Witching hour for those like me, and I'd run out of time. I should've started sooner. The pull of the waxing moon woke me at midnight. I puttered around my room and then reported my ID badge stolen to the wrong number. By the time the faxing department arrived in the morning and forwarded my frazzled voice message to security, I would have already stolen the information I needed.

As ugly as my face was, my identity was secure.

I arrived at the House of Commons grounds, dressed in shoes and clothes I'd never worn in Canada before. My condo building was the first to be built at the edge of the grounds, a convenient place to house Loukin's spy. I used my earth magic again to add a deterrent spell. Those who looked upon me would want to look away, better yet, ignore me. My scent would never take hold in their memory. It was an extra layer of protection if I encountered any personnel inside.

I walked down the protractor-straight walkway of the twenty-five-acre property. The stones reflected the neon hue of the moon, making me feel like a black stain on the craftsman's perfection. Crickets quieted their nighttime symphony as I passed. I checked my cell as any student would.

The arched doorways were carved like Ottawa would be Canada's masterpiece, the weathered steel door and electronic keypad said they abandoned that idea during the Y2K problem. Sticking to my role, a crumpled chocolate bar wrapper fell from my pocket as I searched for my card. I swiped my badge and the door clicked open.

Most of the building was locked down after hours, so I followed the path security streaked on the floor with their rubber steel toes. I made it deep into the central block without having to jailbreak any doors. The security office was ahead. I focused my vampiric hearing, and listened to the voices in the office. The skeleton staff was on break, talking about what they had for dinner, which meant the halls were clear.

I picked a door just before the corner. In view of the camera, I touched my badge to the keypad while slipping my other hand onto the pad simultaneously. I released a flicker of the Light Charm. A jolt of electricity shocked my heart. Heat whooshed down my arm, bringing on goosepimples. A sonic wave thumped into the keypad.

The pad lights flared, then glowed green.

I hustled through the door, and it clicked closed behind me—only seventeen more to go.

****

Employees' personal information was kept in the Restricted Data Center. My student tour concluded when I asked what type of data was kept on our server. I got the message; it was a question outside my role. The corridor had a triple-door entry point, and those

13

who manned the center didn't mingle with other staff. They vanished at the end of the day with the rest of us plebians, which is why I was surprised a heart was beating low and slow behind the door.

Fingers stroked the keys of a computer.

I stood eye-level at the *Access Prohibited* sign, considering two options. One was to wait them out. Two was to hit them with a sleep spell. The hum of the electrical current in the walls felt louder. I'd already loitered outside the door for too long. The subtle lights of the cameras ever present.

I zapped the keypad and stepped inside.

The gentle rhythm of keystrokes ceased at my entry.

The tension this simple act brought propelled me through the second door. The click of the third door closing carried through the air of the still dome-shaped room. Computers and revolving stations surrounded a sunken center floor, blocking my view of the main hub. The single heart rhythm continued its quiet melody at the command center. Their stillness a marking of shock or survival skills.

I called my earth magic. The question was: how to creep close enough for the sleep spell to catch? I lurked from one station's shelving to another, counting the beats of the occupant's heart with each step I took, their pulse quickening.

My vampiric agility flooded my muscles. The pursuit of prey, an action I'd suppressed since childhood, enthralled my senses now. I glided against a ten-foot console, moving without sound. My own heart drummed against the plastic at my back.

With a swift turn, I descended the stairs.

I prowled low to the floor, shadowing the stations into the center. The beat was close enough my fangs slid down from the roof of my mouth. The calmness of the room was overpowered by the peaks of excitement in their heart rhythm.

The chill of gooseflesh cascaded down my arms.

I could scarcely exhale as I crouched behind a desk opposite my target. My heart matched the thudding which filled my ears. It wasn't fear that had their blood pumping. It was far more exhilarating yet unbearably trepidatious. I could feel it in my own trembling body. I didn't use my magic. I rose.

Andre sat in an office chair, staring at me, his breath slow and soundless.

I didn't move. For a moment, I thought I lowered my block on the bond, but a quick change in senses confirmed the icy barrier was in place. Was the bond active on his end?

"Karo," he said, not taking his gaze from mine.

My eyes. I'd forgotten to change my eyes. Like a bucket of water was poured over me, I realized I had the face of a rotten peach. Of course. My dignity was always damned.

I look behind Andre at the computer screen flashing. A USB stick was plugged in, and a file marked employee data was seventy percent transferred and counting.

"You stole my idea."

He didn't turn to the computer. He stayed fixated on my face. "It's like the shell of you withered into a raisin."

"Can we stick to the task at hand, please? I'm going to need those files from you." I closed the gap between us and reached for the stick.

Andre swatted my hand.

A ventilation grate clattered to the floor.

We looked up in unison. Two bodies flew at us from the ceiling dome, their leather coats flapping in the drop. Andre and I dove from the station. The dark-haired men landed with a pounding shudder.

They'd absorbed the shock and swept their arms across the floor. Thick curling blackness wafted from the ground, which blistered my skin. I scrambled back.

"*Gioco da ragazzi*," one man said to other.

Murky clouds rushed my face. I hurtled over an office chair. The smoke storm clipped my leg. I rushed the only Italian insult I knew. "*Vergogna!*"

Andre flashed to the second man in a streak of color, catching him by the throat and thrusting him through the command desk before he could touch the USB. "What does the Italian underground want with Canada data?" Andre asked.

Before I could speak further a wall of black smoke whooshed at me. I rolled on my injured leg and dashed behind a desk.

"We're not underground," the man called out as the sound of furniture hitting the stairs boomed. "We've freed ourselves from our oppressors, like real men. You should try it."

My fangs punctured my lip as I yipped. More smoke bit my ankle as it flowed under the furniture. I sprinted to an area not yet flooded with the Dark Charm but was still only a moment away from being enveloped. I lit my fire in my palms but hesitated. If I misfired, I could damage the computers.

Whooping sirens cut through the air.

"No fire!" Andre screamed.

Thunder clapped, and an inky black blot snaked through the air.

I dropped to the floor.

Heat and static electricity whooshed down my back. The metal wall behind me screeched and shuddered.

A figure emerged from the rim of smoke. The man Andre threw into a desk held Andre's USB key. I could have called the Light or Earth Charm, but my split-second instinct of hunt and prey already seized me.

I leaped onto his back.

His fist glanced off of my mouth, knocking my fangs off course, but I slipped his guard and encircled his neck. Surprise gave me the instant I needed. My legs locked into a triangle. My right thigh bore down into his gut. My shoulders hugged his. I squeezed my biceps.

His throat gave the first three inches like foam. He gurgled. The USB key tumbled from his hand and slid across the floor. His nails raked across my arms. He lashed out at my face.

I pressed against his neck, hiding my head. A punch thudded into my shoulder; the joint flexed, but didn't dislocate. I clenched, my muscles burning to maintain position.

He drove us into the wall.

My skull smashed against the cool steel. He drove us back again. Then again. Metal crumpled against my back. My vision spotted, the pain in my head dulled. Then the floor flew at my face. I released my hold, but my arms still enclosed his neck. I lay huddled on his limp body. I rolled off onto the ground, the siren's screech mimicking my headache.

Screams filled the room.

In the smoke, I could see security guards flailing. I shuffled along the floor to the USB key and pocketed it. Andre appeared and raised me to my feet. We skirted the perimeter of the cloud of dark magic to a gaping hole in the floor.

"Trust me?" Andre asked. His body erupted in his violet electricity, and he took my hand. My skin prickled as his magic encased me.

He stepped off the ledge.

My footing skidded to the edge of the hole, Andre's weight making me teeter. "There's your answer."

"Jump," he said.

Footsteps rushed toward my back, making my decision for me.

We fell. In a whoosh of concrete and darkness, speckled with sparks from live wires, Andre's magic flared at our feet. The fine shreds of violet lightning wove in a dome, their brilliant hue mesmerizing me and warping my perception. We slowed. My stomach flip-flopped from the suspended feeling of falling. The ground rose to our feet, and we touched down like a bubble skirting the pull of gravity.

The dome scattered, leaving us bathed in the red hues of emergency lighting.

I looked up. A small circle of light flickered with shadow. The ring of sirens was now a dim melody. We were at least a hundred feet underground. I was off course with no escape routes. I tuned up my vampiric hearing, and a low-pitched ring filled my ears, one which only select animals would hear. The underground base had a separate security system. A yellow sign hung by a door, its keypad dead to any electrical current. I peered at it, pulling away from Andre. His fingers, entwined with mine, tugged at my hand. He let go, letting his touch glide over my skin.

"It's another restricted center," I said. "We should take advantage of the power being out."

"Most bases' power supply is wired to shut down upon forced entry."

I opened the door. The black screens of the computers confirmed no data could be transferred, yet knowledge of the lab's existence was information in itself.

I opened the closest desk drawer, then the next.

"We didn't know how deep the House of Commons ran," Andre said.

Metal squealed. The drawer I pulled ripped from its hinges. *We.* Andre's loyalty to Loukin, born from childhood, was under his skin like a sickness, unseen but just as lethal as any competing spy. His mission was to gather the intelligence Loukin needed, and mine was to thwart him from what he sought. I riffled through useless papers and perishable snacks. "How long do we have?"

"Not long." Andre used his vampiric speed to clear the desks on his side of the room.

I put my fist into the lock of a filing cabinet. An unopened envelope marked *registered mail property of the Canadian Federal Government* sat on top of a narrow briefcase, the briefcase latched imprinted with the mystic symbol of an eye.

"Security," I said.

Andre turned to the door, and I stuffed the

envelope up the back of my shirt into my bra strap. He stood still, listening for footfall and heartbeats.

"My mistake. We should go before…"

The boom of an explosion and the tearing of steel echoed in the hallway.

I ran into the corridor, in the opposite direction, drawing my vampiric strength into my run. The room blurred. My hair blew back. I skidded to a halt at the end of the straightaway. Like a rat in a maze, I panicked at choosing left or right. "Which way is out," I whispered amongst the stampede of bootsteps.

Andre streaked past me up the left hallway. "Find the moon."

I chased him and pictured my magnetic friend. I focused on the moon's pull, how my skin itched to feel its glow, the feeling I had when I woke from sleep tonight. Like a hand hovering over the hairs of one's skin, I could feel the moon over my shoulder. I ran to it.

Andre and I matched stride. I pushed myself further out of spite.

"You've been drinking human blood," he said.

"And you went on mission on an empty stomach."

We raced through the tunnels, stopping some overnight personnel with the shock of our speed. I hadn't yet guessed what spell Andre cast to hide his identity, but I assumed he eliminated the vulnerability.

He leaped.

I doubled back.

He hoisted himself up through a hatch in the ceiling. I followed, welcoming relief from the video cameras. I trusted my spell to hold for a few hours, and the time was well beyond that now. We charted an air vent into a utility room, which led to a hall, then a second utility room.

We stepped out of the door, and the concrete floors I'd grown used to were replaced by glossy pink granite. A group of people in suits walked past, starting the five a.m. shuffle to work. We merged with them and boarded an elevator up. My head throbbed in the fluorescent lighting. The doors dinged open at the lobby, and it was only then I realised I was in my own condo building.

I reached for a button, and Andre's hand clamped onto my arm. He guided me around the corner into an *Employees Only* room—another janitor's closet.

"I'm beginning to think you have a thing for closets."

"Your friend is here," he tapped on the wall with his knuckles, finding a spot where the thud deepened. "Plus, you can't be seen on video going to your floor in your disguise."

Roman. I forgot I made a date with him to spar at the dojo this morning. *Shit. Double shit.* Andre had already confirmed I was residing where Loukin placed me. Had he been in my condo? The room spun. My legs wobbled now that I wasn't running; standing still, it was clear I sustained a head injury from my grapple with the Italian vampire.

Andre placed his hand over the position of the low thud and braced. A torrent of crackling violet streamed into the drywall. Blackness burned outward like a spilt inkpot. The lights went out. People in the hall gasped. We stepped back from the small plume of chemical-scented smoke. A ball of Andre's magic ignited like a lantern above.

"First thing, you're hurt," he said. "I'll heal you,

21

and you can wait out your spell here while the power is down. When you enter the elevator next, you'll be a different person."

"I'm on human blood, I don't need…" I blocked his hands from coming to my hips. "Don't touch me."

"Oh, I'm sorry," he said. "I didn't realize they had ethical blood centers in Canada; that's where you've drank, isn't it? Because I thought it was morally beneath you to drink human blood. Or have a mere few months changed that?"

"Who I'm drinking from is none of your business."

He leaned in. "Actually, it's relevant to our mission. If you kill a human and attract attention, you'll jeopardize our cover. If you bond with another vampire, you're giving another access to your emotions."

"The fucking last thing I'd want to do is drink from another vampire after I've tasted your putrid blood."

Andre flashed an arrogant display of perfect teeth in a grin.

I never said fuck. Men didn't make me swear like this. *Control. Control. Control.*

"Human blood won't heal you, anyway," he said.

He was right, human blood kept me well-fueled, but only vampire blood had the power to heal. The longer Roman waited, the more his suspicion would deepen. He couldn't see me beat up. Our relationship teetered on a balance of his ruse of not knowing I was in trouble and my ploy of pretending I was okay.

"Bite your wrist," I said.

His lips parted, smug and slow, his fangs slid into view. He held his wrist to his mouth, letting the tip of one fang draw first blood, which pooled like a jewel on his skin.

Then my mouth was wrapped around his arm.

His blood—warm, sweet, and salty in my mouth—made the memory of it seem dull. Like liquid caramel, it slugged across my tongue, the sensation making my body quake and my head tilt back. I sunk my fangs back into his flesh. *Hard.* The endorphins of my bite roused the rapid rise and fall of his chest, which was pressed just below my breasts.

My legs were entwined around his upper torso while I held him against the wall by his neck. My other hand clutched his wrist so hard my knuckles were white.

I let go and stepped back, unnerved that I lost track of what I was doing.

"You'll heal fine," he said. "Your face is already changing. I'd be worried about retinal scans, but your ridiculously long lashes probably covered your irises from the overhead cameras. Can I check?" He stepped forward, and I let him. "Look down, now look up."

I did and met his gaze. His eyes were so blue, bluer than I remembered, and evoked all the hazy memories of seeing only them during the ecstasy of our bond.

"Your face is back to normal," he said.

A feather-light touch grazed my skin just below the envelope against my back.

I blew past him, out the door, and into the stairwell.

Chapter Three

By the time I'd climbed the stairs to my penthouse, I was late enough that Roman and I could have sparred *and* gotten breakfast. I was in the doghouse again with Roman, which was not a good place to be with a werewolf.

The condo was empty, free of foreign scents or signs of forced entry. Ina left a note that she'd enrolled in a new class and would return for dinner. *Step one, look presentable. Step two, call Roman.* I took the letter from underneath my shirt and slipped it into the crack where my dresser top met the base. Then, I showered, scrubbing down—even my toes—with the overpowering floral soap Roman's senses detested. Steam coated my bathroom mirror, but my smooth skin was unmarred in its milky reflection. I called Roman with one hand and yanked my jeans over my hips.

"Hey!"

"Buzz me in. I'm coming up."

The phone line clicked dead.

I peeled my wet hair from my neck, but the droplets had already soaked the neckline of my shirt. I dragged my nose along my wrist, searching for the scent of Andre's touch. Andre once said I'd reeked of werewolf, and since Roman's sense of smell was far superior to Andre's, there was the impending doom of Roman smelling vampire on me. Even worse, identifying Andre's scent.

Roman's knock thudded downstairs.

"Hey," I said, holding open the door for him.

The Charmed markings of my entryway ward illuminated. Roman stepped through, and the golden aura of my earth magic dissipated from the plaque.

"That's strange. It's never lit up for you before."

I worked the spell around those I loved and branched down from there. Those in my heart could enter of their own accord, friends could be deterred, and those I didn't know could be stunned into submission for hours or even have their memory erased. Intruders with malintent could wind up like Kaz for all I knew. I'd let my fear dominate me as I created the ward and poured my feelings about Russia into the spell. I meant to tweak the enchantment afterward, but I simply wasn't ready to change it yet.

"Well," he said.

"I ate bad seafood last night and was puking my guts out. I slept in and am probably going to miss class today. I'm sorry, Ro, I didn't mean to ghost you."

He took off his boots and placed them on the mat.

"That's it?"

I searched his face, which was blank, except for his eyes. Beneath the brown speckles, gold burned through—he was trying very, very hard to prevent the wolf from breaking free. To be fair, waiting over an hour in a condo lobby could transform any man.

The tension in his shoulders grew.

His arms elongated, just a few inches, but the shift blared out like a warning bell.

"Ro…"

He scooped me up and hoisted me into the air. I

soared toward the ceiling, then to the floor. I braced. But his hands coiled around my waist and swung me onto the couch. He held down my kicking legs, eyes glowing, hands shooting out. He tickled me.

I erupted with laughter.

His steely fingers wormed in between my ribs, bordering on pain. Hot droplets pooled in my lashes and rolled down my cheeks. I gasped for air between laughs, and his fingers withdrew.

"You thought you could get away without giving me a hug, eh?" Roman's lips bloomed against my collar bone, their warmth pillowing up my neck. He paused to gaze at me. Then, he licked the tears off the side of my face.

"Auh!" I rolled, and he let me push him back onto the couch. I sat in his lap. "How do you like it?" I licked him from neck to cheek.

"I like it a lot, actually." His arms encircled me, and he kissed me on the mouth. His tongue touched mine. My ribs compressed violently, expelling the breath from my lungs—pressure balled in my throat, blocking my words. I wheezed. One of his arms unfurled to clutch my jaw, his fingers piercing the nerves of my face. "Whose blood have you been drinking?"

I gasped. "You're hurting me."

"Why do you taste like blood?"

I looked into Roman's eyes, expecting to see the wolf free, but they were Țuică brown. Icicles pierced my belly; my stomach curdled. Slowly, I feathered a line down his hand to his fingers. Then, I ripped them backward and used them to turn his arm in the socket. If he were a normal man, I could have torn his arm off.

"I said you're hurting me!"

He released me.

I stepped back into the coffee table. "What was that?"

He wiped his face with his hands. "I'm sorry, Karo, it's just, if you've been feeding off someone else, you're jeopardizing everything I—we—have worked for in our relationship."

"What are you talking about?"

He looked up, and it was like looking at grade-school Roman, eyes wide and sincere, lips ready to kiss any bump or scratch. "Humans are so fragile, Karo, if you lost control while feeding off them, you could kill them. When you drink from me, you're safe."

"I drank a blood bag." I used the excuse of straightening the rug and coffee table to avoid his eyes. *Lies, lies, and more lies.* "Ina hooked me up with a contact which can supply me with blood when I need it."

"Did you not drink enough from me last night?"

"No, I didn't." I didn't know if my deception was rotting my heart through guilt, but Roman's blood tasted more bitter with each feed of late.

"Karo, you should have told me." He went to touch me but paused. "Can I touch you?"

"Not yet," I said.

"I can handle you drinking more. You don't need to hold back with me."

He couldn't. And I did. The euphoria of my bite slowed his heart rate dangerously low when I didn't satisfy myself on a blood bag first. Werewolves were strong and could heal instantly, but they couldn't tolerate the bite like another vampire; the drawback was pure body chemistry.

"Is this a masculinity thing?"

He snorted. "I wish it was. If you think about it, you'll see I'm right. Please, come sit?"

I perched on the edge of the couch.

Roman stood and retrieved his backpack from the door. He took out a white-and-silver photo album and sat.

"What's this? A photo album of a wedding I forgot about?"

"Close." He laughed. "My mom made a photo album for you after your mother died."

I wanted to flinch, to recoil like I had all the times Roman tried to talk about Mama, but I took the book with frigid hands and flipped the cover. There she was, in her twenties, beautiful and laughing. A small bundle sat on her hip; tendrils of dark baby hair splayed over the blanket. I turned the page. The next picture was of Mama and Mrs. Lupei cooking in the kitchen. Roman and I were on the third page, barely two feet tall and holding hands.

"My parents paid for her funeral while you were gone."

I looked up. My vision was wet and cloudy.

"Because you were gone, no one could execute Ana's estate. The card of the lawyer to contact is tucked into the back cover."

My tongue felt like a slug. "There's no way I can repay her kindness; I'll call your mother and tell her the same. To tell her how much…"

"They love you, Karo, and your family. They'd never leave Ana in limbo."

He was talking about her soul. The Charmed

people had a burial custom to lay the dead to rest; Mama needed a token of the four elements and a final token of love. I had just left her. I'd abandoned her body in the wreckage of our burning house.

My face was soaked.

Roman wrapped his arms around me.

I buried my cheek into his t-shirt. "I'll call the lawyer when I'm ready. Until then, I'll thank your mom."

Roman kissed me. His tongue found mine again as he cupped my face.

I pulled back. "I'm sorry, I'm still queasy and just need to rest. I need some time to myself."

He leaned his forehead against mine. "Sure, Karo," he whispered, "I'll give you time."

The sunrise never came. Gray clouds filtered any light that escaped, making even the lightest parts of the sky a muddy beige. My coffee had cooled. The only warmth which remained was in Mama's smile. I lost three hours to her photographs. My feet were cold, and a woolly pair of day-old socks lay on the ottoman, but I hadn't yet stirred myself to movement.

The room illuminated. The wall of seamless glass showcased fluorescent clouds storming outside my balcony. Thunder clapped. The room darkened, except for a small blinking red light on my answering machine.

I wanted to punch it.

My recon mission to collect data prior to operation *Bunny Ears* was botched, thanks to the Italian vampires, but I still had Andre's USB and the letter. I walked over to my eighties-style answering machine and pressed the button.

An electronic voice blared, "key in sequence."

Three high-pitched beeps rang out.

"A. Russia. Equals Z. State origin."

Three more beeps pierced my ears. The message repeated.

The last code I received referred to a person, specially, what I would know about them. *A, Russia.* My father's real identity was the previous answer key and was unlikely to be duplicated. The only other *A* I knew from Russia was Andre. Andre Zima. *State origin.* Surely everyone knew where Andre was from?

"Ukraine."

"Welcome, Dark Eyes."

I shook my head. "You'll have to get a better password next time."

The machine pierced my eardrums with a long tortious beep, bringing me to my knees.

"Assignment. Wreckage Control. Commencement. Twenty-four hours. Intercept Colin Mullins, prior to information exchange. Data collection. Four hours post interception."

The red light blinked to clear white glass.

The dripping sink faucet went from annoying to unbearable due to the bilateral ringing in my head. I turned the water off and cleared away the garbage from when I had made coffee. If the machine slag—the voice from my answering machine—could interject with a silencing beep, it was listening. Which meant Loukin knew all my private conversations with Roman and Ina. How could I be so careless? The frequency buster in my condo kept others from intercepting my calls and texts, but there was nothing to stop my direct hardline to Russia from recording all it heard. My only redeeming action was excluding Ina and Roman from my plans of crossing Loukin.

I went upstairs and slid the letter from its hiding place. Sat down on the bed. Tore the envelope open. I unfolded the accordion of thick paper. The first page was a handwritten letter from doctor to doctor, scribbled in almost illegible handwriting, outlining the information requested from their meeting at a gala in Bavaria. *Germany.* The second page was genetic test results, similar to a DNA forensic report but far more in-depth.

Subject: Female

Sample: Saliva and hair

Origin of maternal haplogroup: species unknown.

Ancestry composition: 88% species unknown, 8% French/German, 6% Scandinavian

She had a supernatural mother and a human father, but her mother's supernatural genes dominated her genetic makeup. I did the math. *102%.* Her totals added up beyond one hundred. I scanned to the bottom of the page. She had an extra set of chromosomes, so the computer system, designed for humans, added up the total to one hundred and two.

The page following the genetic report indicated the woman analyzed was an heiress to multiple diamond mines, including many in northern Ontario. There was no other information indicating the vague reference would be of significance to the recipient.

I always wondered if I went to the hospital as a child if my body would betray my secret. Since Mama had a home birth, tended to by the healing powers of my grandmother's Earth Charm, I didn't even know my own blood type. *Species unknown.* Was this how a vampire's genetic test would show? Ina said there were species lurking around parliament I hadn't yet encountered. Was this one of them?

More pertinent still was the government's underground bunker below the House of Commons; were they aware of supernatural beings? This genetic test indicated they were studying what they could. Was this the type of information Loukin would covet?

I'd hope the contents of the letter would be of assistance with my next mission, perhaps even remove the implied pretense of violence. *Wreckage Control. Intercept Colin Mullins prior to information exchange. Data collection. Four hours post interception.* The machine slag expected us to extract the information from poor Mullins within four hours of collecting him. I'd have to be clever if I didn't want to use violence. If I hadn't botched my recon mission, perhaps *Bunny Ears* wouldn't have turned into *Wreckage Control*. I should have anticipated and planned for the risk of encountering other spies.

I stood and slipped the letter back into its hiding place. I still had Andre's USB stick of employee data to analyze. I walked down the stairs, into the living room, and opened my laptop under the frequency buster. When I plugged the USB in, a window appeared on the screen with the file transfer. I clicked through the files until I found *Colin Mullins*.

He lived down the street.

On the surface, Mr. Mullins was a university graduate who'd finally made it. He'd graduated from the stunning University of Ottawa. A Master of Commerce under his belt, he landed a gig working for the Minister of Finance and married a translator he'd met at the House of Commons. But there was a crack in the picture glass because he'd entwined himself in the game of risk versus reward, and the information he leaked put a retrieval on his head.

I would have to come up with a new spell to conceal my identity if I didn't want to go touting around the face of rotten fruit, or worse, have my shoddy skills expose me and wind up like Mr. Mullins: on a list for extraction. If I could hide my powers from other spies altogether, I could gain an advantage.

My cellphone alarm went off.

It was time to make my third deposit this week into my exit plan.

Chapter Four

I sniffed. The bottle of perfume in my hand sparkled in the bright lights of my bathroom mirror. Scents of sugary licorice, warm spice, tart cherry, and earthy musk cloaked the air. I doused myself and felt the tingle of my earth magic encase my body. Mama's bewitched can of kitchen oil spray—my clothing fire retardant—lay in the garbage can. The dead aerosol can haunted me with the fact it was the last of its kind.

This small change in my life I had tackled head-on, and purchased the most expensive perfume I could find. The bottle was from a niche perfumer on the main shopping strip and cost five thousand dollars. I even tweaked Mama's old spell to last longer. A few sprays may last over a day now.

Perfume became a new hobby of mine. My spending sprees were a deceptive way to squander my Nabokov fortune. I had talked the cashier into providing cashback on my sale, claiming I was allowed to make purchases on my trust but not withdrawals. She wasn't sentimental but had obliged me with indifference, which told me she'd heard the story from her clientele before.

I had a new access point for unmarked withdrawals, and I confirmed the store was popular enough that my perfume scent wouldn't reveal my identity. Now I had to work on hiding my powers, my biological scent, and my appearance.

On a roll of bewitching feminine items, I dumped the free makeup bag of samples I had received with my purchase. A black tube of lipstick gleamed within the cluster on the white marble counter. I slid the cap off. A velvet-smooth stick of lipstick was inside, as black as the tube around it. I held it up. Its matte texture absorbed light rather than reflecting it, making the color seem darker than night itself. Darker than the hate which coiled in my chest.

I sat down on the cushioned bench at the side of the counter and called the Earth Charm once more. Instead of focusing on the details like before, I called out to the Charm in my head. *Hide my scent, my face, and power from all but those who I want to see me.* I poured my feelings into the spell, my fearfulness, my loss, and my need to hide. The vulnerability I felt from all which happened to me in Russian washed over me like a wave, and in the undertow of the spell, left my body.

When I opened my eyes, I felt lighter. The familiar gold aura of my magic diminished around the tube. I had never worked the Earth Charm like that before, but I felt unburdened to a degree, like a sliver of the pain I carried dissipated.

I stepped to the mirror and smoothed the lipstick over my lips. Rather than making my features look stark and gothic, it accentuated the fullness of my mouth. The curve of my cheekbones looked softer, and my large dark eyes were more doe-like.

I stepped away from the mirror. I had until the lipstick wore off to complete my tasks.

Ottawa's chilly winds only worsened as the day progressed, and the morning's stormwater had turned to ice on the sidewalk. The streetlamps flicked on, though sunset was a few hours away, triggered by the bleak overcast of gray. Any moment, the snow could hit, blanketing Ottawa for the next five months. A toying stray snowflake flickered as it glided into a patch of light.

I clutched my laptop bag filled with cash and summoned my vampiric senses, using my agility to avoid slipping on ice. The cold thinned the commotion on the streets, but I listened for anyone approaching at speed. I silently sifted through the conversations occurring for buzz words that would be pertinent to me while I walked.

On my second day back in Ottawa, I tracked down an old apartment building, which still charged a hefty fee for rent. I hinted to the landlord I was escaping an abusive relationship and the woman let me rent under the name Anne Smith. Two of the most anonymous names possible. Telling a half-truth to the woman stung, but I was no longer in a position to be above such things. Plus, my all-cash offer had enticed her into asking no further questions.

My phone vibrated in my pocket.

Andre's spy name, *Smoke*, was on the screen.

—*Licorice or sour candy?*—

I shouldn't have been surprised he was a contact in my phone; I'd already accepted the trap was set for my blackmail long before I caught on; what I was ashamed of was the fact there was a ghost contact list I hadn't located.

—*None.*— I replied.

A few steps further, my phone went off again.

—*Chocolate?*—

Distracted, I missed a shadow crawling up from behind. I turned. The glow cast by the streetlight illuminated empty sidewalk; no figures stalked the shadows, but I was haunted by the feeling of a presence nearby. I doubled back to check the mouth of the alley, which was clear.

—I don't eat candy.—

—God.— He replied. *—No wonder this place is so depressing. The cashier spoke to me like I was crazy too.—*

I arrived at the apartment building but circled around and waited for the foot traffic behind me to pass.

—Why are you texting me about candy?—

—Mission tonight.—

—It's a mission, not a date.—

I entered through the back exit and climbed the stairs. The slight tingle on my lips as I passed the camera in the stairwell was encouraging. I took out my dented key and unlocked the door. Passing through the door ward was like stepping through a wall of quicksand. I had crafted the ward spell with both the Earth and Light Charms using the principles I learned from Miruna's book while making it my own, ensuring Loukin or his minions couldn't disable my security with the information they had.

I flicked my wrist.

Dozens of candles lit on the coffee table, bookshelves, and dining room table. The city lights outside looked stark against the amber flames. Scents of beeswax and honey pooled in the growing warmth of the room. I sank down onto the sofa. Most of the furniture was from a secondhand store across the street, which mainly dealt in reupholstered antique furniture, the ones painted in funky colors and clad in an overstuffed, fun fabric.

I slid the ottoman to my knees and lifted the cushion.

When I had filled the chairs in my master bedroom with cash, I took to filling the ottoman. I added the last remaining layers of the bundles of money. Then I spooned some coffee into my French press. While I waited for the water to boil, I reviewed which piece of furniture I could gut next. So far, Ina's room was untouched since she didn't know it existed. If she did, I was dead, or the wards on my condo were broken. The bench at the foot of Ina's bed meandered to my mind. *Six feet by two. Roughly three stacks per foot in length.* Enough for roughly four and a half million. I pressed my coffee. A few more weeks of cash drops and I may be able to stay put for a while.

I sat down at the dining table. The pastel china and matching sugar bowl reminded me of home. I added two lumps to my cup, sipped it, and added a third. Then a fourth. When it was so sweet it hurt, I wondered what flowers were on Mama's grave.

I downed my cup, washed up, and collected my things. I had a dinner reservation with Roman tonight and hoped my request for space was enough for him to let tonight's plans die. I scanned my bookshelf, selected the next spellcasting volume, then locked up behind me. Memories of spending my nights studying and spellcasting with Mama were as bitter as the cold, so I let them flee my mind with the whipping wind.

The walk home was far from quiet. Restaurant windows lit up the street like roaring hearth fires—

people eating and drinking in the commotion cast flickering shadows onto the sidewalk. Every ten feet, the music would change to a different ambiance. The usual drinking spot for grads and government workers, the Laff, a modernized hole-in-the-wall château, was packed to the frost-battered windows.

With the pull of the moon rising, more people weighed into the street: my kind, or worse, likely along with them. I put more energy into my sense of smell and hearing. If supernaturals were on these streets, there was a tell, a hint, that I was missing.

Ina turned the corner. She was three blocks ahead and had diverted from her usual route home from University of Ottawa, yet with my senses heightened, I could see her clearly. I could also see two men following her.

I walked on the verge of a run, moving swiftly and soundlessly through the pedestrians. I walked three blocks' distance in a minute, but I was still a block behind when they approached Major's Hill Park. Ina stayed within the light of a memorial and then approached the shaded grounds lined with trees. She veered away from the safety of the well-lit street. It was a deadly moment to shortcut through the park, but it also gave me more time. Just as the second man was immersed in shadow, I seized his jacket and rammed him into a tree trunk.

The first man went for Ina.

I shot a bolt of Light Charm into his chest. He dropped to the ground, the lightning streaking along his skin, contorting his muscles.

My forearm snapped.

The man I held against the tree popped my elbow

up into the air, the backward joint bowing my arm. I shrieked and jumped back. He overpowered my hold. I had drunk vampire blood today, but he had drunk more.

A murky fist missed my jaw, but tendrils of smoke from the Dark Charm sizzled the skin of my collarbone.

One-handed, I blocked another blow. Pain birthed a wave of adrenaline. Fire ignited in my palm, but I fought the urge. Illuminating the forest with my blast could draw more opponents or cause a fire. I entwined my one good arm with his next strike and let loose the Light Charm.

Threads of lightning streaked down his arm into his body. He vibrated against me with a grunt. But he kept coming. I hit the ground. He continued to shake but forced my arm against my chest. The crunch of his teeth grinding rose over the hum of electricity. Saliva leaked from his mouth. His second hand shot out from his side and wrapped around my neck. He squeezed.

Shit.

I wrestled with the hold, exhausting my oxygen. I lay still, then bucked. My fangs tore into his neck. The taste of rancid white chocolate exploded on my tongue, followed by a flavor akin to the smell of green mold.

He headbutted me.

My nose pulsed blood down my throat, drowning me on my back. His hold bit into the tendons of my neck, and the pressure in my head threatened to pop my eyes. My precious few seconds were up. I released my fire.

The darkness gathering in my vision occluded the final look on the man's face. The pressure which laid upon my body, the man's weight, evaporated as the heat of flames enveloped me.

I dropped the energy of my fire magic and rolled onto my knees and forearm, my limp, broken arm trailing along. Coughing consumed me. I let gravity pull the fluid from my lungs.

When I looked up, Ina was cowering beyond the first man, who lay half scorched in the grass with hitched breathing.

I wobbled onto my feet.

She scrambled backward.

"Ina, it's me," I said. I'd forgotten about my spell, but the moment I'd said the words, realization crossed her face—*those who I want to see me*.

"Karo," she said. "Holy shit. What did you do to yourself?"

The small taste of vampire blood amidst the grapple worked to repair my arm—the nerves within my elbow sang out with renewed pain with their activation.

"What did I look like?"

"You were a woman I didn't want to look upon, but one I knew was there. It was strange. But when you used your magic, your eyes were hollowed out; I could see that. Instead of fire surrounding you, it looked like a black storm, utter blackness, and the man upon you, he just disintegrated." She shuddered.

I staggered to the man on the ground and kneeled. I held out my wrist. "If you want to live, drink, but you have to leave Ottawa." When I prevented their attack on Ina, I accepted death as a potential outcome, but I had not set out to kill these men.

He bit me. Euphoria followed the sting of fangs. I pulled back quickly enough to prevent him from getting any excessive strength.

"Thank you," he said, his Russian accent prevalent. As his breathing steadied, his eyes flicked open. Darkness spiraled out from a snake tattoo on his forearm. The snake came to life on his skin, gray ink flashing as it slithered from the crest of thorns and roses, winding its way into his chest, and disappeared like a serpent into water. He looked at me like he was about to speak, but instead, he went still. His chest didn't rise again.

I rose, my gaze on the tattoo, on the empty spot where the serpent once was. "What was that?"

"He broke his vow to Loukin," Ina said.

I checked over my shoulder. Our altercation was brief and mostly silent, like most violence. For the moment, we remained undiscovered. "The Eastern Block security camera."

"It was the first thing they took out," Ina said. "All *Ispolniteli* take an oath. When he made a deal for his life with you, it must have broken his promise to Loukin."

I looked down at the body. All *Ispolniteli* bore an insignia spelled with the Dark Charm. "Why didn't this happen to Andre?" Maybe he had not betrayed Loukin's orders. *No.* Loukin was clearly upset at the news of our bonding.

Ina took her keys from her purse, the ripped strap dangling on the ground, and pointed a little laser pointer at the body. "His Light Charm protects him from the spell bestowed upon the *Ispolniteli*." She pressed the button, and a blue stream of light beamed out instead of a red one.

The body of the fallen vampire turned to ash on the charred grass, just like the corpses in Romania after the morning sunlight touched them.

"UV light," Ina said. "A vampire's body is easy cleanup."

The gold chain Ina always wore underneath her shirt hung in view; a small golden paperclip shone in the light of the streetlamp as we emerged onto the walkway.

"A gold paperclip?" I asked and started to wipe the blood from my nose. My tender face squished like an overstuff blood bag, burning with pain from its healing. Chunks of coagulation stuck to my cheeks. I tried to use my other hand out of habit and winced.

Ina looked annoyed by my tone. She pulled a wet wipe from her purse and handed it to me. "Yes, when we administrative assistants have learned the business, we are awarded the highest honor; the paperclip pendant is symbolic of all we have learned. I was in the process of showing the *Ispolniteli* my immunity when you came."

"Oh," I said. "So, you could have shown them your necklace and they would have left you alone?"

"Yes," she said and continued to walk along the path lined with trees.

I followed her. "So, I didn't have to fight those vampires."

"Well, he was dead set on killing you, so I'd say you did. But on principle, no, you didn't."

My laugh came out hoarse. "You flash your paperclip, and then everyone knows you're untouchable?"

"More like, unkillable." We entered the darkness again just before the side entrance to our condo building.

"You don't need me to keep you safe?"

"No."

My cheeks burned. People like Ina were one of Loukin's most valuable assets; of course the *Ispolnīteli* wouldn't kill her. Yet, Loukin had let her leave. The taste of the vampire's blood still flavored my mouth, white chocolate so old it had converted into mothballs. *What did one have to do to have a soul of mothballs?*

"I am still grateful," Ina said.

"Any excuse to kick some ass," I said, trying to rinse my mouth in my own saliva and ignore the pain in my arm and face. I wondered if the small taste of the vampire's blood would be enough to restore me. Then a blood craving crippled me to my knees.

My cell phone vibrated again. I breathed through the thirst and took out my phone.

Another text from Andre. —*I got you caramel. I know you like that. :)*—

Chapter Five

A few hours and a few juicy blood bags brought me to the cusp of mission *Damage Control*. I felt awful, but whoever had donated this blood had the flavor of lemon gelatin. It was too unusual to squander. I finished the last of the bag while I lay on my stomach, watching the end of the romantic comedy Ina picked out. She ate her pizza with a knife and fork, completely unhindered by my choice of beverage.

"I better start getting ready," I said and walked to the garbage to throw out the empty medical bags. A drop of blood fell on the white marble kitchen tile, almost matching the contrast of the red mahogany living room floor. I wiped the splotch with my finger, ensured Ina wasn't looking and sucked the last drop from my skin.

"Mission?" Her gaze was unmoved from the television.

"Should I say I'm shopping or visiting friends?"

She snorted. "It's the middle of the night." She turned. "Your face looks better at least. You should use your new spell for a disguise again."

I looked at my reflection in the microwave. She was correct. I wouldn't need Andre's blood again, and I was dead set on resisting his blood as much as possible.

There was a knock on our door.

I opened it, and Andre stood before me. Seeing him

at my door made it more real he was now in Ottawa and no longer across an ocean.

I crossed my arms. "What are you doing here?"

"I figured we could go over our plans for tonight together." He looked to the side, showing his displeasure at speaking in the hallway.

I stepped aside. "Come in."

He stepped over my threshold. The plaque didn't illuminate as it had for Roman, so I assumed my security system was back to equilibrium.

"That's enough firepower to keep an army out," Andre said.

"Or a snake," I said.

Ina turned from our living room sectional. "Hey, Andre. Oh, your fancy date shirt." She tongued a lollipop pop she just unwrapped, bearing a mischievous smile. "Who's the lucky girl."

"I didn't know you kept track of my escapades around the Grand Hotel, Ina," Andre said.

Ina turned back to her movie. "It's hardly keeping track when you've been everywhere."

I laughed.

"Though," Ina added, "That shirt doesn't come out often."

"Ouch. I'll be in the kitchen nursing my wounds." Andre smiled, genuinely pleased with Ina's barbs. I hadn't considered they might have known each other a while through their service to Loukin.

"I assume you don't want a drink?" I asked.

The vein in his neck throbbed. He met my gaze.

I backed up to the fridge. "We have wine or pop."

"What type of pop?"

"He likes cherry pop, like you," Ina said.

"With ice, if you have some, please," Andre said.

"The nearest thing to human food I've ever seen you consume was blood disguised as wine," I said and got a glass from the cupboard.

"There are lots of things I like." He put his hands in his pockets, but I saw a finger twitch.

I poured his drink. "Tell me about your plan for tonight."

He sat down at the counter. "Well, without my USB, I don't have Mullins's address, but I confirmed he scheduled himself for an unusual graveyard shift at the House of Commons tonight. I presumed we would trail him from his shift tonight and abduct him prior to the exchange."

Refusing to sit down, I recapped the data I had collected from his USB. "When does his shift end?" I asked.

"Three in the morning."

Our stove clock read *1:30 AM.*

"We should go now, in case he spooks, or he is alerted to our mission." *Or any other reason I could think of to get you out of my condo and to stop sipping pop at my counter like we're friends.*

"Okay," he said, catching the urgency in my eyes. "I'll get changed."

I was up the stairs with my back to the bedroom door in seconds. I had not meant to use my vampiric speed. My chest heaved. *He's not craving you*, I told myself. For if he were, it would force me to acknowledge, as his bonded spy partner, that I'd neglected to provide him with vampire blood thus far, putting him at a disadvantage to the ones who had it.

His safety was not my concern.

Neither was the fact he wanted my blood.

I crossed the distance to my master bathroom. My cosmetics were as I left them. I applied my Charmed lipstick and added another squirt of my perfume, noting my last twenty-four hours would soon expire. Since my disguise was a success, what I wore was irrelevant.

Yet, I paused in my closet.

I plucked a pair of faux-leather leggings from the hanger, the ones that defied gravity with their tautness yet moved like spandex. My hand kept going back to a cashmere turtleneck in a shade of pale lavender.

When I stopped before my floor-length mirror, with my dark hair and black lips, every curve of my body was on display. The innocence of the fuzzy sweater turned malicious in the curves of my breasts, waist, and hips. A cruel pleasure took hold as I committed to my choices. I grabbed my black leather riding boots and down-filled trench coat on my way out the door.

Andre looked up when I descended the stairs. I reminded myself I hated him and let this show in my stare. His gaze stayed with me until I stopped before him.

"Ready?" I asked.

Having already put away his glass, he rose.

"Ready," he said.

We walked to the door. I turned over my shoulder to see Ina smirking in the reflection of our windows.

"You two have fun," she said.

We waited in silence for the elevator, and I strategized ways to extract information from Mullins without killing him. The elevator dinged, and we stepped in. Even when the doors closed, I could still feel Andre's gaze on me.

"You're staring."

"Just studying what type of spell you used," he said. "It's letting me in, but there's an energy around you."

I turned to him. "Interesting. What do you see?"

He looked down at my mouth, then met my gaze.

I looked away.

"Just," he hesitated, unsure, "you, your magical energy. When you move, your skin glimmers golden-red and pink at the edges."

A ding announced the ground floor.

We devised a plan to watch the two exits used during the graveyard shift from the cover of the trees a hundred feet away, which meant being perched in a tree beside Andre, who was chewing red licorice. The frosted pattern of the pine tree's bark imprinted in my hand, I was gripping it so hard. After fifteen minutes of crickets and mouth noises, I turned to him.

"You said you brought caramels."

His smile shone in the moonlight that filtered between the pine needles. He pulled a bag from his inner coat pocket.

I took a caramel. It dissolved on my tongue. I took another one and realized how hot I was, how warm my cheeks were. I repositioned myself and opened my jacket to the night. When I looked up, I was two feet closer to Andre. I rolled the caramel in my mouth. It was dull in comparison to his blood.

"I don't want to kill Mullins," I said.

"That's a relief," Andre said. "When you got that Italian vamp in a choke hold, I thought you'd turned into a sadist."

I laughed, and my caramel almost fell from my mouth.

"Your daydreams aside," I said, "I've participated in too much violence lately."

Andre nodded. "I know the feeling. Not to invade your space, but that's why we come in twos. It's easier to share the burden."

"Have you been watching me?"

"No," he said. "I mean, I feel for you with the bond all the time, but no. I heard Meat and Spade were taken out today. My contact said the *Ispolniteli* were given orders to tail Ina."

The image of the vampire's face when he was electrocuted seized my mind. His face while he strangled me. I clutched the tree branch, closed my eyes, and breathed until the memory passed. Andre was no longer an *Ispolniteli*, but he still had access to *Ispolniteli* resources from years of service. The threat he was to me was always lurking, despite any feelings the bond projected.

"Well," I said. "I know which one was Meat."

"Karolina," he whispered. "You don't trust me, I respect it, but I'm going to need the document you took the other day."

I turned to him. "It's very unlike you to ask for what you want."

"Maybe I want you to know the real me. No games."

I laughed and focused back on the doors. "You love games."

He took another bite of licorice. "I do love games, but—"

The eastern door opened. A man with brown hair

stepped into the moonlight. He pulled his coat collar up past his ears, then put on a tweed fedora that might have been fashionable to wear to a beer pong party in university five years ago. His photo didn't do him justice; he looked more weasel-like in person.

Andre put his candy away without a sound and dropped to the ground. I called up my vampiric senses and followed him. We prowled the shadows, stalking Mullins's walk across the lawn. His briefcase looked familiar. I honed in my eyesight on the emblem the latch bore. It was an eye. He carried the briefcase from the filing cabinet I stole the letter from.

I lost sight of Andre.

The tree line ahead kissed the curve of the sidewalk. If I could gain a few meters, I could intercept Mullins. I leaped with each stride; my muscles burned with the control it took to slow each landing into a silent step. I breathed slow and full in rhythm with the rustling of the wind in the bare trees. I hovered within the forest edge. He reached the outer corner of the east sidewalk.

My hand reached out into the pool of streetlight.

His briefcase rumbled in his hand. The eye insignia whooshed out a bluish-white light that encircled the case and my hand.

I retreated with a jump, clutching my hand to my chest, the sting of the eye's magic a shock to my system. Mullins ran to Wellington Street, clutching the case to his chest. The noise of his feet slapping the concrete drummed against the east block of buildings. Just as he passed the statue of Sir Wilfrid Laurier, a dark streak in the air knocked him to the ground. Movement of the blurred figure flashed again and

Andre pinned him to the dark side of the statue. Mullins was limp.

If my eyes couldn't keep up with Andre's movements, I had already exhausted the vampire blood I had consumed. In my next fight, I would be at a greater disadvantage than my last. I advanced, keeping my distance from the briefcase, which was now inactive. "Where should we take him?"

"My place," Andre said. His eyes were the swirling black pools I had witnessed before when he used his hypnotic powers, a specialty ability he possessed from his invocation of Dark Charm.

"Have fun carrying him," I said.

"I attempted to spell him, but when I started, he just lost consciousness."

"Well," I said. "I hear performance anxiety happens to lots of people."

****

Since Mullins was lifeless, Andre couldn't hypnotize him. Instead, he slung Mullins's arms over his shoulders and piggybacked him, Mullins's feet hanging limply at Andre's knees. We walked back into the trees, heading east, when two teens cut through the woods. Andre dropped Mullins to the ground, pretending he was upchucking. They passed us by, and we continued our walk, but it wasn't long. Andre led me to the most famous historical château in Ottawa, right next door to Parliament Hill.

We stopped at the circle of light cast from the towering French gothic hotel. When illuminated in the night, its pointed peaks gave the illusion of stretching into the clouds above.

"Take an arm," Andre said. "We'll pass him off as

our drinking buddy."

"They're not going to let you take an unplanned guest in, let alone a supposed drunk who could puke all over their carpet."

"It's a surprise; you'll love it." Andre thrust Mullins's weight upon my shoulder.

"The last time you informed me I'd *love it*, we bonded."

I shuffled forward with Andre out of the trees and into the covered entranceway. Strands of amber lights on the alcove ceiling led to a set of doors crowned by a stained-glass window, the antique ironwork an original piece of the hotel's history.

Not only did the footman remain silent, but he also timed opening the door for our arrival with perfection.

I looked at Andre.

"Didn't you know?" he asked, and we stepped inside. "I'm the Prince of Monaco."

"Your highness." A hotel attendant said as we walked through the lobby.

Influential politicians and royalty stayed at this château when visiting parliament, but Andre did not resemble the Prince of Monaco. I reached out with my Charmed senses and felt a spell surrounding him, which was completely undetectable until I searched for it. Like his assessment of me earlier, his enchantment let me in. The bond, or the spell itself, let me see the real him. I parsed the root source—his belt buckle.

We stepped into the elevator.

"For the record, it was when I bit you," he said, "and you did love it."

My jaw clenched at word *bit*. It was the only time he'd bitten me.

"Save it." I tilted my head up to the news on the elevator television, studying the highlights streaming across the bottom and not retaining a word.

The doors dinged and opened

I was the first one out, dragging Mullins with me.

Andre caught up.

"Which room?" I asked.

"Here." He flashed ahead of me, and I assumed he took measures for the cameras on his floor. He opened the door, and the three of us entered. His wards were like stepping through a massage chair. The vibration still resonated in my teeth as I bent to take off my boots.

Andre let Mullins fall back into a chair, then caught my hand. "Never take off your shoes."

I straightened. "In case we have to leave in a hurry."

"Exactly. One never expects to be caught off guard."

"That's why it's called off guard," I said while I examined the room.

The hotel provided Andre with a penthouse suite. The walls were paneled in white and cream, letting the midnight sky and Ottawa River color the room like a painting. I clipped my knee on a dark-espresso coffee table on my way to the bedroom. Once inside, I threw open the curtains and confirmed his view of my condo building.

"You weren't watching me, eh?"

"I was here if you needed me," he said, "or wanted to talk." He relocated Mullins deeper into the room. "Drink?" Andre held his wrist out.

I glided toward him, fixated on the veins of his

smooth skin. Metal shone by his hand in the chandelier's glow. He pointed to a metal cocktail bar on wheels.

"I'm fine, thank you." I sat down. "Are we waiting until he wakes up?"

"I'll wake him up in a second." He poured himself vodka over ice. "I need to ensure there are still no holes in my soundproofing spell." He paced the room.

I took a chunk of ice and bit down. The hard crunch was a far cry from skin, its cool shards melting on my tongue.

When Andre had finished, he put down his empty glass and knelt before Mullins. He rolled up his sleeves, exposing the skin where his *Ispolniteli* mark should be—if he did not have the Light Charm. Wisps of smoke faintly glided from his hovering hands. The smoke twirled its way to Mullins's wrists and feet, solidifying into bonds of dark magic that shone like black oil. A faint tendril of smoke was sucked into Mullins's nose.

His head jolted back. "Where am I?" He jerked against the bonds. "Who are you?"

My stomach rolled already. Mullins was an academic, one who likely settled into the convention of married life and attempted to turn his five-figure salary into six. The snivel on his face told us he didn't consider he might lose his life.

"You're going to sit still," Andre said in a low tone, "and answer every question I ask."

"Help!" He screamed. "Help!"

I stepped forward. "Colin, if you want to get home to your wife within the hour, stay calm."

He hushed, his gaze moving between my mouth

and Andre's black eyes.

My fangs pricked against my tongue. I had not felt their descent nor felt my disguising spell diminish. *Could he see my face?* I straightened. "We're not here to hurt you, but we need you to answer our questions, can you hold yourself together?"

He nodded. A single tear glided down his cheek.

"What information are you trading tonight?" Andre asked.

"The research funding for the underground base," Mullins said.

The intel was linked to the secret base Andre and I accidentally infiltrated. "What research in particular? Or are you trading the funding for the base as a whole?"

"They want to know the funding for a special project. There was a break in, and their spies got wind of the fact a letter was sent to a geneticist in the base. I requested the details of the project to approve their budget, but I was denied. I'm only sharing the finance budget, I swear!"

"Who's they? Is there a hardcopy of the information in your briefcase?" Andre asked. Mullins nodded.

Andre picked up the case without issue, but uneasiness made me step back. He hovered his hands over the latch, presumably checking for spells.

"The eye, it—"

"It's fine. I'd feel it if it weren't—"

Bluish-white light blasted from the case. Metal whizzed through my arm. I dropped to the ground shrieking, but Andre's screams overpowered mine.

"You," Mullin's voice boomed into our cries, "cannot interfere with your betters without consequences."

I looked up from on my back into dead, dead eyes. Mullins spoke, but his face and body were slack, void of emotion or any movement other than his limp, wagging jaw.

"Retreat now and live through our wrath."

Mullins stilled. His jaw gaped open. His eyes stared through me.

Chapter Six

Andre's screams continued, uncontrolled and guttural.

I rolled onto the squishy carpet and saw my blood soaking a ring around my torso. Andre was a foot from me, beneath a metal web that pinned him down. The metal that tore through my arm had embedded itself into the floor at each point of the web.

I ripped up the closest strands then shrilled, crumpling over. The web wasn't metal; it was enchanted silver. I recovered. Then lifted again, closer to Andre's arms.

"Hurry!" I screamed.

I held on, keeping tension on the cords so Andre could get his upper body free. He cried out and shoved on the spikes near his stomach. The strands let go. He rolled and rose to his knees before me. I clutched my arm.

Andre took a handful of blood bags from a duffle bag next to a chair. "Bite," he said and pushed one into my face.

I bit down as he tied a cloth napkin around my arm. The flavor of oranges bloomed in my mouth, followed by a chalky taste. I sucked back the blood, not caring if it was human or vampire.

Andre leaned against a sofa beside me, and I joined him.

The stinging of my severed artery, coupled with my blood loss, sent my heart rate soaring. The blood bag crumbled in my hand as I sucked the remaining ounce from the bag. "Was that vampire blood?"

"Human. Why? Do you want to bond with another vampire?" Andre hadn't finished his blood. He was getting paler. "You need to replace your fluid volume, Karolina. Human blood hits our systems quick, but it won't heal the wound."

"Aw, are you skipping out on an opportunity to trick me into your blood? How sweet."

"Thank you, I am sweet." He slumped to the ground.

I hovered over him. "How do you feel?"

He was as pale as the walls now.

"I think the magic of the blast hurt me more than I realized."

"You took the brunt of it," I said. I touched his hand, and it felt as cold as the ice I ate moments ago.

"I'll be fine. I'm just going to sleep here and drink more blood."

I took the blood bag from his limp hand and squeezed it into his mouth. "Why didn't you ask for my blood at my condo yesterday?"

"I'm not going to pressure you for your blood, Karolina."

I lay down beside him and squeezed more blood into his mouth. "Not even when you're vulnerable without it? How long will it take for you to heal?"

"The night, maybe two."

A drop of blood rolled down his thick bottom lip. I caught the droplet with a finger and brought it to my mouth.

He perked up, despite his weakness, watching my face intently.

"That sucks," I said, "for you."

He laughed, breathy but fragile. "You mean for you. I have a great bite."

"Okay, then, show me again."

"Are you asking me to bite you?"

I put the blood bag down. "Yes."

Andre rolled over onto his side to face me. He searched my expression for any sign of sarcasm, but instead, he just caught me in a small tremor from his increased proximity. I let my vampiric senses peak. His heartbeat was thready and rapid. His breathing was shallow and rhythmic. I met his gaze. His pulse spiked with mine. I choked up.

"Bite me," I whispered.

His hand glided up my arm into my hair. Instead of the quick puncture of fangs, his other hand trailed a finger down the length of my neck, pulling back my fuzzy sweater. "What if I said no…"

I couldn't hold his gaze; my lower abdomen was clenched too tightly. "Then you might not have the opportunity again."

The wet of his lips touched my skin. His kiss was warm and sweet, gentle on my neck. Air whooshed up my shoulder as he took a deep breath. The pierce of his fangs was smooth and quick. Euphoria exploded from the punctures, barreling through my body.

My back arched, pressing him against me. I held onto his shoulders and rode the wave his bite gave me. He drank longer than the last time, and each pull of blood brought the sensation on again. My soft cries filled the room. My fangs nicked his skin, and his sweet, salty, caramel blood flowed between my lips. My hips searched for his, but he held me firmly in place.

"Please…" In frustration, I ripped his shirt open and began kissing his shoulder.

He parted from my neck to press his tongue into my mouth. Cupping my face, he kissed me as deeply as I needed.

I shoved him into his back. Then rose to my feet. I had to cross Mullins's corpse to get the ice bucket. I sat down and put a handful of cubes on the back of my neck. *Shit.* I didn't drop my guard on the bond, and I still lost control. *He's a liar*, I reminded myself, *he used you.* But those reminders had not kept me in check.

"Your perfume smells the way you taste," Andre said. "Sweet, spicy, a little fruity."

"Andre, don't." I paced to the window and kept my back to him. "I didn't mean for that to happen."

"Did you mean to bite me back?"

"It was just a graze." I turned. It wasn't just a graze—my fang punctures were there in the meat of his shoulder like a desperate kiss bled into a bite. I may have hurt him slightly.

"You probably shouldn't feed straight from a human, Karolina. At least not until you can separate sex from feeding, and you can keep track of what you're doing when you drink."

I poured myself a glass of water and removed the napkin from my arm. It was fully healed from Andre's blood. "The only feeding I know which isn't from a blood bag, is with sex."

Andre stood.

I didn't look at him, so I couldn't tell if he caught

the implication. Andre and I had not had sex, so my phrasing meant I was having sex regularly with another man.

"You can't run from the way you feel."

I downed my glass. "Don't tell me how I feel."

I walked back over to Mullins and bent down to look at the briefcase. His mouth and eyes still hung lifelessly open. My stomach rolled, and my vampiric hunger shriveled. I despised myself for wanting to have sex ten feet from his corpse. I searched the contents of the case with a hotel pen. There was an excel spreadsheet inside.

Andre stepped to my side and took the paper, but I'd already seen the budget he'd circled. It was a genome sequencing grant. *Base Franklin*. Franklin was a common enough name, but knowing the grant, Rosalind Elsie Franklin came to mind and her scientific discovery of DNA. The base's security system indicated its use was for more than science. Could the government know more about the supernatural community than the underground anticipated?

Andre looked down at me.

"What do we do with the body?" I asked.

"I can call the cleanup crew."

"I don't imagine you have a laser pointer for humans."

Andre pulled out his nineties' flip-phone, the model a telltale sign of a frequency buster in place, and started dialing. "If I had a laser pointer for humans, Karolina, I'd have bartered for my position a lot sooner."

****

Andre opened the door, and two men stepped in at

his invitation. Their hotel uniforms evaporated in shadowy clouds upon their entry. The cleanup crewmen were more Russian *Ispolniteli*. They avoided facing Andre directly, which could have been a sign of disrespect or fear of the advantage of Andre's new position.

The crewmen didn't speak but only assessed their task. They knelt a table length from Mullins and rolled up their sleeves. Snake insignias rippled on their forearms. Black oil flowed out, turning into tendrils of shadow which crept across the carpet.

Mullins lay undisturbed.

When it was clear no further magical traps would be triggered, they started dismembering Mullins and loading him into a curtained trolly.

I retreated to Andre's bedroom, closed the door, and put pillows on my ears. My choice was to take refuge beside his bed, else forever be haunted by the noise. The sheets were folded tightly against the mattress, but the scent of Andre's cologne was on both pillows. Musky, crisp, with a lingering sweetness.

I focused on the bag at my feet. I recognized his overnight bag from the first time we met when I had snooped through his things. His spellbook of dark magic was there, glittering like crushed onyx in the lamplight. From my experience of touching the book, the texture was more like dried blood—prior to the searing pain of the book's poison. I held the zipper open further with my boot. There a brown file slipped beside his folded clothes. I slid the bond down and felt Andre at the far side of the suite. It took a strength I had not yet tested to keep my emotions neutral while the connection between us flowed.

I dropped a pillow and took the folder from the bag.

Inside was a printout of account transfers to a bank in Italy, the largest bank in Florentine history, the Medici Bank. Archivists alleged the Medici Bank was liquidated in the fifteenth century, but this money wire begged to differ. The sender was from an account in Switzerland. Figures as large as my inheritance streamed across the page. At the bottom of the list, a Canadian transaction was logged, one from a mining company.

Andre's footsteps approached.

I cursed myself for letting my excitement slip. The letter at my condo indicated the woman analyzed was an heiress to Diamond mines, including one in Northern Ontario.

Andre entered.

I was caught sitting on his bed clutching his pillow. The envelope stood halfway out of his bag. He almost rounded the footboard until I crawled onto my knees on his bed.

He stopped.

"Are they almost done?" I asked, holding his gaze. I flexed my toe downward, pushing the envelope into his bag.

"They're finishing." He stepped to the edge of the mattress. Even as he towered over me, my hips half the size of his, I felt powerful. His stare hung on me like he was helpless in the pull of my movement.

Like he was at my mercy.

"I didn't mean to wind up on your bed."

His fingertips touched my hips. "But you are."

"What would you have done if I wasn't here?"

"I would have been in a lot of pain, and likely a lot of trouble. Then again, I might have had the information I'm missing had you shared the contents of the letter with me."

"What letter?" I asked, my touch trailing up his back, mimicking what he did to me in the closet. "The one you tried to slip out from underneath my shirt? I don't have it anymore. Maybe you should ask your *Ispolniteli* friends if they have it."

"I'm going to need the letter, Karolina." His tenor shifted; the pragmatic face he wore when he was calculating his next move dominated him.

The outer suite door closed.

"I should go," I said. I was almost at the door when he appeared at my side.

"Too much werewolf blood isn't good for a vampire," he said. "If you drink enough of it, it plants a breading target on your back for wolves."

"I don't think you need to be troubling yourself with what I do with Roman."

The hum of the electricity in the walls grew like Andre was drawing energy from the room. His hand flexed, then closed. The lights flickered. For a moment, I wondered if he was angry.

I collected my coat.

"Just promise me you won't follow this any further without me."

"Andre," I said. "I won't promise you anything."

Chapter Seven

My condo parking garage was dull and empty, making my intensified senses hard to ignore. This was the longest my vampiric sensations had stayed heightened after seeing Andre. I sat down in my SUV and waited until just the very human pulse of excitement remained. The leather seat creaked as I pressed the ignition button and then touched the radio icon on my dashboard screen. The new-car smell reminded me of my objective.

My interactions with Andre today showcased the advantage his connections gifted him. *His contacts*, he'd said. I had contacts too. I wiped my lipstick off in the mirror. The Charmed folks of Ottawa were people I could trust. I remembered I, too, had a community. If my answering machine truly captured all which was said, my handler in Russian would know I wasn't home to receive my next mission.

****

When I entered my hometown, I had not intended to visit my mother's grave. The darkness of the storm made the fading night linger. I looked down at my hands on the steering wheel, trying to recall when I passed through the cemetery gates and parked the car. My hand hovered over the reverse button. Discussing Mama's funeral with Roman yesterday was painful, numbing even. I didn't have the strength to open the car door, yet my hand did it anyway. The short, clipped grass swished underfoot. The groundskeeper had overwatered it, a sign Mama's grave was well taken care of.

Fresh daisies were in the vase under her name. Decaying rose petals from Mrs. Lupei's garden were scattered across the mound of frozen dirt. The fresh sod had washed into the earth before winter frosted over.

I knelt down. Mama's name hung at eye level. The cold ground pulled the heat from me like her grave could leach the energy from any life which touched it. Daring the earth to take me too, I placed my hand on the headstone.

The ground rumbled. Light twinkled across the frost, then flowed up before the grave. I jumped back but hesitated when I saw the figure taking shape. It was Mama, a whisp of her physical form, lighting up like a white flame in the dreary creep of dawn.

"Karolina," she said.

"Mama!" I swung my arms to wrap around her legs, but I passed through her.

"I'm a message, darling, not the real thing. A piece of myself left behind before I crossed over at my funeral."

"How is that possible?" I asked. Her image looked to be made of tiny strings of electricity, which warmed the surrounding ice. I ran my fingers through her again, feeling the pleasant heat I had felt when Auntie Miruna healed my legs in Romania. "You sparked the Light Charm when you sacrificed yourself for me."

She nodded.

"Don't you dare smile," I said. "If you invoked the Light Charm, you had a choice between life or death.

Are you saying you chose to leave? You chose to leave *me*?"

"I saw the future, Karolina. I saw a moment which broke my heart and choose to forfeit my life force for when you needed it. Did you not feel my presence in Russia?"

My cheeks were suddenly soaked. "I heard you," I said. "I heard you whisper my name."

"One's child is the great treasure one will ever admire, but never own. You are the part of me that transcends time and carries my love with it." She hovered her hand on my cheek. "I lived a good life, Karolina; it's your turn to find love and purpose."

Tree branches rustled and scratched against one another in the wind. Dawn burst forth from behind a wall of bare oaks. Patches of sunlight beamed down from the clouds, lighting up Mama's daisies and the twinkle of frost.

"I love you, Mama."

Her image started to evaporate. "My estate wishes are at the Lupeis, make sure you read the document."

"Really?" I wiped my eyes. "Your message from beyond the grave is to remind me about your estate paperwork?"

I looked up, and she was gone.

****

The sunshine continued to beat down through my windshield. I took the turns and curves of the road into town without thought, letting familiarity guide the way. The quaint main strip had the eerie feeling of the opening scene of a horror film because I knew if I kept driving, I would find the dilapidated ruins of my burnt-down home. I pulled into the occult shop run by another

Charmed family in town. *Déjà vu* set in as I checked my makeup in the review mirror. This shop was the last place I visited prior to Mama's death. Yet, the ornate Charmed markings carved into the wooden sign above the store's windows glimmered at my presence like they were beckoning me back into the fold.

The door jingled as I entered, and the force of an electric fence made my Charmed senses ignite. The store's wards had been reinforced since I was last here. Frankincense saturated the air like a second security spell. Artur, the store owner, stepped through a beaded doorway while carrying jars of incense and dried herbs. His pace quickened when he saw me and he put down the jars on the nearest table. I noticed him going in for a hug, and my arms hung awkwardly at my side.

"I'm so sorry about your mother," he said.

I patted him on the back, then looked for a gap to slither away through. "Thank you," I said.

He looked at me with the scrutiny of Auntie Miruna. "You've changed, very much."

"Fighting for your life will do that."

He nodded and walked back through the beaded door. "It will indeed. Come, I can offer you help."

I followed him.

"Time moves quickly—cell phones, children moving out of home, but we, the Charmed," he turned to me, "we always take care of our own." He sat down on a stool in front of a weathered wooden table. The knife, the coin, the cup, and a white flamed candle looked like Mama's teachings reincarnated.

I batted a bouquet of crows' feet hanging from the ceiling, and sat down on the stool opposite of him.

"Dip your hands in the bucket of water by your

seat."

I dipped my hands.

"Then rub them with salt," he said. Only after I'd given it my most enthusiastic try did he produce a deck of tarot cards. "Blow."

I complied, then held my hands on the table as Mama taught me, channeling my energy into the wood. It's a fine art, inserting your will, your destiny, into the reading without overpowering the energy of the dealer.

The first card he flipped after I cut the deck was the Lovers. The shiny gold card of two bodies entwined was illuminated in the candlelight. The next card which crossed it was the Queen of Swords. She was a bitch; there was no disputing it. The Five of Swords, a man attacked at all angles. *Betrayal*. The crumbling Tower of Disaster. Then the Devil card. Men and women danced with the perception of being chained. Aside from the Lovers, the only blessing in the deck was the Knight of Cups. After all the disaster and treachery which laid before me in the cards, he crowned me with the Ten of Cups card—bliss achieved with one's true love.

Artur then cleansed his hands in a bucket beside him and dipped a finger in a blow of salt. He drew a line of salt down the middle of his forehead, then seized. His legs kicked mine under the table, but I kept my hands planted. It was over in seconds. When he opened his eyes, they glowed gold. His mouth relaxed as he channeled the power of the earth, our mother and protector.

"Those in your life whom you want to love are not what they seem. In addition to this, there is a great, dark magic haunting your steps, looking to devour you. You escaped it once, but it now lurks in your shadow, chased by the power of the wind. Its whispers are seductive. It has already crept through your defenses. It craves your future blood, and absolute power." With a final jerk, his eyes cleared.

"Well," I said, my tone flat. "It's nothing I didn't know already."

Andre had committed to Loukin's bidding to sway me to spark the Dark Charm, to give up a piece of my soul. The seductive powers of the bound I knew all too well. The bit about the wind gave me a slight chill. I had forgotten about the foreign magic I encountered a few days ago until now, but its magic was not Bronwyn's. I went to rise, but he caught my hand.

"This is a darkness you do not expect. In my premonition the thought was clear, you are vulnerable to this threat. It takes you by surprise."

I sat back down. "What I need to know is how the mining industry is connected to the Undergrounds." I would not mention diamond mines nor the contents of the letter. Bronwyn's tracking spell had started in this very store.

"I imagine it's connected the same way the Icelandic publishing industry is connected to the Dyads. Or how the foresting industry is connected to werewolves. Which underground are you referring to?"

"Just mines in general. Which communities use mines as an income? Did you know the Dyads expanded their enterprise from Greenland into Ottawa real estate?" I hoped Andre had told the truth when he told me this over a month ago, and I hoped Artur would elaborate if the Dyads were involved in other operations.

"I'd just heard," he said. "You are catching on quickly, Karolina. Although Ana kept you sheltered, she taught you well."

I couldn't tell if he circumvented the question on purpose or was distracted by his thoughts of Mama. "Thank you," I said, "but going back to the underground. What are the Canadian Gypsies involved in? The Canadian vampires?"

"Canadian vampires are not from North America originally. Their income is based on foreign trade, commercial goods, and high fashion. Money, glitz, glam, and luxury travel."

"And us?"

He began packing his talismans and tarot cards away. "That should be easy for you," he said. "I'll give you a hint. It was Ana's greatest talent."

"Healing?"

"Medicine. The indigenous people of Canada have a magic of their own; they are skilled healers, but when the Charmed immigrated to Canada, our healing magic was the commodity we could offer, along with defensive magic. When Canada was established as country, over a hundred years ago, agreements were struck among the supernaturals."

"More like two hundred," I said.

"You should be proud. May of the Charmed folk studied medicine and contributed to the universal healthcare we have today. My wife says, when insulin was discovered for diabetes, it was a Charmed lab assistant who lit the secretions of the cells for Dr. Banting to find. So, without our people, my wife wouldn't have the medicine she needs today."

I was proud. Months ago, I thought the Earth

Charm was boring, but it healed and protected people. After seeing the depths of tragedy around the world, safety and wellness now held priceless value. Plus, I'd used the Earth Charm for defense more than my fire magic over the past few days.

"Tell me more about the agreements," I said.

"When the Canadian government struck treaties with the indigenous people of Canada, so did the underground factions. The Charmed people only asked for immunity from violence, in exchange for our contribution to the medical field."

"Mama was killed."

"Yes. Your mother's death changed everything. You were not here, but communities mourned Ana. There are whispers saying the Dyad enforcement was too heavy-handed. Some even question why they were at your house to begin with."

The insidious feeling I swallowed during Bronwyn's escape in Russia crawled up my throat. "Bronwyn—"

He held up his hand, silencing me. Warning glared in his eyes. "When protected people die, the accords among the supernatural societies seem not so permanent anymore. I was called to represent the Charmed at the next meeting of the communities."

So what? Talking about an abuse of power was not going to bring Mama back. Nor would it safeguard the next person who stood in the way of Bronwyn's objective. I gripped the back of chair I rose from; the wood creaked, threatening to break under pressure. I circled back to the question he didn't answer. "Which faction is involved in mining?"

"Not a specific one. Mining is a business for the

government and aristocrats."

Artur was from a different generation; when he said aristocrat, he meant what millennials coined as the "one percent." I pictured my university roommate preaching from her beanbag chair; though a sliver of her concerns was merited, her words resonated with me now. *Wealth runs the world. Banks fund the governments only to pit them against one another. They don't want you to pay attention to the man behind the curtain.*

At the time, her intensity made her sound like a cult leader, but I couldn't help but wonder how deep the supernatural influence ran in our world if a hidden society controlled the earth's mineral wealth. For it would mean their influence could devastate currencies while strengthening others, sculpting the globe to their objective. Yet, in my investigation, it wasn't a man but a woman 'behind the curtain.'

"Thanks for your time, Artur."

"There is a friend of mine you could speak to," he said. "He owns the pawn shop in the next town, northwest from here." He looked at me the way Mama had before she tested me on an earth spell. "But you must conceal your identity before you ask questions there. Secrets come and go, and he may ask for some in return."

"Thank you, Artur."

He nodded. "I'm sorry my shop was not safe for you the last time you were here. My ward was tampered with, then Ana died. For the record, it was after she was dead that I went back and retraced the breach to find a tracking spell was placed on you at my store."

Artur knew more than what he was saying. If he

retraced the tracking spell, then he knew it was a light-magic user who tracked me. I met his gaze and understanding hung in the air between us. He'd been general in answering my questions, but he'd given me the lead I was looking for.

"It wasn't your fault," I said.

I stepped through the beaded door once more, and the beads kept jingling as I crossed his ward. The resonating energy of the protection spell disbanded as I searched for pawn shops on my GPS. There was only one on the fringe of the town Artur spoke of. I put my black lipstick on and started the engine.

****

I expected a store similar to Artur's, but when I drove to the location, a busted sign looked like it would fall on my roof. I passed the parking lot entrance and parked at a packing depot half a mile down. I walked to the store. The exertion was calming, ideal for reviewing the details of the letter and Andre's list of account transfers in my head.

I arrived at the parking lot. The slick asphalt gave way to dirt halfway in. I stepped past a patch of frosted weeds, and the ground slithered before me. Rocks shot up. Mounds of earth snaked through the dirt, crisscrossing and wreathing into a circle around the shop. I jumped back, hovering at the fringe of the defensive magic. My identity spell must have triggered the enchantment.

A man's face came to the window.

I cocked out a hip, gave a beauty pageant smile, and waved. I hoped my identity spell would adapt to my intent, as my smile sure wouldn't work if he were looking at the face Ina saw.

He came to the door.

"I'm looking for a special piece!" The wind blew my hair over my face, and I took the opportunity to playfully pull it away with a laugh. "A friend sent me. He said it could only be found here."

He opened the door, and the circle of twisting earth parted for my entry.

I took one step and spread my Charmed senses out, feeling my way closer. It appeared the spell had parted. I stopped before the door. "Is it safe to enter your wards?"

"Yes. Come in. You're letting all the heat out."

The shop was a hoarder's delight. Small children could get lost in the maze of boxes that occupied the floor. The shopkeeper walked along the glass encasements lining the perimeter of the shop, and I followed.

"Thank you so much for letting me in." I struggled to keep my knees from shaking after the vibration of his ward, but my foot twitched.

"Cut the shit, cupcake," he said. "There're only a few reasons why a Charmed comes here disguised, and usually it's for information." He paused. "One for one, that's the deal."

I squared my shoulders. "One what?" I hadn't finished feeling around the shop for spells. Thus far, I counted seventeen traps.

"Gosh, you're not a bright one. Questions. One for one."

"Deal," I said.

He waited, and in his frustration at my lack of response, I upped my count to twenty. The closer the traps were, the harder they were to notice. The nearest one was only a few feet away.

"Which supernatural faction is involved in mining?"

"None."

He had a poker face. His gruff demeanor didn't fluctuate, but his heart rate did. He struggled to slow it under my stare, but he did. He was trained to lie.

"This question is easy," he said and met my gaze. "Why do you want to know?"

"I won't answer until you respond to my question truthfully. I had it on good authority this was the place to come for information, and I doubt you want your reputation to cease."

"Who are you to say I haven't answered you honestly? Give me your reply or get out of my shop." He stepped through a slot between the counter.

"Truthfully?" I smiled and placed my hand on the glass counter to lean in. "My mother is dead. That's why I want to know."

He didn't recoil but shifted down the showcase. "Would you like to see something special?"

I avoided the trap I had ferreted out and stood opposite him.

He looked down to some gemstones in the case. They were rubies, in similar shape and style to the one I wore around my neck. The oval shape and three-toned braided gold pattern were so similar, my hand almost clutched my necklace. I placed my wrist on the counter instead and reminded myself my spell was in place. He had already confirmed I appeared to him as wearing a disguise.

"They're very pretty," I said.

"They are knockoffs. The real gem is very

precious, and in higher demand the farther north in Ontario you go."

"Really? How fascinating," I said. "Do you supply diamonds from northern Ontario as well?"

His pulse spiked uncontrollably, and this time I could observe him physically restraining his impulse. I paused to let him compose himself. Within a few breaths, he calmed.

"It *is* a very interesting gem," he said, "but it's the lore around it that people find *most* interesting. There are pictographs detailing its creation over ten thousand years ago."

This was not fitting into any threat or message I could deduce. It felt factual and relevant to the gem I wore around my neck. Yet, it was almost like he was stalling for time.

A sonic boom shook the ground.

I braced. Then I turned to the windows. A dome of fluorescent white electricity fell to the ground, surrounding the shop and parking lot.

"I rescind your invitation," he said.

The wards of his threshold pulled at me like a magnet. I clutched the curved glass of the showcase, but my body whipped across the room. I hit the ward like a ninety-foot drop into water, then smashed into the frozen earth outside.

Eight Dyads approached me. Their metal armor, branded in never-ending twines of rope, shone within the pulsing light of the dome. Heavy footsteps crunched along the frozen dirt as they encircled me, their battle weapons adding to their weight. Many of them carried axes like Lukas. Others had a sword on each hip, one as tall as me, and the other as short as my arm.

"Can I help you?" I asked.

"Identify yourself," the blond in front of me said. His face was shielded behind his helmet, but tips of wheat-colored hair hung out the sides.

I rose. My limbs already pulsed where I would have bruises, but I stood in a half lunge, ready for an attack. "No."

"If you give us the information we require, you may walk free," the blond said. Noting he was the only one who spoke to me, and the others waited for his direction, I assumed he oversaw this team.

"My identity is mine," I said. "You do not police my kind, but," I held my hand out and sparked the Light Charm within it, "I'm of no threat to you, nor to what you stand for."

"Lower your hand," he said, "and drop your spell."

In unison, all their hands glowed.

"I will not."

Beams of light burst forth from their gauntlets. My fire magic ignited, called from the instinct of battle, but I had already lit the Light Charm within my hand. The spark exploded, forging with my fire, and solidified into a shield.

I hit the ground.

Surging beams of electricity pummeled into me. The force drilled me deep into the earth, blackening under flames and raw white-hot energy. I screamed as I watched the soil diminish beneath me. The sheer weight of their attack pinned me down. Deeper into sediment I pressed, encased by my magic in the darkness. I needed a counterweight. I split my focus on the Light Charm. Maintaining the shield, I gathered all the essence of white magic I had to spare and blasted the rock beneath me.

I soared into the air, almost colliding with the Dyad shield above the shop.

The currents of magic from the warriors followed me, encasing my fire. When I hit the ground again, my counterblast kept me from sinking, but it was fleeting. I walked forward, pushing a third lightning blast into the magic of their leader.

"I'm not here to fight!" I screamed, and in my release, the light within my hand thickened, shooting out into the leader's face.

His helmet shattered.

With the force I exerted into the Light Charm, my fire diminished. The leader stepped forward through the torrent of light. Among the sparks, I saw a glint of his ax. The blade clipped my coat behind my back, just missing my skin. He spared my life, but the arm of his axe shattered my collarbone. I crumpled.

Before I hit the ground, he stepped in and clutched my shoulder. Electricity seized me, just like the *Ispolniteli* I had cooked back at my condo. My breath stilled, and I froze, looking up to his face. His milky-blue eyes held no malice, only purpose. He released me from the electrocution. Then there was nothing but force and air beneath me.

My hair blew back. The ground gave way to clouds. He clutched me around my waist, and the gravitational force kept my cheek pinned to his chest. I saw the edge of northern Ontario, the Arctic, then the Labrador Sea.

All Dyads had the Wind Charm, not just Bronwyn.

I held onto his shoulders, terrified he would let go.

Ahead, a sphere of light shone. We entered it, only

to emerge in the sky once more. Labrador was now a distant strip in the sea at our feet. The clouds grew dense. Moisture drenched my clothes and hair. The peaks of Greenland pierced a blanket of fog. We skimmed above frosty white hills speckled with brightly colored houses, only to catch an updraft alongside a cluster of mountains.

A province-wide crater appeared.

We flew over the ridge and into the mist—the air smelled of rock and honeysuckle. Like the clouds were restrained by the wind rotating along the crater edge, a thermal oasis stood at the bottom—bathed in sunlight. Volcanic springs steamed palm trees. Wispy tendrils crept between flowering shrubs and green hills.

We touched down in the courtyard of a fortress in a gust of wind.

The ancient stronghold battled with the domination of glass and steel. A shimmering triangular building halved the stone fort. It sloped skyward, capturing the noon and western sun. Regular civilization claimed a section of the acreage; amongst the tropical growth was an airport with transport planes and a tower.

I found my footing on the grass and pushed away from Dyad's stomach to part. The pain from my broken collarbone immobilized my left arm. I bore the discomfort and stepped back.

He looked down at me, allowing a foot's distance. "Please comply," he said. He was good-looking, with a thick, square jaw. I stepped out of his hold within the circle of his squad and noted they were all fine-looking and just as formidable.

"Why am I here?" I asked.

A Dyad whose eyes glowed as bright as the helmet

he wore approached. The light shining from him was like a small sun to my retinas. I tracked his movements by staring at his armor. The squad parted for him.

Blondie straightened. "Jarl."

"*Drotten* Arie," the Commander said. "Who is the renegade?"

Drotten was what the Vikings had called their warlords. Jarl was equivalent to earl. The Dyad who detained me was high in their chain of command and far more lethal than he displayed during battle.

"She has refused to identify herself. I believe it's more a case of stupidity than defiance. We picked her up from a trigger trap. Some sequential words were mentioned, likely by accident."

"Where?" the Jarl asked.

Arie paused, and his team noted his hesitation. "At the weasel's," he said at last.

"Bring her in for questioning," the Jarl said.

Chapter Eight

"I'm not a prisoner," I said. "I was taken against my will. I have rights. I demand to be brought back to my country."

Arie laughed. "See, stupidity. I can deal with the misdemeanor."

The Jarl approached me, and I squinted. "You do not have rights," he said, "when you do not identify yourself." The tone of his voice made me imagine the seriousness of his face. The truth of the circumstance stood out in my mind, as it likely did in the Jarl's; a civilian would have identified themselves, an operative would not.

"I lost my memory when I walked into the pawnshop," I said. "I do not know who I am."

"Yet, you know what country you are from?" The Jarl asked.

"I watched us fly away from Canada."

He leaned in, causing me to turn my head from the light. "If you remember nothing, how is your spell still active?"

It was true. My identity spell shifted with my intent. Most skilled practitioners, especially ones who could craft an identity spell, built them that way. If I had lost my memory, I would no longer hold the intent to stay concealed.

My pause validated him.

I analyzed the different pleas I could make, but none would assist me now. I had walked into a corner, and there was only one way out of it. "I am only authorized to speak to Lukas," I lied.

He pulled back, giving my eyes a break.

"May I remove my coat?" I asked. "It's hot down here." Rather than waiting, I slowly slipped my limp arm from my cut sleeve, accentuating my injuries. I arranged my coat over my good arm and waited. When the Jarl remained silent, I looked to Arie.

"Her fragility is a ruse," Arie said and stripped an armored glove from his hand. "She melted a hole into the earth with the Fire *and* Light Charm before we captured her, and she cracked my helmet." He paced in front of me, muttering, "Your black flames aren't fooling anyone." He addressed the Jarl. "If I had to guess, I'd say it's the Earth Charm keeping her hidden, and judging from the amount of strength she displayed, she's not fully human."

I kept my face blank.

He stepped in close, so close I could see the pulse of blood in his neck. My exhaustion from battle went to war with my thirst for blood. I pressed my tongue against the roof of my mouth, discouraging my fangs from release.

He smiled down at me. "My guess is vampire genes, but I couldn't confirm without starving her for a week."

"If I didn't know you Dyads any better, I'd say you have a vampire fetish," I said.

"Last chance," Arie said, "comply and drop your spell."

"Enough," the Jarl said. "Get her inside and call for

Lukas."

****

They led me to the old building. Arie and the Jarl directed the way while two Dyads guarded my back. As we approached, I noticed the swirling carvings on the fortress stones. The markings reminded me of Viking runes, yet they were not like the ones I'd seen in history classes, or in any documentary or book. One in particular resembled a star-like pattern plummeting to the ground. Dyads made a home on our earth thousands of years ago, but the planet or moon they originated from in our solar system was a mystery. Looking at the ruins now, I wondered if they knew their history but kept the information private.

Arie and the Jarl stepped through the threshold.

I stopped, and the Dyads behind me walked into my back. "Is it safe—"

They shoved me through the ward with strength equivalent to a vampire's. I hung midair in the magic of the threshold. The electricity shocked me into submission, but from within my chest, the Light Charm broke forth, sensing its kin. I hit the smooth, cold floor, twitching in the aftershock. I wondered how many volts I had just experienced and how much more my heart could take.

"See," Arie said. "Stronger than a human."

We continued down the hall of the ancient stronghold, and I gathered as many details as I could. Their base was protected by light magic, just like the wards at Kazimir's—the ones forged by Bronwyn. I reached out my senses and saw luminous strings, like gridwork, encasing the building in my mind. She must not have told the Dyads I collapsed Kaz's wards. *Why would she?* It would have exposed her allegiance to him and her betrayal of her own. Yet, this stalemate of ours left her people vulnerable—I could dismantle the Dyad wards.

When we passed into the modern part of the building, the halls swarmed with Dyads. Many were Caucasian, but men and women of all ethnicities came and went, some in street clothes, others in armor.

We stopped at the elevator, and when Arie pressed the down button, I worked to control my heart rate. I hated basements. They reduced my escape points drastically. When a fight ensued in a basement, the chances of the victim emerging were slim. The only way to boost one's odds was to avoid entering such a place or taking the position of the aggressor.

To run or to fight?

I would not make it off the island without assistance. Even if I managed to steal a boat at the shoreline, it would take me days to hike the mountains—and I was not dressed for the Arctic cold. My identity spell bought me time to scheme. Time changed all things. I could gather intelligence on the Dyads and try to uncover why their keyword traps were targeting Canadian diamond mines. When my time expired, I would have to attack by surprise.

The elevator dinged.

Four floors below ground, Arie led me into a modern, sterile-looking room. The floor had large vents in the floor; the type meant to drain the fluid from a power washer. *Not good.* There was a thick metal desk and some chairs in the room, but the hospital bed in the center was another air-horn warning.

"May I please speak to Lukas now?" I asked and

claimed one of the chairs at the desk. Maintaining proximity was vital; I wanted to stay close to the door and far, far away from the bed. I wanted to deescalate thoughts of torture or violence.

"You seem uncomfortable?" the Jarl asked.

I laughed. "Usually, Lukas arranges for me to stay in a room with a view."

They hadn't taken my coat yet, and I hadn't yet been searched. I still had precious moments. I hoped my contribution to Lukas's prize battle in Russia would soften his unwillingness to listen to me. I summoned my vampiric sense and listened.

The air reeked of old, coagulated blood. Water dripped in the vents. The smell of rust and damp iron followed. Our three hearts echoed in the room, mine spiking when my concentration shifted. I pushed my senses farther. The other rooms were empty of life. The elevator down the hall rattled and clicked with its weight and counterweight mechanism.

"Drop your spell." The Jarl made no effort to censor the impatience in his tone.

I focused on the floors above. Two floors up, I caught heartbeats, faint but audible, like a whisper. One was strong and rhythmic, excited. The other crunched. It was as if glass was ground down with each beat, then crystallized again in the heart's refractory period.

Arie shifted closer.

"I cannot drop my spell, until Lukas speaks the safe word." I lied. "When he is here, I'd love to work with you."

"Lukas isn't coming," the Jarl said. "Lukas doesn't work in intelligence, he's not a handler, he's an enforcer. Spies are not given clemency, nor are they allowed bargaining chips—"

"I'm not a spy."

The Jarl stood. "You will drop your spell, Miss. Whether I must strip the Charm from your corpse, I will have your name!"

Electricity sprang from my chest, exploding into an orb around me.

The Jarl flipped from his chair. There was a large ping from the warping metal of his breastplate; then, the heavy desk crushed him.

Arie closed in, his eyes glowing. His punch came so fast; I hadn't seen it until I flinched. His blow glanced off of my ear and tore into the wall. Metal screeched as he retracted his hand.

Ear ringing, I blocked his next blow with my forearm, but the force of his attack threatened to break my remaining functional arm.

"I'm sorry," Arie said.

"No, I am."

His other arm reached for my neck, twinkling with light which would shock me into submission but I sprang and wrapped my legs around his ribcage. My fangs punctured his shoulder. His blood was like swallowing liquid nitrogen, so cold. The sensation numbed my mouth and throat.

His fist collided with my kidney.

There was no electrical pulse like before, only a dull impact, which was soft compared to his last attack. The next hit was feather-light. His blood had no flavor. My mouth was void of sensation. The pull in my belly alone told me I was sucking, and I had lost track of how long.

I tore myself from his shoulder, and the room spun.

The lights spotted my vision neon. I sank to a crouch, and the soft skin of Arie's forearm grazed me, the touch feeling so, so good. He was slumped on the floor, his breathing rapid and shallow.

"Holy shit," he said.

I continued to stroke his arm, and a bluish aura trailed my touch. I giggled. "Why is your blood different?" My hand continued to wander up his thick bicep onto the emblem of his armor. An entwined sea serpent biting its tail writhed and came to life in a glimmer of a rainbow.

He took my wrist. "You smell really good."

I looked down at him, and his heart rate picked up, irregular and weak. My inky lip imprint stood out on his thick creamy shoulder. I shivered. Whispers carried up from the puncture marks, echoing in my head like his blood was goading me back for more.

"What the hell is in your bloodstream?" I asked.

He reached to pull me to him, but I blocked his hand.

"What will your bite do to me?"

My defense reminded me I had a plan. "Nothing it hasn't already." I counted the beats of his heart. He would survive, but I took a lot of blood. Blame it on being impaired or that he was looking at me with puppy eyes I put another lipstick imprint on his forehead.

He sniffed my hair.

I rose, looking for the button to open the door. I stumbled through the steel wall like it was aluminum foil. The screeching of metal was swift but echoed down the hall. Movement stirred on floors above, where I had detected heartbeats before. I looked for the stairs, bounding upward to intercept them before they reached the elevator—except I flew through the ceiling. I leaped again, through the second and third floor, then slid into the hallway.

A figure turned the corner. It was an old woman. Her wrist was slit, and cobalt blue liquid dropped into the floor.

"Agatha!" A woman called.

The old woman's hand glittered when it went to her mouth like she held a handful of tiny stars or diamonds. She chewed, and her skin was coated in blue light like mine. Her figure crystallized, cracking the concrete floor. Her eyes hollowed into black caverns, then filled with light. She charged me.

Be it the substance in my blood or instinct warning me, I turned and ran. The elevator mechanism clicked on its ascent. Its sensor caught my approach and dinged open. I put my fist through the console and grasped the steel line. In an instant, she was almost upon me, and I crushed the counterweight's anchor line.

My back hit the floor. I clung to the steel sides so I wouldn't go through but flattened into the floor with the magnified pull of gravity. Floors flashed by the gaping hole like a movie reel, and I was glad the console was dead, no floor numbers were flashing on the screen. Seconds ticked by. Waiting for the impact with the roof of the shaft brought on adrenaline akin to battle.

The ceiling flew at me.

My arms and legs spread wide, dispersing my weight. I blasted the floor and ceiling with the Light Charm, hoping the counterforce would keep me from crushing to death and ricocheting through the floor and plummeting down the shaft.

I embedded two feet into the elevator frame, the

Light Charm buzzing in a protective coating surrounding me. As I climbed out, the puncturing of metal sounded out like a drum roll in the shaft below. The woman climbed the shaft at rapid speed.

I stepped into the hall and dashed by an aerial view of Greenland. Music thumped from a door down the hall, the drumbeat primal. Mist swirled against the glass, forming ghoulish faces that let out throaty yips as I passed. They trailed outside the seamless windows, following me as I headed to the door, to the din of the party. I entered, disbanding the Charm and handling the door with a paper-light touch.

My blood zinged like the substance within it was the key to entering through the ward in place. The penthouse was packed. Dyad armor was strewn across the floor. Men and women danced, some shirtless, others in plain clothes. A kaleidoscope of rainbows bounced off the mountains, through the panoramic windows, and into my eyes. I stepped into the safety of the crowd.

Agatha's steps softened outside the door, but she did not enter.

For the moment, I found sanctuary.

Colors zipped along my skin. I stepped deeper into the throng and swayed with the drumbeat. I recognized the Sami drum in the music, but the high notes were an instrument foreign to me. Long resonating notes overlaid the music, resounding in my chest. Then an electronic symphony of beats blended with the Viking melody. There were no speakers. The music came from the air itself.

A shirtless Dyad carrying a bottle of vodka bumped into me. He smelled of cherry throat lozenges, which were dropped into his bottle. He rocked with me, touching my hips, and gliding his hands up my sides. My head tilted back with the feel of skin on skin, and he poured some lozenge vodka into my mouth. I stepped away, savoring the fruity burn in my throat.

A circular white leather sofa was at the center of the room. I traced my hands along the men and women who occupied it and joined them. We sat around a coffee table piled with small cobalt shards. They pulsed in the light, and I felt a lure akin to the pull of Arie's blood. *Arie*. He may recover and alert the others.

I gasped and clutched the upholstery beneath me. My head rolled. My awareness shrunk to my immediate vicinity—my hands, my feet, the music. Fear tensed my muscles, shooting me upright. I did not know if the substance in Arie's blood had peaked, or if I would debilitate further. Worse, the hard droplets on the table were whispering, and in my unawareness, I reached for more. I leaned back into the sofa and kept going, going, and going.

I was immersed in darkness. My senses dulled, and in the empty void, only the bond remained. An icy wall swelled and rumbled in my mind like it wanted to dissolve. I shattered it.

My cellphone vibrated in my coat slung across my lap.

I laughed.

My back broke the concrete when I leaped through the floor, and the Light Charm encased me in the elevator, but the fact my crappy cellphone survived seemed ironic and hilarious along with my extortion. I laughed until my eyes watered. *Miruna*. I put a spell on the phone to protect it from damage because my orders were important, as Miruna depended on me. I unzipped my pocket and took out my phone.

Andre texted me. *Where are you? What's wrong?*

I replied slowly. *The belly of the beast. You?*

I'm outside your place.

I laughed. *Well, you won't find me there.*

Where are you?

I felt the presence of eyes upon me, uneasiness in a room of people at ease. *Greenland*, I typed.

His reply was instant. *How bad is it?*

Like Romania, but worse. I wish I had wings. The mountains are so beautiful.

Karolina, get to an isolated room. I'll walk you through what you need to do.

A woman sat down beside me. "Nice phone," she said.

I turned.

Bronwyn smiled at me.

Chapter Nine

"Thanks," I said and positioned myself on the edge of the sofa.

"Are you having fun?" She asked.

Her eyes swirled like the sky outside, but it did not stop me from wanting to pummel her into the floor. She was taller than I remembered, scrawny rather than nimble. Her form had withered to skeletal one instant then filled back out once more. I shook my head.

"Are you okay?" She laughed, and her voice matched the pitch of the music. Hearing the sound of her melodic voice again rolled my stomach. A chorus of murmurs rose from the crystal pills on the table, like they sensed my intent, like they craved the violence brewing inside of me. But survival was my goal. If my odds plummeted then I could consider a final act of revenge, but I'd likely not succeed in a room packed with Dyads.

"I am," I said, "but I think I'm going to be sick. Where's the bathroom?"

"The main one is over there." She took a sip of her drink and pointed, "but you can use mine."

So, this was her penthouse, her party. I was not surprised she had schemed her way to the proverbial top. Sitting next to me, she looked like a partying university student. Why sell out your own? To what purpose?

"That's a very interesting phone you have," she said.

My phone. She knew I was a Russian Spy. She knew how Kazimir's enterprise was operated, and likely Loukin's.

"I'll be back." I rose and stumbled sideways into the coffee table, knocking some pills off the table. They jumped and hissed along the floor. I stepped back, and it felt like I was floating in midair.

"I'll help you," she said.

I made it around the sofa before she closed the distance. She reached for me. My fangs plunged into my tongue. Fire burned in my throat, and I felt my spell swirl around me. Before she could correct the gap in her guard, I thrust my hand into her sternum.

She flew back and shattered a potted plant, wheezing from the blow.

Light flared at the door. The pills on the table disappeared like a blanket of invisibility was yanked across the pile. Lukas and Arie entered the penthouse with an armored unit.

Bronwyn's hands lit up. Rather than a lightning bolt, a circular ring of light raced at me, just like the portal Arie created.

I dashed to the bathroom door, dodging a nearby man. The contents of my unzipped magical pocket spilled into the floor. I looked back as I slammed the door closed and saw my spelled lipstick roll into the ring as it barrelled to me. The enchantment shuddered against the wall, then a blast of lightning splintered a corner of the door.

I threw up the Light Charm in a shield as drum-sized holes were blasted into the drywall. I looked at my phone.

Okay, Andre, type fast.

The crystal light hanging from the ceiling shattered from a bolt and crashed to the floor.

Andre's text glowed as I crouched in the shadow, positioning my shield to the blasts.

Cut your hand and think of me. Think of how I make you feel. Keep the bond lowered. And, Karolina, be honest with yourself.

Six holes blew into the wall at my side. Then an ax. Yet, my fangs hovered at my wrist. Lukas was here. I split my focus, dividing my shield in two. My magic shrank, but I darted to a makeup bag at the sink, plucked a sparkly pink lip-gloss from the bag, and wrote: *Lukas, Bronwyn is a traitor.*

A barb of ice impaled the glass, shattering my canvas.

But the message was still there.

I dropped beside the toilet and bit my wrist. Blood trickled onto my sweater. I thought of Andre, and smoke unfurled around me, creeping up the vanity like a shadowy demon. More gaping faces ghosted at me in wisps. I closed my eyes, and Andre's touch at the hotel grazed across my skin once more.

The noise of splintering wood pulled me back into reality. Metal glistened like falling rain in the light of my magic and the haze of the smoke. *Axes.* The Dyads were chopping their way into the room.

I disappeared into my thoughts, panic numbed by the substance in my system. How did I feel? How did Andre make me feel? Sunshine poured over me in shades of caramel and orange. I knew this dreamscape well. Andre's blue eyes contrasted the red sun reflected on his face. We were back on deck in the Black Sea. Except we were not at sea at all.

Inky-blue waves warped into darkness, swirling around me. The orange sky faded into dead leaves. Then I was falling. My stomach whirled. Twiggy branches flickered by as I plunged toward snow.

I sat on the cool leather passenger's seat of a black SUV.

Andre held my gaze as he squeezed my shoulders. "What happened?"

"I followed a lead," I said and gripped the console dash, not believing the vehicle was real. "I'm high."

"No, it's the magic of the bond, you astral traveled. Between spy partners the bond actually holds benefit."

"No," I said, "I am *really* high." The smooth seat texture changed to the tiny ridges of snakeskin and wreathed underneath me. "I drank Dyad blood!"

"They have blood, Karolina, like we all do."

"No!" I grabbed his collar. "There is a substance in their bloodstream. They were partying, but I think they were all hopped up on these shards of…I think it's blood, alien blood. The alien's blood sounds like crystal, like glass in the vein, and she glowed blue like the shards. There was a coffee table full of them at Bronwyn's party, and they whispered to me!"

He shoved his forearm into my mouth. "Drink, then talk."

I bit and expected yet another shift in my reality, but with his blood, my vampiric acuity resurfaced. The coolness in my mouth dissolved. The warmth of Andre's blood ran over my tongue, its sweet flavor awakening my taste buds. I pulled back before my hand slipped farther up his arm.

The tree branches behind his window were bare and snow-covered, but I recognized the pattern. I turned my head. The wooden sign engraved with *Dalca* still stood beside the cobblestone walkway Mama and I made, but it led to a charred crater. Timber beams were reduced to coal piled atop the rubble. Foot traffic had cleared a path where Mama's body was extracted.

"Why are we here?" I asked. "You said you were outside my place."

Andre bit into a blood bag.

I waited and stared out the window. My breath fogged the glass, blotching out the wreckage.

"I am outside your place," he said. "When you left, I had a feeling you would be following a lead."

I shook my head. "You saw I went through your bag, and you trailed me."

"I lost track of you at the Charmed store in town. The owner's security system almost wiped my memory when I approached. I figured this may be one of the places you would visit after."

So, he did not know about my visit to the pawnshop.

I faced him. "Why would I want to come here, huh? To be reminded of the awful way my mother died?"

He sat back. "I guess I thought you might be looking for closure."

"I'm not."

"Okay," he said. "Tell me what happened."

"Everything I said was true, minus the pills whispering, probably."

His eyebrows rose. "Aliens?"

"You said before you didn't trust the Dyads' 'rah-

rah cheerleader crap.' Well, you're right, at least to some degree. I was abducted while following a lead, and I accidently encountered a woman with bizarre blood. I could hear her blood crunching in the vein. I think her blood is fed to Dyads, but it's a secret." I explained Bronwyn's party, her wards, and how the pills disappeared when Lukas entered. "Also, when the woman pursued me, she didn't enter the party, which made me think she wanted to remain undetected."

"Woman or alien?"

I shifted. *Agatha, she'd been called Agatha.* "She was an old woman, who ate…" I did not want to share the connection to diamonds. "She transformed into a crystalized being of sorts. But before that I bit a Dyad *Drotten*, and the substance in his blood *felt* like it had come from her."

"Which *Drotten*?"

"His name was Arie."

"That's not good. He's one of their lead strategists and the head of special operatives. If you encountered him, you intersected one of his assignments." Andre sighed and brushed back his hair. "Okay, so you are telling me there is an alien at Dyad headquarters whose blood turns into pills that get you high."

"And give you strength, stronger-than-a-werewolf type strength."

"Which get you high and give you powers, and you know this because you managed to bite Arie?"

My breath hitched. "Yes."

"Yes?"

"Yes. I know it sounds like I was drugged, but I was not. I bit Arie in the midst of battle, and substance in his blood intoxicated me and made me hallucinate. Luckily, he'd never experienced the euphoria of a vampire bite before."

Andre snorted. "How do you know that?"

"Because he was...cute...and kind of scared but wanted me to bite him again."

Andre's amusement vanished.

"The thing is," I continued. "Judging by his fear of vampire euphoria, I don't think he would have knowingly consumed the shards if he knew what they were. The woman wanted to remain hidden from those in the party. The Dyads could be drugging their operatives and select groups of enforcers against their will. Which means the shards may not affect Dyads the same way they affected me."

"Walk me through your first encounter with Arie?"

This was tricky. I already mentioned my abduction, but I would not mention the pawnshop or that Canadian diamond mines were keywords to Dyad trigger traps. I paraphrased what happened sensibly. Now that the shock had worn off, I relayed the details I was willing to share.

Andre ran his hands down his face, then gripped the steering wheel. "You're still not trusting me, Karolina."

"Yes, I would have the IQ of a rock if I did, Andre. You tricked me into drinking your blood which resulted in a vampiric *marriage*. You tried to lure me into losing a piece of my *soul*. What did you think? Because of the bond and my new occupation, I would comply with telling you everything when you asked it? Maybe even open my legs for you too?"

He laughed, looking like I had struck him. "Oh, you've had me wrapped between your legs long before we bonded, just after we met in fact."

At the University of Carlton dorms. I shoved the recollection away before it could form.

"Yeah?" I pressed my face into his comfort zone. "Then get my legs the hell out of here, and you won't have to see me again."

"You'll have to see me again, Karolina." He didn't lower his gaze, but it softened, and for once, he seemed his age, all ninety years of it. "I didn't plan on tricking you into bonding," he continued, "*you* tricked *me* and then poisoned yourself when you rummaged through my things. The opportunity for a blood exchange presented itself, and I took it. I'm not proud of how we bonded, but I did not plan it."

I strained to ignore the warmth surrounding me through the bond, making my voice drop to a whisper. "Your opportunistic streak continued, Andre."

"I can explain my actions with Loukin if you let me. I've been scheming, and I think you will approve."

"Just get me away from the cremation site of my dead mom."

Silence ensued as Andre reversed out of our driveway. It was a long and daunting view of what once was, but the tears in my eyes kept the details blurred.

"Where should I take you?" he asked.

"Roman's."

****

The drive was peaceful and offered me quiet reflection. Andre was correct in the sense I had no closure, at least not until I visited Mama's grave, and it still wasn't enough. Had he followed me to the graveyard? Had he seen me cry? My eyes burned and welled up again at the thought, at the vulnerability on display. I continued to stare out the window and saw where the woods diverged for an old storm drain. Roman's house was ahead.

"Pull over here, please," I said.

We cruised to a halt at the edge of the road.

"You can't make it through life numbing, Karolina. At least, not a vampiric life. When you numb, you block out the positive experiences too, and it's feeling the good which makes surviving the bad worthwhile."

His hand stroked mine, and his touch was a sensation I wanted to fall into. I wanted it to envelope me. I wanted to lean into him and breathe in his musky, sweet scent. His affection seized me through the bond, and my toes curled. I squirmed under the heavy, warm weight of his empathy.

"I will prove myself to you and we will be free," he said, "you just have to trust in us."

I was out and into the woods before he could talk of 'us' any further.

A twig scratched my cheek, and the sting of the wound sweetened the sense of being alive. The chorus of forest life chirped in the rustle of ice-covered trees. I broke into a run, heading down a woodland trail familiar from my childhood. I was here. I could feel. But not with Andre. My stomach swirled when I thought of his name. *He can't be trusted*, I reminded myself and pushed my run farther. I slammed the bond into place. Then trembled as I slowed and emerged into the clearing where the Lupei house sat.

I approached the backyard, taking in the expanse of the land and, in the distance, the flagstone walkway leading to the patio lined with Mrs. Lupei's prized roses. When I arrived, I noticed the rot of the dead rosebuds seeped down the stems and into the hardwood above the root bulbs. They were not trimmed and winterized for the frost. The neglect gave the stone-and-timber home a strange feeling. Like it was cloaked in more shadow than usual, kissed by the hint of decay. But the back patio was neatly swept, ready for any snowy backyard function.

I tried the glass slider on the far side; it was unlocked, as always. I slipped inside and found the great room warm and quiet. Sunbeams drifted across the southern sky, sprinkling the room with the twinkle of dust in the air—the accumulation of dust, another rarity.

"Hello," I called. I removed my boots and was puzzled at the continued silence. "Hello?" The nearby office was empty, so I proceeded to the base of the stairs. "Mr. and Mrs. Lupei!"

When there was still no response, I headed into the kitchen. The white marble counters of the double island were glistening clean, but no fresh-baked cookies were laid out. Coffee was there for the grinding, but I opted for the raspberry tea Mrs. Lupei and I always drank together. To sit down with her now would feel like gaining a piece of Mama back, and I still hadn't thanked her for Mama's funeral.

I made a pot of tea and poured a cup. On my way back into the great room, I tried a cookie I foraged from a container in the cupboard, but it was stale. I sat down on the long squishy sectional, and the scent of coffee drifted to my nose. A cup of black coffee sat on a side table to my right. I picked the mug up; it was cold, but the scent of honey was present. Roman was here maybe twenty minutes ago. Andre and I would have just missed him on the road.

I called Roman.

His phone rang a few times, then went to voice mail. He was busy or ignoring me. I reached up and pulled a soft blanket made of alpaca fur over myself, the ones many Indigenous Canadians sold at local trading posts. I sipped my tea.

On the coffee table, atop the lower shelf, there were spare photos of Roman and me sticking out from a photo album. I reached for the pictures and disturbed a cloth covering a copper box. It was long and thin, the shape of a safety deposit box one would find in a bank, but Mama's Charmed markings were etched into the shiny copper casing. The corners were blackened, like the magic within had charred the metal. It could not have endured the fire that consumed my home, or else its center wouldn't remain untouched. Did it contain the documents Mama's spirit spoke about? Did the Lupeis try to open it to execute Mama's estate?

I felt with my Charmed senses and confirmed that there was no hostile magic awaiting me as Mama's intent would have secured. I slid the box into my lap, and it opened with ease.

Inside was a copy of Mama's will. I clutched my tea mug, warming my chilled hand. The paper felt feather-light compared to the weight settling in my chest. I made it to the second sentence before I folded the document and slipped it into my coat pocket.

The next note compelled me forward into the fading light. It was handwritten on thick paper, yellowed by time. It was an agreement, not the one Artur spoke about, but one between Mama and a famous Anishinaabe chief.

In exchange for the Dalca's refuge, for as long as it remains undisturbed, by their actions or of a people not our own, Karolina Dalca will return the Blood of the Creator to its rightful owner on her twenty-first birthday.

I triple-checked Mama's signature. What the hell was the Blood of the Creator? She had never mentioned such a thing, and if it had occupied her potion cupboard, it would have perished with the rest of our belongings in the fire. I put the paper in my pocket with Mama's will. Roman's parents would be home soon, and I would have the answers I sought.

The sun's amber-and-scarlet rays slipped into the darkness behind the forest canopy. I finished my tea and lay down on the couch, letting my mind catalog any items that could fit the description within the note. What object was so valuable it could secure my family's protection? Had this agreement not been violated until Bronwyn attacked our home?

The shadows of the forest drifted across the frost-tipped lawn beyond the back patio, sinking into the creeping twilight.

I focused on a three-wicked candle on the coffee table. Then I dropped my guard on the Fire Charm, allowing my magic a fraction of relief. The wicks ignited. The warm glow of the flames illuminated the center of great room, but gusts of wind, the rustle of trees and shadows, bore down on the wall of windows. The cold outside seeped in, crawled through the paths of darkness the light did not touch.

Shadow raced across the patio stones outside, too fast to be tree branches moving in the wind. The room chilled so much that the hairs on my arm stood erect. I lay still, focusing on the window when I caught movement. A black shape edged the windowpane. I focused on the candle flames, picturing their energy source, and imagined them snuffing out.

The room fell into darkness.

The gray-purple hue of twilight bled through the windows. Speckles of snowflakes whirled by, reflecting the silver light of the rising full moon peeking through the trees. I lay still. My pulse beat in my ears, and I awaited another quick blur of darkness. Minutes passed and adrenaline built into a panic attack within my chest.

A long shadow crawled across the glass.

I tensed, wanted to recoil through the sofa.

On all fours, a large, dark figure crept onto the patio.

Chapter Ten

The shadowy form outside the glass slider was more wolf than man. Its smoky outline was akin to dark magic, but the bone-chilling cold that licked my skin screamed a warning that this magic was far more sinister.

I felt with my Charmed senses, to get a sense of which magic was before me, and to discover how the Charm could be manipulated in such a way. Yet, it was void of the Charm, empty like the vast glacial landscape of Canada's northern-most hemisphere. The foreign magic reminded me of the message I witnessed days ago on a gust of wind and forested leaves,—a message that spelled my name. I could not identify the origin of the magic then, and it was just as anonymous now.

My breath fogged in the frigid air.

The phantom snapped its head in my direction.

With my heart pounding as prey ensnared, it took all my control to move painstakingly slow. I slithered back between the arm of the sectional and the side table. Then I retreated into the hallway, keeping the wispy beast in my gaze, unblinking.

Yet, it was gone.

The coldness was suddenly above me, shooting down my spine like a bucket of ice water. I looked up to the thirty-foot ceilings and stepped into the hall.

It followed me.

I paced to the security system and armed Roman's home. As the beast continued to track me into the center of the house, I pulled out my cell and dialed Mrs. Lupei's number from memory. It went straight to voice mail. If the apparition outside could enter, it would have. This meant I was safe inside, but Roman's parents were not safe returning to their home. I crept past the basement door and felt the hum of magic. I placed a hand on the door, and strings of light glowed in the hallway. The door was warded with light magic, similar to Bronwyn's wards in Russia. Perhaps Mrs. Lupei was a far greater practitioner than I knew? Or perhaps Roman had dealt with this new threat before? Had he taken precautions for his family and contracted one of the Charmed to create a magical safety bunker?

I wouldn't confirm either scenario until I spoke to them.

I entered the front hall. In the pitch-black darkness beyond the glass doors ahead, I could sense it watching me. My skin, rather than recoiling in fear like before, now goaded me on toward the stalking predator. There was one way to find out what it wanted.

I sparked the Light Charm in one hand, then used the other to key in the security code and opened the door. The cool night air fell over my shoulders. Dead leaves covered lightly in snow crunched beneath my socked feet, and I silently cursed myself for forgetting Andre's advice regarding my shoes.

My instincts alarmed at the darkness to my left, so that's where I prowled, along the side of the house, just before the corner. I spun.

"Boo." A young man thrust me up against the wall and plunged his fangs into my neck.

My forearm made it to his throat before the euphoria hit me. My back surged into the wall, and my head tilted up into the motion light shining upon us. I hammered my fist into his ribs.

He dropped me.

My vision was spotted from light exposure, but my eyes adjusted quickly, and I watched him stagger back. His pupils dilated to the size of pebbles.

"You've been bad," he said. "You missed your intel deposit. What species did you drink from? And what the fuck have they been taking?"

I went for his wrist to detain him. He evaded me, and I fisted his coat instead, ripping his sleeve clean off. The snake insignia of the *Ispolniteli* slithered on his forearm. He swayed, experiencing what I imagined to be the latent effects of Arie's blood. I expected him to strike again, but he leaped to the woods, blurring out of view with the knowledge of another species in my bloodstream. Perhaps even a species the Canadian government obtained genetic data on linked to payments from Canadian diamond mines.

I charged after him.

If Loukin discovered I was withholding information, my plan would die. Would he hurt Miruna? He promised he would. Adrenaline, the waning substance in my blood, and all my vampiric strength launched me at the vampire's heels. He wasn't used to running in these woods like I was. His senses were sharper, being a full vampire, but he was unaware of the ditch hidden by shrubs before him.

He fell.

I landed on his back, slamming him into the frozen dirt. He moved to roll me off, but I gripped his shoulder and slipped my leg around his other bicep. I hit the ground, spread beneath his back, shoulder to shoulder, immobilizing his arms. A chokehold would have incapacitated him, but I needed him conscious. He whipped his head back to headbutt me, but I was stretched across the broad length of his shoulders and clear of his attack.

He rolled down the valley of the ditch.

I took the impact until a rock struck my spine. My hold jostled.

"Be still! If I wanted you dead, you would be!" I yelled.

He stood, charging backward out of the ditch, and would surely strike a tree; the impact could break my back. I released the Light Charm, and he dropped to his knees. Within seconds of improvisation, I recalled the bonds of the Light and Dark Charm I'd been at the mercy of before. As I pictured them, the electricity which streamed from my hands condensed.

He grunted, and a moan vibrated from him.

Light balled at his hands and feet, and I feared letting the magic flow any longer. I cut the current. We were immersed in the darkness, moonlight, and glow of the bonds. I focused my senses so my eyes would adjust and dropped beside his unmoving body.

His breath fogged the air.

"I had heard you were hot," he said, "but truly I had no idea."

The pun spurred a surprised laugh from me. The vampire could be my age for all I knew, forced into servitude just like Andre or Tod. "Hotter than a live toaster in a tub of gasoline."

He grunted.

I listened to his heartbeat, which was stringy but steady. *Another tank.* "Look," I said, "My feet are freezing, and I know what the *Ispolniteli* mark will do if you talk."

He pressed his lips together and waited.

"I have a proposition for you. I will wipe your memory clean and drop you off at a motel in town. You have to be still while I enter your mind with the Earth Charm." The night air was calm and frigid, unnaturally quiet. I tensed, noting the shadow wolf could still be lurking.

"I'm not saying yes," he said, "but hypothetically, I'd want to pick up a pizza along the way, and you'd be buying."

"I won't say 'deal,' which I think you appreciate," I paused, rearranging my words in my head, "but I'll look forward to heading into Vinny's Pizza tonight. I'm hungry too."

He lay still.

I hovered a hand over the bonds on his legs. Putting more energy into the bonds would strengthen them, so instead, I imagined retracting the magic I'd summoned. Almost at a trickle, the light bonds at his ankles dissolved.

"Can you walk?" I asked.

"Yes."

He rose, took one step, then dropped.

I rushed to his side. The snake was already missing from his tattoo; it burrowed up his arm along his bicep. I scratched at it, trying to block its path, then pushed down on his muscles like a tourniquet.

He gasped like the snake had burrowed deeper.

I held his cheek. "Where are you from? Who can I

contact for you? Where's—"

His eyes fluttered then stopped moving, like they were glued into place, staring over my shoulder. I turned and saw the full moon streaming thick yellowy light on the trees. Branches whipped in the cold wind, filling the forest with movement and emphasizing the lack of motion at my knees.

The vampire's body was still warm beneath my hand, like the remnants of life remained. I didn't have to give up yet. I held my hands above his chest and loosened the Light Charm. Electricity crackled between his chest and my hands. I stopped and waited for a heart rhythm, an inhalation, any sign of life. I breathed into his mouth and zapped him again.

Then again.

When I lost my count, I ceased and folded to the ground. Like a dam broke inside of me, tears flowed down my cheeks. I continued to sob when I found his wallet and cellphone, and I sobbed when I discovered he was American, like Tod. I cried into the earth as I dug a hole for him, and I cried as I positioned one hand on the surface of the dirt for the sunlight to touch in the morning. Tears still dribbled off my chin as I returned the shovel I borrowed from the Lupei's garage.

"Screw this shit!" I threw the shovel, and it clattered across the concrete. Then I collapsed into a ball outside the garage door, my frozen feet tucked beneath me. I took out my phone and dialed Roman. Still no answer. "Fuck this."

I walked back inside the house, disarmed the alarm, and looked through the front hall closet. I needed an object that was Roman's. In the corner, I found his lacrosse stick. *Perfect.* The more the object was used, the stronger the spell's connection. I clutched the worn wood in one hand and summoned the Earth Charm. My feet hummed with the flood of magic, and I channeled it up into the stick.

"Find him," I whispered.

The lacrosse stick lit the room like a giant golden matchstick, pulling me in the direction of the front door. I looked to the key rack. Roman's SUV was in the driveway, so he had driven his company vehicle. Yet, both sets of keys were missing from their hangers. I checked the dish on the front hall table, then opened the other door to the basement movie room. I felt no ward as I went down the stairs but saw the door that connected to the basement cellar sparkled with the same woven strings as the door that connected the cellar to the great room.

I walked to cushy sectional, our usual snuggle spot for movie night. Roman's keys were sticking out of the folds of the couch. On a throw pillow, a sparkly smear caught my eye. I held the cushion, examining what appeared to be lip-gloss. I pulled up my vampiric sense of smell and was punched in the face with the powdery scent of flowers. Mrs. Lupei often offered the cleaning ladies coffee, and I wondered if they had rested down here instead of in the kitchen.

The golden glow flowing around Roman's lacrosse stick started to dim.

I hurried upstairs. The sound of the key in the lock was crisp in the deserted night air. No animals stirred, and the wind ceased. I dialed Mrs. Lupei again as I got into Roman's vehicle but hung up when I received her voice mail.

Shadows crawled across the driveway, spilling into

the lawn.

I threw the SUV into reverse and peeled down the driveway. The vehicle dipped into a ditch, and I fishtailed into the road. I didn't look back. I drove ten kilometers over the speed limit down the dirt road and broke onto the highway. Roman's lacrosse stick hovered at the dash, gaining momentum as I headed southeast. After twenty minutes, the stick nearly impaled my ribcage, slamming into the driver's side door.

Rather than guiding me south to the Lupei's distribution centers in Ottawa and Gatineau, the magical compass pointed at the eastern fork in the highway. Within a few minutes, I entered Québec. The stick struck the dash once more when the car realigned. Roman's family owned an old lumber mill adjacent to a hydroelectric power plant in Waltham, but it shut down when we were children, and I was sure the water table from the underground basin flooded the facility.

Yet, it was where the spell led me.

The moon was almost at peak rise, so the sign on the metal fence gleamed through the windshield. It read: *Ne Pas Entrer*, commanding me to comply. My vehicle rumbled as I held my foot on the brake. The grounds were dark, and the windows were shuttered. I honed my senses in on the building, not picking up any traces of life.

But the lacrosse stick, sure as a compass needle, remained at the dash.

The wind rustled the trees, their whispers trying to taint my thoughts like an insidious force had gathered here. I dialed Roman one last time and hung my head against the wheel when the call clicked over to voice mail.

I backed up.

Then I put the pedal to the floor.

The fence broke like water against a rock.

I skidded in the dirt and gravel, spinning out a few meters from the main entrance. With my adrenal chemistry already pumping, I kicked down the door.

The hall was dark and quiet. A glacial gust of wind barreled at me. I waited for movement, an attack, a heart rhythm, but my only company was a rattling pipe and the occasional rat. Vermin stayed where there was food, then moved on. I focused on my sense of smell and the pungent scent of decay flooded my nose. Not wanting to linger in the stench of death, I followed the direction of the cold air. I crept silently, regaining any disadvantage I created with the fence and door. The Dyad blood I'd consumed was now exhausted. Not wanting to sacrifice my strength for my other senses, I kept my hearing at the level it was. The main processing cavern stretched upward like an ocean of darkness, I proceeded with a fraction of my scotopic vision, avoiding the outline of machinery in the dim hue of the dark. My path narrowed. The darkness stretched on. I felt like I had lost myself in a pitch-black maze when moonlight touched the floor ahead. I braced against the corner, listening to the soft murmur of voices like the buzz of nocturnal insects in the night air.

I peeked around the corner.

The back of the mill was blown open, exposed to the wind hurtling down the inky mouth of Lake Robinson and up over the dam. A blackened circle was carved out of the earth from an explosion which took a half-mile to level with the forest floor. Speckles below moved about; eyes reflected the moon like the sign out front. I channeled my senses to my vision. There were wolves among the people, thousands of them. Far too big to be timber wolves, too grotesque to be considered beautiful.

My encounters with Roman's wolf form were terrifying, and seeing them gathered in masses now, raised the hairs on my skin higher than the rushing wind.

A low growl echoed behind me.

Still as a statue, I shifted my gaze.

Not one, but six werewolves had surrounded me while my senses were redirected. My only escape was down. On the brink of an altercation, it was difficult to move in subtle degrees. My muscles screamed out for movement. To strike or to run.

I inched to the ledge.

The ground below quieted, and I knew the eyes of those who gathered in the crater were stalking my back. My heel shifted off the ledge. I balanced there, planning my drop to the floor underneath.

A wolf, like a silver bullet in the moonlight, launched at my leg.

I dropped and reached for the floor below, but missed. I fell four floors before my fingers caught an edge. My shoulder torqued, and I dangled from one hand. Howls erupted from below, some far too close. Air stirred at my feet with the noise of jaws snapping.

I looked down. I was only three stories above ground. The werewolves streamed into a mound in the darkness, jumping up and biting at my legs.

A reverberating snarl boomed over the land.

In unison, the wolves dropped, hanging their heads

and burying their tails between their legs. They moved forward in a bow, encircling a lone werewolf in a colosseum-wide gathering. The lone wolf reared onto its hind legs, stretching to the night sky. Its eyes glowed an iridescent amber, emphasizing its godly height as if three wolves had forged into one. The grass at its feet emanated swirls of gold like the earth was siphoning energy into the beast. Magic wound around the now towering figure, lighting it like a king among monsters.

Its skin liquified in a change I knew well.

I dropped from the ledge and approached the assembly. The wolves growled at me as I passed, but they remained submissive.

Its grisly form melted away into the silhouette of a man, and Roman's side profile was visible from this distance. He stepped toward me, completely naked, with his jaw and shoulders so tense, he looked ready for battle.

"I thought you were in trouble," I whispered.

"It's okay," he said, then raised his voice louder, projecting. "As my mate, you are welcome here. It's time you were introduced to my pack, as my family."

Howling erupted like a hurricane. The sheer volume and mass of cries were enough to vibrate my bones. I did my best not to flinch or cradle my shoulders, terrified any sign of weakness might spark a chain reaction of hunter and prey.

Roman extended his hand to me. "Do you accept?"

Chapter Eleven

I stopped where I was, my hand outstretched to Roman's. If I rejected his offer of immunity, would his pack attack? Could he keep the werewolves at bay? Roman knew I had bonded with Andre. If I accepted Roman's offer, would I enter another magical pact? Would it override my bond with Andre? The stir of water and wind coiled in the quiet, like tension within a spring.

I took his hand. Then leaned into his chest and stood on my tiptoes. A vampire's senses had inhuman acuity, but I imagined a wolf's hearing was sharper. I lowered my voice to the most inaudible level possible. "No," I whispered.

"She accepts!" Roman shouted.

The choirs of cries smothered my hearing, I gripped Roman's arm, and the light surrounding him enveloped me too. The magic looked like my own version of the Earth Charm, but its texture slugged across my skin like a leech winding around my forearm.

"Meeting adjourned," Roman said.

Bodies rippled into view, and just like that, I was surrounded by thousands of naked men and women. They talked amongst themselves while others remained in wolf form and darted to the woods.

Roman transferred my hand from his arm to his hand, pulling me into the crowd.

"How will they all get home?" I asked.

Roman didn't laugh; his jaw was still taut and pulsing. "They'll shift and run through the woods to wherever they came from."

I thought of the first time I'd met Roman's wolf form. He had been camping in the middle of the backcountry.

Rather than taking me through the mill once more, Roman guided me around it. He faced forward and pulled up me hill like I was on a leash.

"That's enough," I said and yanked my hand from his.

He spun. "How could you embarrass me like this?"

The pink flesh of a naked man emerged from the bushes. "Sire, I brought your truck to the lot, but your other vehicle is here as well."

Roman glared at me. "Can you please drive my company truck, Sébastien?"

A few more gathered with them, and I stepped around Roman's nude minions. Roman followed me into the parking lot.

I wanted until Sébastien drove away. "How did you expect me to get here, if not by driving?" I asked.

He opened the driver's-side door. "Maybe something more befitting of a vampire spy crashing a werewolf gathering where outsiders are slain on sight."

I sat down in the passenger's seat. "Oh, really? I thought that as your mate, I was welcome."

Roman stopped putting the shifter into gear and gripped the steering wheel. "How could you show up here smelling of vampires and Dyads? Smelling of *him*?"

How could I have forgotten to cleanse my scent? I

went too long without refreshing my perfume. I checked my reflection in the mirror; my lipstick had worn off, which meant Roman's whole pack knew my identity, my scent, and the scent of those I'd come into contact with.

"And then tell me *no*?" Roman's knuckles had turned white.

"I told you I needed time," I said, "partly because of my new occupation, yes, but I'm not here on a mission, Roman." I clutched his elbow. "There is a messed-up energy surrounding your house."

He turned to me. "What do you mean?"

"I went by your house. No one was there, but there is a strange entity brewing there, I can't identify the source of its power, but it gives me the creeps, Ro. You need to call your parents."

He took out his phone.

"It looked like a wolf," I continued. "Not like you, or your pack members, but one made of shadow. I think it was hunting, and I felt like it was playing with me."

"No answer." He hung up. "They're out on a date. Let's go check the house out before they get home."

"Your house felt…wrong. Your mom's roses are dead. Aren't your cleaning ladies dusting? When did you reinforce your basement cellar with a ward?" Had it been that long since I'd visited Roman's house? He came to the city for most of our dates, and the few times I came to town, we'd had the house to ourselves. All I wanted to do right now was give Mrs. Lupei a hug.

Roman took my hands into his, stroking my wrist with his thumb. "My parents have been busy helping me with the expansion into Québec. My mother

Charmed the cellar to keep important documents there. Did you hear anything? The furnace has been rattling."

"No." I took a deep breath. "Can you tell your pack I was on a mission for you?"

"You want me to lie for you?"

"I only came here because I feared for your and your family's safety. Otherwise, I would have showered and waited for you at your place."

He leaned back against the seat, holding my hand. Clouds wisped across the moon at its peak; its magnetism had me tracking it across the sky. I closed my eyes. The moonlight felt warm and liquid, pouring over my chest and soothing my heart. Roman's hand felt cold, like a shell, an impression of our connection before. I looked up at him.

His eyes were glowing. "Other Sires have been usurped for less than what you ask, Karo. I cannot look weak. The only way I can protect you—"

"Roman, please," I whispered, "Don't."

"Is for you to accept my offer of mate."

I pulled my hand back but couldn't free it from his grasp.

"It's the only way I can maintain power during the Québec expansion. We can have it all, Karo. You'll lose your vampirism, your fire, but it will pass to our heirs. You'll be everything you ever wanted. Loukin won't be able to use you for your abilities, you'll be free. The only thing you'll have to worry about is our family."

"You're not respecting my answer."

He shook his head. "You're not respecting me. Or the work I have put into us. I can end the torture you're going through. Ana didn't want you to be a spy, she wanted you to grow up happy and free—within my family's protection."

"I…"

I wasn't respecting Roman. Not in the way I should have. I shouldn't have started our relationship on a lie. Roman lied to me during our friendship, and it caused me to run. When we'd returned to one another, I'd continued his pattern. Maintaining the constant deception of my involvement in Loukin's operation was like a peg in a log; one tap with the head of an ax, and it would split in two. I turned cold, shivering in my seat because I knew, though we hadn't left each other yet, it was only a conversation away. We were irreparably split from the moment I chose to live a lie.

"Commit to our future, Karo."

I wanted to. I wanted to be what we were when we were young, a team full of love and security. But now, it was a shallow love because we built our romance on deception.

*And…*Orange and black fluttered across the hood of the car. The fuzzy antennae of a bird-sized moth caught the moonlight. Its wings slowly flattened, illuminating the dark eye-like pattern on its terra-cota wings, reminding me of moth totem folklore.

Repressing one's inner desires.

I had deceived Roman in my heart because I had slept with him when another man broke it.

"I can't commit to our future. Not when we're at odds, and not when I've deceived you. Maybe when this is all resolved, we can rebuild." *But I'll never give up a piece of myself to be your mate.* I wanted to say the words out loud, but I got caught in his honey-brown eyes and in the reminder of all we once were. Like he knew I was on the cusp of actualizing my feelings, he let go of my hand and put the shifter into the correct gear.

"We can talk about it when we're home," he said. He backed up and over a pothole, not paying any care to the creature on the hood. It jostled but stayed with me, bearing down for a windy ride.

"There's a dead body buried on your land, by the way."

Roman didn't seem surprised but tensed as if we'd be attacked as we drove down the highway. "Where?"

"I was flushing out the wolf apparition and one of Loukin's spies took me by surprise."

He relaxed. It was the most honesty I gave him in months.

"I tried to work around his oath to Loukin, but it didn't work. I buried his body with one hand above ground for the sun." I closed my hands in my lap, clutching them. "I'm so sorry I did that on your property." My eyes burned, and I clenched my jaw. I couldn't bear crying again. "I'm so sorry all of this happened." I gasped for air, trying to pull back the tears brimming my eyes.

"I can end all this pain for you, Karo. You won't have to go through this anymore."

"You're not respecting my answer," I said, my voice clipped.

He focused on the road. "We'll talk about it at home."

No. He would not accept my answer. He never would. And this was the problem with Roman. I overrode his sovereignty to save him when we were kids, so it was acceptable for him to do the same to me now. Accepting his form of saving was to strip me of who I was and fit a mold of who he wanted me to be.

"How many times do I have to tell you *no* before you get it?"

He turned to me. "Get what? That you want to throw away our fucking future for the naïve impression of taking a stand? You want to play with the big boys, Karo? You have no protection from my pack. How does that feel? The truth is you fucking need me, and it's about time you respected your position."

The moth let go.

It fluttered up and over the roof, along with my stomach.

In the headlights ahead a cloud hovered, except it was moving, flickering. Thousands of moths flowed up and over the vehicle in the airstream, each one just as beautiful as the first. I clutched the seat, watching the eyes strobe by in a flit of wings. Scarcely able to breathe, I heard the moth totem in my mind, a gentle whisper among the rushing air. *Desire coming to light.*

I was not owning what I wanted. I had not faced it yet.

"Holy shit," Roman whispered.

"Pull over," I said.

In shock, he slowed the car onto the gravel shoulder.

I opened the door, and the moths flowed around the metal, touching down over my shoulders. "You and I are done."

I slammed the door before he could respond and turned to the woods, the moths swarming around me. I dropped the bond and ripped open my palm with a fang. I then thought of Andre. By the time Roman rounded the car, I dissolved into the eclipse of moths.

****

The ether felt warm. Trees in shades of midnight spun around me. My feet dropped into the earth, and I fell. While falling, I was weightless—the experience feeling like an embrace, like hovering in a moment in time. Euphoria gathered around me. My chest ached; my belly clenched. The warmth rose from my toes like a wave, dissolving at my crown.

I dropped into my body, resting upon a cushioned bench. A screen shielded the private booth I occupied from the bar. I recognized the elaborate hotel entryway visible from the door. The bond brought me to the famous historical château, the hotel Andre conned himself into which catered to diplomats.

I felt Andre's presence and spotted him sitting at the bar with his back to me. I trembled. In the afterglow of my travels, my skin tingled along my lower stomach. The want that brewed within me was unsatisfied, and my body goaded me into approaching him. I veered to the door midstep, blocking the bond once more.

Andre didn't turn, but his shoulders tensed. I had no doubt he felt my arrival through our connection, but if he was surprised I returned to Ottawa so soon, he didn't show it. He took a sip of his drink as I left the room.

Then I was in the lobby and out into the crisp night air. The city noises dimmed on the other side of the trails of Parliament Hill, and the damp air quieted further as I passed through the park before my condo. The lobby felt barren as I entered in the dead of night, the solitude suffocating rather than soothing. I rode the elevator up, avoiding my reflection in the doors, and crossed my threshold. When I reached my bedroom, the restraint I had on my emotions broke, and salty liquid rushed down my face.

I dropped stomach first into my bed and gasped, the pain I worked so hard to suppress flowing out. The pain of losing Mama. The sad state of my life. The demise of my relationship with Roman. Time passed slowly. While I cried, my bedside clock clicked over to four thirty. In an hour, my morning alarm would sound, telling me to bottle up this agonizing release to endure another day.

Slippers shuffled along the floor beside me.

My dresser light ticked on, and I turned to see Ina hovering above me. "You cry anymore and your eyes are going to swell shut." She swatted my hand inward and sat down beside me. "What's up?"

"Well," I said, voice hoarse and nose stuffy, "Roman and I broke up, and I really dislike the person I am right now." I summarized what Roman said to me and acknowledged my lies to him.

"I've seen worse."

I laughed. "Not that comforting."

"Well, you have to learn to love yourself, Karo, because if you don't, no one will."

"Yeah, I think I know what the 'no one will' part feels like."

She held my gaze. "Does it hurt?"

"Like a bitch."

"Yeah?"

"Yes," I said, barely able to see her through my puffy eyelids. "Why are you doing this?"

"Think about it, Karolina. Most of your family is gone. In your lifespan, one day, all you care about may disappear. How do you think one finds the strength to continue?"

"They focus on the love they had?"

"To live a life of melancholy and nostalgia? No."

Her point was so depressing that it stifled me.

"You have to love yourself. When you do, you are open to life, to love, to possibilities."

"I can't even think—"

"You'll meet new people, Karolina. You think you'll go a thousand years without friendships and love? If so, you'd die of a broken heart long before you approached middle age."

I opened my mouth to speak, but Ina cut me off again.

"What if you had a child? With a few hundred years of sex, it's a very real possibility."

I laughed, but it was more of a wheeze.

"Vampire children may only happen a few times in a lifetime, but they *do* happen. How do you give endless support and guidance to a child if you haven't been able to give this to yourself?"

"I don't know."

She rose. "You won't be a spy forever, no one is. They die or they retire. Forgive yourself for the mistakes you've made. You don't want to take them to your grave, and you don't want them to haunt your life. If you were a shit person with Roman, own it, and most importantly *grow* from it. Only a fool repeats the same mistakes twice."

"You're right."

"Of course, and that goes for him too. If he continues to act a fool, your disconnection will allow you both the opportunity for growth." She took my hand and squeezed it. "But he may never grow, Karolina."

"I'm done denying what I want, and it's not him."

"What do you want?"

My mind went blank as if a reset button was pressed, like it couldn't fit any more emotion or contemplation in my brain.

"Do you want to blow off class today and have a girls' day?" I asked.

Ina looked down at me, cocking a hip out, but her face told me she was considering my request. "My next assignment is due in two weeks. You've caught me at a good time." She smiled. "Where are we going?"

I wiped the tears from my face, pulled off my sweater, and headed to the closet. "Anywhere but here."

Chapter Twelve

Ina approached my vehicle ten minutes after I left our condo, a new record for her morning routine. She opened the door and sat down, her wet hair smelling of flowers.

"Dare I say you are excited?" I said.

"I even packed snacks."

I backed out of my parking spot. "Why don't you give mine to me now, then the rest of today will be my treat."

"I thought you didn't like leaving paper trail for Loukin?"

I laughed. "Open the glove box."

She did, and stacks of money thumped onto the floor mat, one clipping her ankle. "Ouch!"

"You okay?"

"Yeah," she said, rubbing the welt.

I frowned. "Sorry. We should probably buy you some hiking boots."

Ina handed me a granola bar with the package half unwrapped so it would catch the crumbs. "Is hiking our activity today? I'm more of a lounge-around-a-pool type of girl."

"You'll have the best of both worlds, I promise."

Once clear of the city and the surrounding suburbia, the highway became encased by the woods. Each hill we peaked and coasted down brought new awe from Ina. At the fifth hill, I turned on the radio to tune her out. Halfway through our drive, she settled into silent wonder, and I didn't blame her. The first layer of frost on the city was ugly, the maple trees stripped of their leaves, frozen rain leaching into concrete. But as we ventured north, the temperature dropped, and snow-dusted pines dominated the land, green, vibrant, defiant, and energizing.

Ina rolled down her window. "Why do the shaggy ones all point in the same direction?"

"White pines always point east." The rushing air smelled of cold, crisp, wet earth with a hint of baked dough and sugar.

"You're making that up."

I slowed down, scanning the side of the road for an opening. "Something to do with the wind, or maybe the rising sun." Gravel spanned a short strip ahead. I braked hard and swerved up the driveway. We passed a brightly colored sign, and Ina raised a brow.

"You'll love it," I said.

We walked up to a trading post, but just before the door, we passed a food truck. The sweet scent of baked dough wafted out, misty in the cool air, the fryer crackling inside.

"Ever had a beaver tail?"

Ina stepped beside me, snow crunching underfoot. "Not unless I want to gain five pounds."

"Where we're going, you'll burn it off in five minutes." I turned to the truck's order window. "Two, please."

I opted for classic cinnamon sugar, and Ina selected the same piled high with Nutella, banana, and whipped cream. She juggled her purse in one hand and the onslaught of carbs and fat in the other. We entered the exchange—the room smelled of freshly cleaned carpet and pine timber. Ina glided to a table of moccasins as the door jingled closed behind us.

There was no ward, at least not one which I could detect, guarding the building. Those who owned and worked in the shop were regular civilians.

"The quality is amazing," Ina said and stroked the rabbit lining with her purse hand.

"Sure is."

"I feel bad for the rabbit, though."

"I do too, but I also think it's more environmentally friendly than plastics."

"Still, poor rabbit."

"Yeah..." My chest ached with guilt. Ina wasn't aware of my favorite non-human blood source prior to vampire blood.

We drifted to the next table, which held stacks of woven blankets in intricate patterns and colors. One blanket was spread out over the others. Its threads were in shades of black and purple, fading to a silvery shade of mauve, only to burst into a buttermilk yellow at the center. The three phases of the moon were outlined in black and white against the starburst, along with three female figures. One, slender, danced beside the waxing moon. The other, full and pregnant, stood against the full moon. Lastly, a third woman with a hunched back kneeled before the waning moon.

"The maiden, the mother, the crone," the trading post cashier said as she approached. "Beautiful, isn't it?"

"Gorgeous," Ina said.

I nodded in agreement, still taking in the simplicity

of the concept. As predictable as the womanly progression was, it still felt transformative and powerful like the wisdom of each phase gained momentum for the other,

"It's made of alpaca fleece," the cashier said. "No harming of animals, just a haircut, and they are on their way."

"Alpacas aren't local to the area, are they?" Ina asked.

She laughed. "No. Farmers brought alpacas to Ontario in the nineteen eighties. My family just chose to adapt while keeping our traditions." She turned to me. "But we're not the only ones to change after tragedy."

I backed away. "You sell the goods from the surrounding area, no?"

"Yes, we all work together; there is strength in numbers, and this is how we prosper."

Maybe I received too much cryptic advice in the past few days, and maybe she was just being friendly because we were all close in age, but I felt uneasy. It felt like a setup, as if the conversation was forced. Yet, the cashier didn't have a hint of a threat, and the whole shop was void of any magic I could detect.

But I'd learned to trust my gut.

"Can we grab a pair of the hiking boots behind the cash register?" I glanced at Ina. "What's your size?"

"Nine and a half," she said while she flipped through the blankets one-handed.

"I think you've reached Amazonian status at your size." I took her dessert and placed it on the counter with mine while I paid.

"Yeah?" she asked, her eyes alight and playful.

"Then, I want two of these blankets, one per foot."

I smiled, despite my uneasiness. "Badass."

"Alrighty," the cashier said.

As I took out my money, I turned back to the blankets. "Can I add in the moon blanket too?"

"Sure."

We said our thanks and left. The sun still hung low in the eastern sky, but its bright rays beamed down unfiltered by any clouds. Swaths of light made the snow sparkle between the gaps in the trees as we continued north. It was perfect conditions for winter hiking, but saying so felt like a jinx. Only when we passed the sign that read *Algonquin*, and I was sure the perfect weather would last, I told her so.

"Alright, so I've highlighted our route here."

Ina duplicated my line on her copy of the map. "This is your idea of fun?"

"Trust me, you're going to love the surprise at the end, and if we leave right now," I tugged the map from her hand, "We'll be there for lunch."

She leaned against the hood. "It's going to be a long three hours."

"Four," I corrected her.

The trails were wide and worn, but where we headed soon narrowed into rooted footpaths. Crisp, slick snow remained undisturbed, except for the occasional chipmunk footprint. I plowed ahead, carving out spots for Ina to step. The further into the woods, the quieter it became. The density of the snow in the trees buffered the woodland sounds, except for the crunch of our steps.

Instead of the quiet feeling suffocating, as it did in my condo, it felt like a cocoon over my aching chest. I breathed with a peace I hadn't found since my last hike. I was a different person then. Though I may be broken now, I'm far more real. I'd lived in a reality that was contrived for too long, and the future Roman offered was another attempt to cloister me.

But Roman's proposition was more insidious than Mama's white lies. I couldn't imagine stripping myself of my powers; they were just as much a part of me as my autonomy was. I wasn't going to play house with a partner who wanted me to *know my place*.

Roman's actions felt surreal.

Our moment in the car felt like I was watching it from my bed, like I was caught between a dream and waking. I felt as though I was watching the scene unfold, detached from what was too painful to bear.

But the moths were real.

Roman's words were real.

And so were Andre's. *You'll have to see me again, Karolina.* I could imagine the smug look on his face from staring at the back of his head at the bar. Through the bond or my dreams, I couldn't evade him. I wanted to loathe him for it. Animosity boiled under my skin. Yet it soothed when I saw him, then stoked when he looked at me, stoked when he touched me, and stoked when I wanted him to touch me. *What do I want?*

A twig snapped.

I looked back to Ina, who lagged meters behind me and toppled into a thicket.

"You, okay?" I doubled back.

Ina rose. "You looked like you were walking off some serious angst."

"Sorry," I rubbed snow off her elbow, "At least I'm transparent to one person."

Ina laughed and took the lead. "You're likely transparent to Andre too. One thing I know from being around him is that perception is a talent of his."

"He's older than us, wisdom is his advantage."

"Yes, and his looks can fool people into thinking he's less experienced, because he certainly knows how to get what he wants."

"That, I know."

"But," Ina paused, "he has a kind side. He always protected the staff from other vampire spies when he could, like you did for me."

I combated the glimpses of his soft side from resurfacing. The qualities Ina was hinting at blurred the indignity I felt. The more aspects of his personality I discovered, the more the barrier between us dissolved.

Ina glanced sideways at me during my delay, and my hesitation stretched on during our ascent uphill. We were both sweating now despite the cold.

"How do you feel about Roman now that you've vented, and cried all night?"

We reached the top of the rocky outcropping. The canopy opened, revealing a steaming lake. A geyser boiled up from the center, turning the lake topaz blue, leaving an icy brim along the shoreline. Condensation wafted among the trees, sparkling in patches of light.

Ina stopped beside me. We both gazed at the view.

"I think Roman and I don't know each other anymore."

Ina sat down on a fallen log. "Does this mean you want to fix things, or you want to move on?"

I thought of his words and how trapped they made me feel. He treated me like I was lesser because my wants weren't as important as his. His wishes consisted of me living in a paradigm that wasn't real, a contrived version of his utopia, and he wasn't afraid of bullying me into submission.

"I think we can only be ourselves separately now." The words, spoken aloud, cracked what commitment I had left to Roman. My eyes watered. "It really is unfortunate."

Ina took my hand. We descended the hill, letting the bubbling water fill the gap in our conversation. I closed my eyes and absorbed the surrounding sounds. For a moment, I let the peace fill the hole inside of me I'd just created, but it was superficial because there was no bottom to a void.

"It's eleven," Ina said. "We almost missed the moment of silence."

I forgot today was Remembrance Day. War brings loss, which has a rippling effect that changes all it touches. Ina was right. I had to love myself; doing so was the only way to close the chasms that heartbreak and loss carved out of me.

But it was easier imagined than done.

I stared out at the water. Just because a task was hard did not mean I wouldn't try. I made a habit of attempting impossible tasks as of late; this was a simple addition. Isolating myself from my emotions was a defense mechanism, a temporary fix, but it only hurt me in the long run. It was hurting me now. I didn't want to be unfeeling, and fighting how I felt only made the pain worse.

Acceptance and love. It was worth trying. Mama's message from the grave came back to me: *One's child is the great treasure one will ever admire but never own. You are the part of me that transcends time and carries my love with it. I lived a good life, Karolina. It's your turn to find love and purpose.*

I'll try Mama, I thought, *starting now.*

A gale barreled across the lake, billowing the mist, which reminded me of Greenland. The trees along the shoreline rustled like a heavy object was carried in on the breeze. My senses enlivened like my body perceived a threat before I was alerted to its presence.

"Ina." I stepped between her and the woods. "Stand back."

Shadows swirled within the depths of the trees. Mist blew a light screen across the area, but movement stirred beyond. A tall, dark figure stepped from the tree line.

Ina placed a hand on my shoulder. "You made it," she said and stepped forward.

It was Ben, the gentleman I met in the elevator on his way to the Anishinaabe water protection meeting held in my condo sky lounge.

Ina approached him in a hug, and he wrapped his arms around her, kissing her forehead. She turned to me. "I hope you don't mind, I asked Ben to meet us here after he was done with work."

"I was taking some samples nearby and thought I would try to catch you ladies. Karolina, right?" Ben stretched his hand out to me. "Nice to formally meet you, banter aside."

"Nice to meet you too," I said. "How did you find us?" I shook his hand. He had a firm grip, not too tight. Within our moment of touch, I summoned my Charmed senses further. Rather than feeling the touch of magic within him, there was an absence of it, like a hole drawing the flow of energy. I released his hand.

"I sent him a picture of our map," Ina said.

The mist retreated, and I shielded my eyes from the sun. "The more the merrier."

"Actually," Ben said. "I still have a few more samples to collect. I'll leave you ladies to the rest of your day."

I was going to grill Ina when I had her alone. Ina never talked about men, so if she had invited him, he was special. Did they know each other prior to my introduction to Ben on the elevator? If not, their connection was just blossoming. Though Ben's touch was foreign to me, it was not an indication of a threat. He was just an unknown and was as magical as the trading post we'd entered…or the message of leaves I'd received a week ago.

"Why don't you join us for lunch in a few hours?" I asked.

"Really?" Ina asked, eyeing my expression for signs of falsehood.

"Of course," I said. "We'll be at the main hotel, in the spa."

Ina's face lit up.

"Oh, nice, girl time," Ben said. "Okay, I'll see you two for lunch."

Ina and Ben parted, and we set out on a western trail. When we had hiked a few minutes out of human earshot, Ina took me by the elbow. "You didn't have to invite him to lunch," she said. "I just wanted him to pop by and say hi."

Within the supernatural hearing range, I still had to filter my thoughts. "Honestly, it's great you like him. I'm happy to have lunch with you guys; you and I have chatted, and I've had my time to think. Getting to know

Ben as your friend is a welcome change." I spoke true to my feelings, but I didn't yet give up on trying to deduce if Ben was a threat.

"Really? That's sweet, Karo. Though, I know you will secretly investigate him."

I laughed. "True. But you're a good judge of character." She was, truly. My suspicions were a precaution that a spy depended on for survival, and I'd already made mistakes I couldn't afford.

We reached the hotel before the sun was directly above us. With the knowledge of a spa ahead, Ina hiked at double speed and bounded up the steps of the building only to sit and wait in dirty boots. Chimes played in the lobby, the music a mix nature sounds and peaceful rhythm.

A staff member entered with two robes and slippers.

We followed her through the hall into the cucumber-scented changing rooms, and we soon sat in the waiting area, sipping lemon water and skimming a treatment brochure.

"Sixty-minute relaxation massage," I said. "Do you think I can get three?"

"Not unless the masseuse wants her hands to fall off." Ina peeked over the paper in her hand. "When was the last time you had a facial?"

"Never."

Ina's smile turned wolfish. "I'll teach you how to spend money."

"We have to be on time for Ben."

She topped up her glass from the pitcher on the side table.

"He can wait."

My face was scrubbed, slathered, and soothed, but it was the head massage that plunged me into tranquility. I maybe even groaned. I lay on the table conscious but sleepy, submitted to bliss and repetition. My Charmed senses swirled within me, not raging to be let loose, but in a uniformed flow, like my magic was once again realigned in synchronicity. I relished the feeling.

A bell dinged.

"Flip," the lady above me said. She left the room, and another woman entered, smothering warm, sweetgrass-scented oil on my back. She smoothed the knots between my shoulder blades, and my magic ebbed and rolled with each stoke. I sank deeper into my restful state. My tensions and anxieties, along with my fears, drifted away. Yet, within my serenity, I felt a distant, nagging feeling. In the darkness of my closed eyes, I reached out with my senses into a vast lacuna. A beacon lured me deeper into the abyss, and as I approached, I sensed Andre.

He was worrying.

If I could have laughed, I would. *What did he worry about?* Joyous energy bubbled from me, disturbing Andre, casting his worries aside. Meeting me in thought, he absorbed the waves of energy I released, then oozed his own. Concern flooded me, warm like an embrace or a plunge into hot water. Thoughts broke into mine like clips of a movie. *Me*. Andre was thinking of me. Dread took him; he was worried about me. Angst plunged into my chest and seized my heart. I floated into him, releasing a piece of myself, and the peace I'd found at the lake. The peace I found within myself now. The fear released me, but Andre's spirit didn't. We held each other, drifting; there was only our warmth and the quiet unconsciousness.

A bell dinged again.

Our masseuses gave us instructions and left the room.

"You fell asleep," Ina said on the massage table beside me.

My cheeks were flaming hot. I flipped over and stared at the ceiling. "Yeah, I did."

"Well, you're going to hate me for the next treatment." Ina slipped out of the blankets and into her robe and slippers.

"I've seen worse villains."

"Not like this."

****

Whoever invented waxing was a pure sadist. It seemed counterintuitive to engage in such an act after hours of relaxation. It ripped away the façade of security I'd achieved and restored me to my awful state of hypervigilance, which was my best chance of survival.

We sat down at our reserved table for lunch thirty minutes late. The dining room was filled with light. The timber ceiling came to a peak at the south, allowing a wall of windows to capture the warm afternoon sun. The scent of cedar drifted from the table centerpieces, a lit candle surrounded by evergreen. Ben didn't say a word about our lateness and greeted Ina in the same warm fashion I'd witnessed in the woods. Ina and I exchanged a guilty glance.

Ben laughed. "You can't be the best of the good-bad girls if you're not late for lunch once in a while."

"Just keeping the element of surprise," Ina said

after I explained the reference. "Won't happen again."

Our waitress cleared her throat, and it almost seemed in disapproval of Ina. She bore such a striking resemblance to Ben that I looked at him and expected him to introduce her as his sister. But he didn't. I reached out with my senses and knocked a napkin off the table, letting my arm graze hers to pick it up. I felt the same sensation I felt with Ben.

Either my magic was changing, or there were types of humans I didn't understand yet.

We ordered three plates of smoked salmon with poached eggs, a fruit plate, salad, quiche, and reuben sandwiches with extra sauerkraut. Ben brought his appetite to the table, making me feel comfortable in his company. Ina, who was usually dainty around men, was her ravenous self, which meant she had no pretense with Ben.

A tall blond entered the dining room. He was dressed in the same uniform as the dining room staff but didn't attend to any guests or enter the kitchen. He walked toward us.

The wards. There were no wards here. There were no wards at the trading post. I hadn't felt a ward since we'd entered northern Ontario. Algonquin Park served as the boundary line between southern and northern Ontario, and the absence of the magical shields lured me into a false sense of security.

I braced for a magical assault.

The man bent down to my ear. His voice was less than a whisper, confirming he wasn't human. "You're late for a date. You didn't check your messages, and now your dance partner is dancing alone."

I had not checked my answering machine since my

last mission, and I'd turned my cellphone off. My absence was noted, and it seemed Andre carried on without me.

"Show me your forearm," I whispered back, almost inaudible. Ina and Ben looked at us. Ina assessed my face but she carried on their conversation without alarm.

He slid his sleeve up a fraction of an inch, and the tip of the *Ispolniteli* insignia peeked out. "I'm here to escort you to your next mission."

"And if I choose to stay?"

"It would be fatal to both of us to have an altercation in this neutral territory."

Cryptic. My mother's treaty flashed into my mind. Then the body of the last spy who died in my hands. I stared into the candle flame and wondered how Loukin tracked me down. If he ordered a tracing spell on me, or if he'd found me through other methods. I looked to Ina; the chain of her golden paperclip was visible around the neck of her blouse. It was hard to place my trust in a trinket.

My belly dropped to the floor, and I jerked in my chair. *Andre*. He smashed through the wall between our bond. Pain erupted at my fingernails. Desperation screamed through our connection, and Andre's fear seized me.

Chapter Thirteen

I looked to Ina, and I knew she could see the intensity in my gaze. She had her necklace and spent time with Ben, thus far unscathed. I trusted Ina, which meant I had to trust her judgment.

"I'm sorry, I have to go. It was nice seeing you, Ben." I scooped up one last smoked salmon and poached egg on toast on the way to the door, but the flavor was like cardboard in my mouth. My stomach twisted into my throat. *Andre. Andre, Andre.* His name repeated in my head like a mantra.

"I'll drive you to where your partner was abducted," the vampire said in the same low frequency as before. We stepped outside. "They won't expect a second operative to attempt an extraction so close to Smoke's attempt."

My breath hitched. I stopped. The *Ispolniteli* weren't planning on retrieving Andre.

"No," I said.

The vampire turned, but I'd bitten my wrist and dissolved into a wisp before his hand came. Then I was spinning. The earth beneath me felt like it shattered with the ferocity with which I was traveling. Andre's call, the pull of our connection, felt like gravity, like the strings of matter itself. An aerial glimpse of two men standing on either side of a body flashed.

I plummeted onto hard stone.

There was a clatter and crack. Softness gave way beneath me, warm and wet. One man's cracked skull was a foot from my shoulder, pink and splattered. I'd collided with him upon entry. Snapping the Light Charm around me, I rose.

The sterile room smelled of burnt flesh. Andre was screaming. He was flattened bare chested onto a table by a sliver web, just like the hotel, but his eyelids were cut off. His mouth gaped, one fang missing. His fingernails and toenails were removed, pooling blood onto the metal table. A man stood over him with forceps. He looked up at me over Andre's body, and his eyes glowed a blueish-white like Mullins's, except he consciously reached for a blade from the table.

I flashed beside him and drove my Light Charm-coated hand into his ribs, releasing my power. The blow should have electrified him and broken his ribcage.

His blade, glowing like his eyes, plunged to my belly.

I pivoted, uppercutting his jaw. He dropped but used his momentum to roll. He produced a second blade. He stood in sword stance as if he lived in that position like training with those blades was the task he completed all day, every day, since he first drew breath.

I summoned my fire.

He butterflied the blades into the inferno, attempting to lop off both my arms at once. The swords and his body withstood my flames. I dropped to my knees and rolled, but he countered the slashes in the opposite direction within an instant. The tip of a blade caught my flank, and white-hot pain seared through me, like my tolerance for light magic was weakened. The floor cracked under the heat and exposed the earth beneath. *Another basement.* The room was below ground. Smoke cloaked the crown molding and ceiling. I rolled around the table and up the other side.

Extinguishing my fire, I thrust a palm into the metal web pinning Andre, unlatching a corner. The touch of silver blinded my senses, but Andre's whimpers were far more disturbing. My screams joined his for an instant.

Both swords plummeted toward Andre's chest.

I flipped the table, shrieking as I ripped the rest of the webbing off of Andre. The skin of my hands bubbled. Andre fell across my middle, his large body pinning me to the ground.

The man leaped over the table. The magic of his blades swept over his body, making the gleaming edges look like an extension of himself.

I projected a blast of fire with one hand, masking my other. I drove his fallen partner's sword through his chest. He fell forward, his weight adding to Andre's as his blood gushed over me. I struggled to rise, my hands sliding in the warm, sticky mess. My fangs descended; I wanted to feed, but the human piece of me shivered from the spectacle of such gore. I'd just killed two men, but Andre's safety won the war for dominance in my mind. My pulse hammered in my ears as I surveyed his injuries.

Andre stirred, and his fang plunged into the man's ankle.

I focused my senses on the surrounding Victorian doors of this doctor's-office horror scene, listening for heartbeats or approaching footsteps. The rooms attached were empty, but they wouldn't be for long. I heard an alarm sounding in the distance. The building was old, perhaps a historic medical college, before it became an operational base for supernaturals. Footsteps stormed our way.

"Smoke, which way is out?"

"I can activate my home beacon." His voice was hoarse, a weak whisper.

"Do it now."

He reached for me. "Hold my hand."

I gripped his fingers as if he might slip from my grasp, like the feeling of his touch was an illusion. Yet, the panic that seized me since he broke through the bond subsided.

He rubbed a spiral marking on his wrist against his shoulder. Smoke swirled from the symbol, entwining around him, cascading along his arm and around my body. With a crack of violet electricity, we fell.

The toss of the astral travel whipped our bodies apart, save where Andre's fingers turned to steel, but his grip slipped. We collided again, and I clung to his shoulders. We entwined as we spun. I pressed my cheek to his chest, not wanting an inch of separation.

We hit the concrete in a heap. My wind-whipped hair laid limp on Andre's abdomen. We were in an alleyway. Rats scurried from the commotion into the shadows of the garbage. I recognized the sign on the door, a poster for the Wednesday special at the Laff. We were outside the bar's back entrance, halfway between my condo and my secret apartment.

"Some home you have."

Andre struggled to rise. "Never put a home beacon at your place of stay; if you're using it, your identity has likely been made." His wrist was now clear, the magic spent on our travels.

I reached down and heaved him to his feet. He slumped against my shoulder, which was difficult given how short I was. I'd left my bags and purse with Ina, which meant I was without my replacement lipstick. "Do you have enough strength to shield us?"

He nodded, and smoke wafted around us in a cage.

I could walk us to my condo or to my apartment. To invite Andre into my personal life or not? How much trust could I afford?

A man walked by the mouth of the alleyway. With our identity cloaked by Andre's Dark Charm, the smoke pulsated and darkened at the man's presence. He lingered as if sensing the magic around us. If the *Ispolniteli*, or other operatives using the Dark Charm, were combing the streets of our neighborhood, they were watching my condo. It was no secret to Loukin's staff where Ina and I resided, and my recent absence was noted.

If Andre and I remained undetached since our last mission, Loukin might assume we were still attempting the extraction or were held captive. It might buy Miruna time from Loukin's wrath.

"I have a place," I said in the lowest frequency I could manage. I stepped forward, watching my step so as to not disturb the trash. The man who felt our presence still lingered to the right of the alley's mouth. We crept painfully slow, my muscles straining to hold Andre's weight.

Andre didn't speak as I led him down the street. He moved with me, watching the man now at our backs. The dark magic encircling us waxed and waned depending on who appeared on the street. There were far more Dark Charm users than I anticipated, or perhaps operatives were out in force now. What was Andre attempting to extract?

Andre's nose fell to the nape of my neck. "You're brooding," he whispered.

We turned east, blocks away from my apartment. Those who stirred Andre's magic were sparse now. "You have that effect on women."

He breathed a laugh.

When I approached the back entrance of my apartment building, my knees weakened. The slash on my side was a raw, coagulated mess. If my blood had left droplets, it was in the alley with the trash. I'd have to work an obliteration spell to destroy the traces at Andre's drop site. But first, I had to get us upstairs.

I dragged Andre to the door, hoping his spell would work on the security camera. Five flights of stairs remained between us and safety. "Hang onto the handrail," I said and hauled Andre up the steps. An electric stock traveled from my wound up my back. The stairway spun. I looked down at the gash. My skin was milky white and lacerated like it was covered with white mold. My hand flexed and spasmed.

"How far?" Andre asked, his voice barely audible.

"Just help me as much as you can." I summoned all my vampiric strength, holding onto Andre's torso, and bounded up the steps. I made it up two and a half flights before my senses dulled. The more I exerted myself, the more the toxin seeped from my wound. When I stepped onto the fifth floor, I staggered and dropped Andre. *Keys.*

I'd left my belongings with Ina when I went with the *Ispolniteli* operative. It was the type of hasty reaction I thought was behind me now, but Andre had

149

that effect on me. I crouched beside him and looked ahead to my door. There was a brown box.

I dragged him to the doorframe.

The box was addressed to Anne Smith in Ina's handwriting. The wards on my condo were broken, which meant that whoever attempted the break-in was dead, and my spelled message found Ina while she was with Ben. Though I feared Ben might have also seen my message—formed in the dirt with earth magic when Ina's feet touched the ground—I was grateful she wasn't alone.

I plunged my fist into the box.

Ina thought to drop off the belongings I had at Algonquin. Though I often poked fun at her thoroughness, I appreciated it now as I pulled my keys from my purse and opened the door. *How did it get here so quickly?* Then I shoved the package inside. I leaned over Andre and parted the hair from his bloody face. "Please, come in," I said so he could pass through my wards.

"I'm trying."

I sighed, hauling him up, stumbling back, and letting him fall on top of me. His sticky face nuzzled against my neck, but I was coated in enough blood to not care. "Drink," I said.

The wet of his mouth encased my artery. The sting of only one fang came, and I yearned to kill those two men again. Euphoria took me, and I held him against my chest, one hand entwined in his hair. I held off biting him, letting him gather his strength. The toxin depleted any remaining energy in my muscles, but I knew his exposure was far worse than mine. His arm slid down my lower back, then firmly gripped where my thigh met my butt, pressing me into him. The second prick of his fang came.

I gasped, then arched my head to his shoulder and bit.

His sweet flavor never tasted so good. Warm and thick, his caramel blood rolled over my tongue—the salty aftertaste pulling me in for more. I rolled my hips against him, wrapping my legs around his ribcage. His hand slid into my hair at the back of my head. Then I was on top of him, looking into his eyes, which were intensely blue as if he were crying.

I kissed him.

I kissed his nose, his cheeks. I felt the toxin dissipate but held him still, exhausted from the torture of seeing him so mutilated. His lips pillowed along my neck as I let him roam and hold me in kind. Andre kissed me deeply once more. I then fell asleep within the tide of his breath.

****

I awoke to honking on the streets below. The room was dark, but even darker shadows lingered on my walls from my furniture and the city lights beyond. I sat up on Andre, flicked my wrist, and focused my Fire Charm. The clusters of candles speckling my apartment sizzled to life—the room filling with a warm amber glow and the sweet smell of beeswax. I looked down at Andre and saw his eyes were already open, and he was staring up at me.

"I woke up before you," he said.

I slid down on the cool wood floor. "Well, it's not much, but this is my hideout. You and Ina are the two people who know it exists. It's warded with the Earth and Light Charms."

He rolled, popping up from a push-up. Pacing between the living room furniture, he trailed a finger on the colorful fabric, taking in the details. The candles cast shadows on the muscles of his back, then the curve of his lower abs as he walked to the kitchen counter. He lifted the edge of a teacup an inch off of the drying rack, the one I'd drank coffee from the last time I was here. "This reminds me of my mother's china," he said. "The flowers and the pastels." He turned to me. "It's cute."

"Easy now." I rose, meeting him by the table, and stopped, playing with the edge of his jeans. "It feels like home, to me at least."

He took my hand, his light touch making swirls on my palm. "It does."

Trepidation and excitement shot through me, too much to hide. "So," I took my hand from his and placed it on his chest, "that's the world you live in? That's all you have known since you were eight? Working for Loukin, being an *Ispolniteli*?"

"It wasn't all bad when I was young." He smiled, but it didn't touch his eyes. "When I got older, the traveling was glamorous."

"Right before you met me, you were looking for a way out."

"Yes," he said.

I needed to know what Andre was extracting and the details of our latest mission. I hoped the letter hidden in my condo was still secure; it was the link to the transfers from the diamond mines, I was sure, and it was the piece of information neither Andre nor Loukin had. I needed Andre to divulge what he knew and his schemes to free us.

But none of these questions spiked my heart rate.

A request bounced back and forth in my mind, making it impossible to move my gaze from Andre's chest.

"I'm going to take a shower," I said. I rose my gaze to his, then felt ensnared. "Would you like to join me?"

Andre's fingers touched my hips. He smiled, warm and true, touching his forehead to mine. "Very much."

I moved toward the open bathroom door, letting his fingers trail along my pelvis as I walked. He shadowed my movements, meeting me at the sink. He kissed my cheek, gentle, almost polite, but the gesture made my stomach swirl, more so as he lifted the edge of my shirt. The blood-soaked cotton was almost rigid as it rose over my head.

I reached into the shower and turned on the water.

Andre wiped the dried blood off the tops of my breasts, then undid the clasp on my bra. The lace fell away. His lips touched mine, lightly, barely there, a tease. I chased his kiss, but he clutched my breasts. His tongue swirled over my nipple. I gasped. As he did the other, I noticed the room filling with steam. I yanked at his pants, and they dropped around his ankles.

He dropped to his knees, his eyes on my stomach and zipper. He unzipped me, and I shimmied my jeans around the thickness of my hips, trying to speed things along. He clutched my hand, stilling me. Then he kissed my hipbone, sliding my panties down, painstakingly slow. We backed into the shower, and I was shaking with the anticipation I felt earlier, yet tenfold.

Hot water gushed over us, momentarily colored red, then running clear over creamy skin.

He kissed me, light and exploratory, then rolled his

tongue against mine. My pelvis clamped so hard my knees tingled, and I let out the faintest of whimpers.

"Why does it feel this way?" I asked.

"Because it's love."

He plunged his fingers into me, pressing up against my belly. My voice broke into a breathy cry. He continued, and my chest rose in rapid succession, panting. He held my face with his other hand, talking to me, coaxing me into the rapidly building climax. My replies were incoherent. I searched for something to clutch and settled for the shower bar. His next finger stroke tipped the scales, and I buckled.

I rose, kissing his stomach, finding my way to his mouth. He picked me up and carried me into my bedroom. I kissed him as I had in my dreams, but he pushed me down onto the bed, his palm running down my neck. He kissed between my legs, his warm tongue twirling against the cluster of nerves and skin. I arched, "*Fuck.*"

"Mmm." His tongue was so slow and sensuous I let out a number of curses before my body went rigid again. I looked down, his face watery in my glassy vision, but his eyes, blue as ever, kept me fixated. I went mute and shook harder this time, then released.

Before I could recover, both of his hands clutched my hipbones and lifted my hips into the air. He buried himself into me. His hard touch hit the very depth of me. I cried out. Thrusting, he stroked the soft spot at the very back of my vagina. Fluid dripped from me onto the bed. I pulled at my hair, then roamed my hands over my breasts, spreading my legs as far as I could. I tried to meet his thrusts in kind but couldn't with my hips suspended.

He dropped me onto the bed and pulled me above him. I pumped up and down, each drop a hot caress from pelvis to spine. Andre clutched my face in his hands, whispering to me. Every word matched a stroke deep within me. I moaned in reply, my rhythmic breathing robbing me of my voice.

He gripped the hair at the back of my head and thrust rapidly from below. I felt so good; I couldn't move. I couldn't breathe, caught in the suspense of pleasure, I climaxed again, screaming.

Andre smiled, delighting in my cries and complete loss of control. Rising to his knees, he kept my hips pinned against his muscular abdomen. He held me midair by my butt, burrowing his face into my breasts, driving into me with a force that made him groan. His arms wrapped around the curve of my back. I linked my arms around his shoulders, hanging on like we were astral traveling.

"Drop the wall," I cried.

He did.

An explosion of emotion flooded from my chest to my toes. My brow felt like fire. Heat rolled in waves over me. Then love, true, bright, and shining, held me there suspended, floating, in an abyss. Pure joy met me, and it was coming from Andre.

His joy was mine.

And for an instant, it stretched on into infinity.

Chapter Fourteen

The city streets were quiet now, in the deepest hours of the night. The soft cotton sheets and Andre's warmth encased by my duvet made it hard to leave. Yet, I was too sticky with sweat to fall back asleep. I placed a gentle kiss on Andre's bicep and slipped from the sheets.

The floor creaked as I entered the hall, but Andre lay undisturbed. Peaceful. The candles clustered around my apartment were extinguished. I didn't know if the flames had dissipated with the release I experienced or if Andre had blown them out.

The bathroom was dimly lit by the waning moon. I left the light off. A shower would be noisy, so I filled the large clawfoot tub at a low trickle. I lowered myself in, and the water gathered in a hot pool around my ankles.

Apprehension hit me. I gave myself to Andre. I submitted to the bond, to my dreams, and all of the feelings I fought to numb. But I vowed not to numb. *Because numbing is drowning you*, I reminded myself. I took a deep breath and reviewed the facts.

Any operative could obtain the information the government collected on supernatural beings. Why did Loukin need me? The bathwater rose, along with my anxiety. Gerel's words came to mind; *he wants it*. He spoke about my necklace, but what did my ruby offer other than magical immunity? Why not demand my necklace in exchange for Miruna's book? Was he testing the necklace's effects through me? What and who had I been in contact with because of my missions? *A species unknown, strange magic, diamond mines, and Dyads.* The water crept around my collarbones. Strategizing for my freedom seemed hopeless if I was five steps behind. Panic constricted my throat.

Long legs of shadow danced across the water.

I looked to the window above, spotting a black spider descending the windowpane. It reminded me of Mama's tarot reading one evening. A similar spider touched a card—the Devil card, which depicted a couple dancing in chains attached to nothing. Mama said what bound them was the illusion of being trapped.

I felt stuck, but this mindset would keep me entrapped.

I breathed deeply in the warm water. I had confidence in my will; I needed conviction in my decisions. I rejected my feelings for too long, fearing another mistake. It was time to allow my feelings to influence my choices again. If not, the result was impulsivity and less control than what I was desperately clinging to.

The floor creaked again.

Andre crossed the hall into the kitchen.

I reached for the water and turned it off before the tub overflowed. I heard the striking of a match, and the kitchen glowed with soft light at the end of the dusky hall. Andre was puttering around the kitchen. I leaned back and closed my eyes, taking my last few moments of solitude to clear my head.

Andre entered with a wooden tray in his hands. He'd made coffee with my French press, arranged my china cups around a group of candles, and made jam on toast.

I beamed up at him. "Thank you."

He put the tray on the stool adjacent to the tub, then jumped in. Water splashed my face and sloshed onto the floor. He smiled at me from the other end, and I realized the tub was made for two.

"We can't plot our freedom without coffee," he said.

I took the pink teacup into both hands and sipped. It was a perfect cup. I watched Andre over the brim, enjoying the sight of his nakedness in the water and drinking coffee. "I'm surprised you found food at all; I didn't plan on using this place for a while."

"Why? You wanted to stuff more furniture with cash?" He tapped my breast with his foot, and I swatted his ankle. "Your bedroom chairs almost broke my back."

I laughed. "How did you know which room was mine?"

"The pink," he said. "I always knew you were the type of woman who secretly likes pink."

It was true. I sipped my coffee coyly in response. Before I could crawl up his body and kiss him, I refocused on the task at hand. "Okay, are you ready for an interrogation?"

He settled against the edge of the tub with the dainty teacup in hand. "Ready."

"Why did Loukin want me to spark the Dark Charm?"

"Loukin would never share his motives, but

deduction is a powerful thing. He was researching your family's crown jewels, and there was a journal I managed to read about the succession of power bypassing those with the Dark Charm."

"So Loukin doesn't have the Dark Charm and cannot risk sparking it." The way he used others to kill his brothers supported that reasoning. He even used me. I hadn't known at the time how close I'd been to sparking the Dark Charm. I killed Kazimir. I only had to desire the Dark Charm while I did it.

"Correct," Andre said.

"Gerel said Loukin wanted my necklace. Loukin said it was a crown jewel." It wasn't the only time my necklace was coveted. I remembered the pawnshop owner's words before the Dyads abducted me. The jewel I wore was relevant to the area as well. Then there was Mama's deal with the Anishinaabe chief. *Karolina Dalca will return the Blood of the Creator to its rightful owner on her twenty-first birthday.* I may be indebted to yet another person if the blood was destroyed in the house fire, but I was also only nineteen.

"I am assuming he does want your necklace, yes."

I clutched my ruby. "Why did Loukin make me a spy? Surely others could complete these missions. Why not just ask for my necklace in exchange for Miruna's book of light magic?"

"Succession-of-power spells ensure the object be handed over willingly, or bypassed through ineligibility. He cannot blackmail you into giving it up, and you sparked the Light Charm, so you will never bear an *Ispolniteli* mark, which would force you to oblige Loukin's wants. You don't have the Dark

Charm, so the necklace remains yours."

Hurt cut through me. "Did you ever second-guess yourself in your task to influence me to invoke it?"

Andre leaned forward. "There is no world in which I would let you destroy part of yourself, Karolina. I was stalling for time with Loukin. Bond or not, I didn't have to care for you. Those feelings are real. There are vampires who have bonded only to find they hate each other." He laughed, a dark twinkle in his eye. "Some have even offed themselves out of desperation."

The glimmer, his words, made me feel like Andre had contemplated hurting himself in the depths of despair. But before fear churned my stomach further, I reminded myself he was sitting before me. He found resilience and had enough grit to plot and scheme his way to me.

Andre took my hands. "I lost part of myself for so long, and I hadn't even known it was missing until Miruna healed me. I used finding you to my advantage. You bonded with me without knowing the consequences, which changed my position in Loukin's hierarchy. But I told you before, I don't regret bonding with you. I never will."

"Careful, you're close to confessing your love again."

"Definitely," he said. "After eighty years of floating through circumstance, I finally feel present like I'm living my life again."

Part of me wanted to discredit what Andre said in the shower last night *because* it had felt so raw, so real. It felt that way now. I dropped the bond and probed. Warmth, hotter than the water around us, enveloped me. Not only was he genuine, he no longer put a wall between us. When I thought of it, he hadn't since he arrived. *Had he been waiting for me?*

I jostled my teacup into the saucer, then steadied my hand when I placed it down. I didn't block the bond; instead, I curled up on his stomach between his legs and let his arms encase me.

"Why make me a spy?"

"This, I'm still considering. My first thought was the job might break you down. A slow erosion, and the blurring of lines between right and wrong. Again, it's easy for him if you invoke the Dark Charm."

I nodded. "It's an effective strategy. I'm at my breaking point, and it's only been a few months. Your stronger than me to last eighty-three years."

"Wow, you did the math," he said. "The way I see it, you're tougher than me because you won't tolerate it."

"Apparently, I will if I don't find a way out." I didn't focus on what Andre had to endure or how many times he might have been tortured; it was too sickening. Nor did I focus on what I did to save him. I especially didn't focus on the fact if I had not rescued him, he might not have escaped. I clutched his arms.

"Is Loukin trying to test the necklace through me?"

"Yes, that is my second point. I think he might be testing the powers of your necklace through our missions, but in turn, our missions are an indication of what he wants to obtain through your necklace. If we determine what he wants, we can barter our freedom."

Andre wasn't the type to barter with an opponent. Coercing was more his style.

"My necklace offers immunity." I thought of the genetic report on the unknown species I found at *Base*

Franklin, the alien-like species at the Dyad headquarters, and the shards of its blood. I was definitely affected then. So, what didn't affect me? Werewolf magic. *What else?*

"Who were the men who tortured you, and what were you extracting?" I asked.

"They're *Custodes*, supernatural hunters. Their magic should have overwhelmed yours, Karolina. You should have been rendered unconscious."

That's how Andre wound up on the table. My necklace promised me immunity from this other type of magic, yet the Charms I possessed couldn't overwhelm the *Custodes*. "Tell me more."

"The first *Custode* started in Florence. Before the Common Era, a person with the Light Charm transformed into the first *Custode*, and more sprouted up from there. The rumor is *House Custode* is funded by the Medici Bank."

"You had a list in your bag of account transfers between Switzerland and the Medici Bank." *And a Canadian diamond mine*, I thought. "Is the envelope protected in your hotel room?"

"The envelope would be destroyed if my wards were broken."

"I didn't tell you before, the woman, *Agatha*, who I thought looked like an alien, she ate diamonds before she changed."

"If that's true," Andre said. "You may have encountered the hidden plutocrats of supernatural society. It's never been confirmed, but it's suspected those who control the Medici Bank control *House Custode*—and who they hunt. I've been investigating the link between the diamond mines, but I've seen nothing which could confirm a Diamond Eater's existence. So far, they are a rumor, a fairy tale. Are you sure, Karolina?"

His inflection on my name implied he thought that I was really high at the time, and I was. "Is that what they're called? A Diamond Eater? The shards of blue blood came from her, I'm sure, and Bronwyn was feeding the shards like candy to the Dyads at her party." I summarized the contents of the genetic report I'd found on my first mission with Andre.

He quieted, considering my words. Then he lowered his mouth to my temple, where I felt him form a smirk. "That was the letter you had up the back of your shirt."

I fought the urge to turn and kiss him. "What did you attempt to retrieve on your last mission?"

"Loukin's missions are following the diamonds and their connection to House *Custode*. I was extracting a briefcase like Mullins's, but this one held an artifact."

"Where's the artifact now?"

"Back at the *Custode* base in Ottawa."

I wondered if the *Custodes* were the ones who enforced the rules of the underground, the ones Mama had warned me about all those years.

"Are you going to attempt to steal it again?"

"No."

This time I turned up. He caught my lips, stroking my chin as he kissed me. "Why?" I asked.

"Because, little vampy, I took an imprint of it with a reconstruction spell."

****

We washed, had sex, washed again, and were finally getting dressed. A few outfits hung in my closet.

I opted for a burgundy-and-pink patterned shirt with jeans; underneath was a full lace number. The pink was a wordless jest in response to Andre's comment, and the lace was our secret, a memory I'd carried with me from our last journey.

Andre approached from behind, shirtless and wearing the only pair of jeans he had. He slipped his arms around my waist; his jeans were still damp from the washing machine. "You look nice."

"You too," I said. "Nice shirt."

He laughed, his breath hot against the skin of my neck. He rested his head in the crook of my shoulder.

Looking in the mirror, I applied my black lipstick. The familiar tingle of magic was present on my lips. I reached down and absently felt for the textured glass of my perfume bottle. "You may want to stand back."

"Does it smell like you?"

"Yes."

"Then I'll stay where I am."

I sprayed down my clothes with Andre attached, and the scent of sugary licorice, warm spice, and tart cherry cloaked us. "Maybe you could use a little magical fire-retardant."

"Clever."

I turned around, tilting my head up. "I'll collect the letter from my condo as quickly as possible and pick up some supplies on the way home."

"And I'll get started on the reconstruction spell."

Andre told me his clothing size, and I made a mental list of items while I gathered my cell phone from my purse. I slipped it into my pocket and left the remaining belongings from Ina's package on the sofa, then headed to the door.

Andre moved, blurring across the room to meet me there. "I'd say be careful if it wasn't a jinx."

I smiled. "Maybe I should promise I won't?"

He kissed me, filling my mouth with his tongue and sliding his hands around the back of my skull. I cupped his hands in mine. Taking my time, I absorbed each stroke, each press of his lips. When he pulled away, I reluctantly reached for the door.

"See you soon," I said.

Then I was out into the hall before my resolve dissipated. The stairwell was clear, but I summoned my Charmed and vampiric senses to detect the presence of magic or heartbeats. Once I knew what I was walking into, I pulled out my cell phone and checked my messages. My hand tingled from the spells on my cell phone, surveillance by Loukin's operatives in Russia was still blocked on my phone, but the Machine Slag forwarded my coded message from my condo to my cell. I skipped it, not wanting to go through the details of Andre's last mission yet. The next twenty messages were all from Roman.

Cool air froze my breath in my throat as I stepped outside.

I scanned the immediate vacinity My lipstick proved more than proficient at obscuring my identity, but, as of late, I had been introduced to many forms of magic I didn't understand. I walked down the sidewalk, tracking the heartbeats I approached.

My fingers traced the buttons on my cell phone. When I considered how to respond, my mind went blank. After I approached the park outside my condo building, I texted, —*I can't talk yet.*—

My phone vibrated instantly. —*When?*—

Two heartbeats traveled with me as I headed to the lobby doors. I pocketed my phone. I looked like a bystander; how I acted determined if I was a threat. The lobby traffic was sparse, the usual woman at the desk was absent. I boarded the elevator and pressed the button to the sky lounge. At the last ding, two women boarded the elevator with me just before the doors closed. Their forearms were bare, but my spell picked up a tinge of magic at their proximity. If I could sense their magic, they could sense mine. But having the Charm didn't reveal my identity; I was one of many with the Charm in Ottawa.

They got off at my condo floor.

I exited the elevator one floor above, and a quick sweep of my senses confirmed I was alone. I channeled my vampiric agility and crept without sound. Within seconds, I stood on the balcony that hovered above my master bedroom.

The terrace below was empty, and so was the room attached. Gripping the frozen railing, I lowered myself down in the barreling wind. The frost blanketing the balcony patio lay undisturbed on the way to the door. I hovered. The beats I detected were at the front door. The women separated, one entering the elevator again and traveling up to the sky lounge.

I shoved the slider handle. There was a quick pop, and I slid inside.

My bedroom was destroyed. The pillows were torn apart, the contents of my closet scattered on the floor. My drawers were emptied, and the dresser mirror was shattered to reveal the backboard beneath.

But the wooden side of my dresser was not yet smashed.

I crossed the room in calculated steps, leaving the debris undisturbed. The woman at the door didn't stir, but the acuity of her senses was unknown. My heart pulsed in my throat; I outstretched my hands to the wooden siding and gently pulled back the wood, just before its breaking point. The letter was there.

A heartbeat thumped steadily above me.

I slid the letter out from the crevice.

The beat at the front door blinked off my radar. Then my bedroom door blew from the hinges. The woman soared toward me, eyes glowing like the *Custode* I slew.

I bit my wrist.

Glass shattered behind me.

I dodged a blade gliding toward my collarbone, sensing a swift strike fishtailing at my back. A glowing sword cut through my shin, and would have lopped my leg off, were I not already a wisp of vapor. Four swords cut my shadowy imprint to ribbons, yet I was already falling through the astral plane.

****

I missed the sofa and made contact with the hardwood floor.

"Ouch," Andre said with one eye peeking open. He sat cross-legged on the floor, a stream of violet electricity crackling and winding around him like thorns. The circle of magic expanded and shrank around his middle with each pulse of energy. A hunk of meteor hovered before him, which rose and fell with the tide of magic. The meteor looked like it was made of platinum. An inscription ran in a band along its center, with clusters of white gems at its poles capturing light and casting prisms around the room.

A light so pure and refracted, its rainbow of colors seared my eyes, exploded into the room.

Chapter Fifteen

I shielded my face. The air within the room retracted into the meteor, pulling me along with it. Cushions and candles uprooted in the gale, only to swirl around the stone's perimeter like a tiny planet. As I entered its orbit with Andre, the small windstorm ceased. The debris fell. A kaleidoscope of colors twirled around the room, and tiny glowing orbs hung suspended in midair.

I held my hand out, and an orb winked through it. "Do you have any idea what it is?"

"*Convoca mihi omnes de petra durissima, sed cavendum desiderio.*" Andre twisted his fingers, and the hunk of rock turned. "It's Latin for 'Summon the hardest of rock but beware your desire.'"

I stilled. "We shouldn't summon what we don't know."

"It's a reconstruction spell, so we can't use the artifact to its full potential" He peered at a fleck, and I realized there was the faint outline of a continent stretched through the air.

I rose, circling Andre and watching the lights twinkle on the map of our world. I found Canada and knelt. The closest orb hovered around Montreal.

And Greenland.

"What is its full potential?"

"Its purpose is to summon, but I can't say with

confidence what, or who, the stone will retrieve. Since the artifact we have is a shell of the real thing, we can only see what is before us, the magic which powers the actual summoning is missing."

"What are the flecks on the map?"

"That would be our mission to solve, but I have a theory."

The stone glittered like a Dyad, and I stared at it while I searched my brain for information on the strongest stone known to man. "What's the hardest stone now? Graphite?"

"Maybe, but you want to think of the hardest known stone when this inscription was laid—a diamond."

I looked at the map again. We were getting warmer with the Diamond Eater conspiracy. "They move. The balls of light move."

"Suggesting that they are beings, or objects carried," Andre said.

"My report of the woman eating diamonds is starting to look more viable."

"It is." He squinted as if he was trying to see the orbs' true form. He then relaxed and waved his hand. The artifact's light collapsed in on itself and dropped to the floor with a thunk, except it was no longer a hunk of rock but the shiny blue paperweight from my coffee table. "Or maybe she was just holding them, and you hallucinated."

I elbowed him.

"I trust you," he said. "I just don't want to draw conclusions too soon. Diamonds are more likely their operation's income rather than food."

I turned. "I didn't think you trusted anyone, but

you trusted me to come for you yesterday."

Andre didn't avert his gaze. "I did."

"You don't block the bond anymore," I said. "You haven't since you came to Canada."

"Yes."

I struggled to meet his eyes for too long, but I pushed through the discomfort and returned his gaze. As I explored the patterns of yellow flecks throughout his crisp blue irises, I felt a release, slow like a trickle at first, then sweet and blissful like an intimacy I'd never known. My bottom lip trembled. "Then you might be getting sloppy."

He smiled, lowering his head to kiss my collarbone. Gooseflesh traveled up my neck, arcing my back. I slid the letter between our lips before they touched.

"Let's see." He took the envelope and read it in the time it would have taken me to read it four times over. Finally, he lowered the paper. "You and I do not have an extra set of chromosomes."

"Are you sure? I was wondering if all supernatural species had one."

"No."

"But have you ever been to the hospital?"

He shook his head. "We don't have an extra set." He stood, still holding the paper as he began to pace.

I rose and sat on the sofa. The box from Ina was beside me, and I unpacked its contents while Andre worked over his thoughts. A few of my belongings had spilled out of my purse. I unfolded the blanket and laid it across the cushions. The beautiful imagery of the three women reminded me of the trading post, which then reminded me of Mama's agreement with the

Anishinaabe chief. I located the document in my inner coat pocket.

"Do you know what the *Blood of the Creator* is?"

He sat down. "No idea, but the more I think of your journey to Greenland the more I want to visit the Dyad headquarters."

"If it weren't for our ability to *evaporate* to the other's location, I would have been detained." I explained the agreement Mama had secured.

"I don't see a connection."

"I can't find one other, but the agreement keeps coming to mind, and I keep experiencing things that remind me of its words." I stroked the blanket. "And I continue to encounter another type of magic or lack thereof. It feels like a complete emptiness of magic."

"The indigenous peoples of Canada have a magic of their own, that could be what you're feeling. The agreements they struck with the supernatural communities limit us to which parts of Canada we can occupy. It sounds like your mother had special permission to be on the land your family inhabited. The magic you described could be a ward line you crossed, or maybe you met one of their guardians."

"I grew up just south of the northern Canadian border. I've never experienced a ward line, just wards on shops and homes."

"I don't know what to tell you, I've never encountered them myself."

I looked over Mama's agreement again. "I think I need to get more information directly from the source."

Andre ran his fingers over the back of my hand. "Do you want me to come with you? The last time I interfered with memories of your mother, you pushed me away."

"I think," I moved his hand aside to straddle his lap, my hands finding a home on his chest, "I need to do this on my own." I kissed his neck. "But that doesn't mean I won't be wishing I was back here."

"Yes, but—"

I plunged my fangs into his artery.

****

Clouds gathered in force at the horizon, just below the low-hanging sun before it was devoured by an early sunset. I had driven back to the northern Ontario border, skirting the east Algonquin gates. Since navigating by instinct was my strength, and it seemed my sole option, I parked my SUV and ventured on foot.

The crisp wind swirled dead leaves at my heels. My hair gusted forward, creating the illusion of a shadow over my shoulder. I looked back. Darkness gathered in the trees like phantoms. A leaf rattled along the ice at my side. My muscles jumped in my skin, and I swirled around. Leaves patterned the snow ahead, almost pointing north.

I followed the direction. Gray light filtered through the towering ninety-foot pines, turning to dusk as it met the shadows creeping along the snow. A chirp broke the quiet like a snapping twig. A lone chickadee sat on a thorny tree branch.

A gust of wind hit my back, sending a cascade of goosebumps up my spine. Alarm struck me harder than before, and I glanced over my shoulder. A shadow crawled, sentient and feral. The dark shape formed into the outline of a wolf, rivaling the size of my vehicle beyond. The dark wolf did not stalk me like before; it broke into a run.

I sprinted.

My vampiric strength flooded my body. The earth crumbled beneath my feet. The trees blurred. The hairs on my back stood at attention, screaming out the ghost wolf was upon me.

Yet, the chickadee stayed.

I focused on the little bird, dumping all the power Andre's blood gave into my run. The dirt felt hollow under my steps. Energy prickled my skin in an invisible flash, startling me and knocking me off-balance. My feet splintered through tree roots, and I tumbled into a roll. Lying on my back, I saw the dark wolf approach but stop, ten feet from my boots, sniffing the air.

The shadow wolf howled. Its call, a long, painful cry, shook the ground and rustled the trees. But it didn't cross the line of splintered wood, the ley line where I felt the rush of power.

A howl echoed behind me. Then another. Sixty, perhaps one hundred calls answered unison, the type of yips and cries one heard when wolves caught their prey. I froze, not wanting to take my eyes from the ghost wolf, but an undeniable presence gathered behind me— the quiet stirring of paws in the snow, soft breath expelled from snouts.

I turned.

Luminescent eyes pinned me down, too many to count, and closing in. Fear clawed at my skin, goading me to flee. Eastern wolves were shy, nomadic creatures, but here they gathered in extraordinary numbers, getting brazenly close. Terror came in a rush, and I fought the bodily instinct to shake. The nearest wolf licked the air. Tension gathered between my shoulder blades. I weighed the speed of the wolf's lunge against how fast I could bite myself and abort my plan.

The chickadee landed between us.

At a little chirp from the bird, the fluttering of its wings, and the expansion of its chest, the wolves retreated. I chanced a glimpse behind me. The shadow wolf was gone. Birdsong united as the chickadee dotted along the snow, its path cleared by the fleeing wolves. Soft breaths remained present in the shadows of the forest, signaling the packs did not yet disband.

The bird flew to a nearby twig and joined its brethren.

The atypical behavior of an animal, especially its defense of me, was the telltale sign of another totem. I followed the chickadees. They hopped from branch to branch, guiding me north—their birdsong piercing the rustling fury of the wind thrashing the tips of the ancient trees. The pressure of luminescent eyes on my back, ever-present, added momentum to my hike.

I climbed smooth hunks of granite protruding from the snow. Baby white pines scattered between the rocks, but their roots were secure; I clutched them. The elevation rose, and rocky cliffs gave way to plateaus of forest. Nightfall had seeped through the trees. Light from the half-moon reflected off the birds' feathers. One chirped, redirecting me back on course.

I lit a small flame in one hand, lighting up a wall of rock before me. I hoped the fire would keep the wolves skirting the outer ring of darkness, but I doubted they would continue to follow me up to such bluffs.

I dug my other hand into the earth and rock. Finding my footing, I hoisted myself up the wall—the chickadees perched above me on outcroppings of stone. I climbed freehand and smooth. My vampiric strength aided my grip, but I was careful about the pressure I exerted not to crush the stone. Ice crested a jut out of rock ahead. I lifted my glowing hand and watched the water dribble away, but my climbing hand grew slick and cold. A few more moments, and my path would be clear. I adjusted my hand to stretch and slipped.

I punched my fist into the stone. My elbow hinged, but I stopped my free fall. Then I did what any free climber would tell me not to do. I looked down.

The eyes of the wolves spotted the ground like a swarm of fireflies, sixty feet below. Though there was no connection between them, the scene below felt like déjà vu, Roman's pack waiting with anticipation for me to fall.

Flexing, I slowly raised one foot into a crevice. Then the other. I kept my eyes pinned on my next handhold. When my feet were planted and my legs taut, I yanked my hand from the cliff and pounced. I clutched the rock, once again welcoming the cold against my fingers. There were twenty feet left of climb.

The flames in my hand swelled, and I saw the edge of the next plateau. I climbed with new zeal. As I approached the top, pictographs scrawled across the rock. Dark spirals swirled below a wolf, which then tripled in size. Other animals flowed into its mouth while three humans stood behind a spear. The humans attached through flowing lines. In the next image, the wolf was pierced, an aura encasing its body. The aura then filtered into the land and trees. *Energy never dies.* It was a theory spanning cultures, science, and theology. Mama's spirit was this case in point.

A chickadee landed on my shoulder.

"I'm hurrying," I said.

I passed by the images, careful not to touch the archaeological treasure. The edge above was rocky and sharp. I found a firm grip on a sturdy piece of stone, and drawing my strength, hauled myself up. I had long since exited northern Algonquin. In the dim lunar light, I looked out. Clouds wisped by the tips of the snowy reflective pines onto the cliffs of Mattawa.

I sat down briefly on the flat land, considering my journey down. If the wolves were devoted to tracking me, they'd lose time venturing around the highland. Persistent chirping called me onward. It would be hours until we reached the basin of the hill. I took a step, expecting to plant my foot on the firm earth, but my foot kept dropping, taking me with it.

I fell like a stone through thick white mist, tinged by midnight blue, then collided with water. The liquid was cobalt in patches of firelight, stygian in the darkness. The roar of a waterfall carried across the surface, distant in the night. I moved from the light into the shadows. The water was warm, equal to a lake in the peak of summer. Torches were mounted along the edge of the shore, rocky and treacherous. The mist parted on the wind, revealing the curve of the river, akin to a moat.

I swam to the edge of the water, surprised to find the shoreline bottomless. I hoisted myself up onto the rocks. The area was veiled by magic, or it would have been discovered long ago, but I couldn't detect the Charm. I walked along a crushed-stone path, which glimmered in the torchlight. As I grew nearer to the flames, I saw they weren't flames at all but flickering orbs of golden light. The torches were steel with inscriptions running down their length.

The condensation thinned, and structures emerged in the distance. In the darkness, I could see rough timber and the angular sheen of glass on the buildings. I approached a solid granite wall. The rock was completely seamless, save for the opening in the center. I didn't know how one could move such gargantuan slabs of stone or if the barrier had been carved from the ancient rock surrounding the Mattawa fault line.

I approached the entrance, and dark clouds whirled into view at either side of the opening, the clusters fluttering in the air like thousands of obsidian wings.

"Who seeks passage?" asked a man's voice, sounding bored, like he was disinterested by the monotony of his task.

"I'm Karolina Dalca," I said. Sounding crazy to even myself, I added, "Chickadees led me here."

"I'll check," another voice said. Then one of the flickering black clouds rocketed into the sky, arching over the village and down.

"Nice night," the first voice said to me. In the enchanted encampment, it was likely always a nice night.

"Sure," I agreed and took off my soaking wet coat. Rather than letting my mind fill with dozens of questions and strategies, I focused on the rumble of the waterfall. I found calmness in the slow rhythm of my breath. I didn't feel threatened. As if it was leaking from the earth, the essence here felt like a refuge, like security. When I focused on the strange new being before me, I sensed the same vacancy of magic I'd felt before.

There was a rustling, not unlike the sound of

leaves, and the cloud of black wings returned. "You are granted entrance, but I will escort you to your destination."

I passed through the gap in the wall, and he followed at my side. Lights from the houses lit the ground in abstract shapes. The few people out for an evening walk were dressed in regular clothes. One couple, outfitted for a romantic dinner, ventured from the stone slab sidewalk onto a path leading to a central park. The park wasn't what one would find in suburbia but a dense cornucopia of the natural flora and fauna of Ontario. Thick white pines, birch trees, mint, berries, cloves, an array of flowers, and medicinal plants. Historians have argued that the Amazon was once a garden, pollinated by its sister garden in Africa across the ocean air currents. It felt like that principle applied here. It felt like a self-sustaining garden that housed the secrets to nature and longevity.

My guide led me onto an irregular walkway. Smooth stones inlaid with symbols were spaced out in the dirt, curving around the garden. The stones glowed when I stepped on each one. My magic awoke, vibrating with fervor within me. I summoned the Earth Charm. As my magic filled me, golden figures rose from the ground. Like Mama had appeared before me, a wispy shell of her human form, the figures hovered along our path.

"These are the spirits of our ancestors," my guide said. "They are guardians to our home and those who live here. Please keep in mind, a strike against any inhabitant here is an act of war and is punishable as such."

"The intent of my visit is friendly," I said, "but

consider me informed."

He laughed, which felt like a re-enactment of an old vampire movie, a voice emanating from a floating cloud.

We passed over a bridge spanning a small cranberry bog that flowed into the central garden. The stones continued around the northern face and then curved to a house styled like the others. Two more dark clouds rustled outside the door, blocking out the warm light leaking from the windows.

"Karolina Dalca," the guard said.

An arm formed out of the dark, writhing mass and opened the door. Light fell onto the stone from inside. I crossed the threshold and finally felt the hum of both earth and light magic. I wiped my feet on the mat and examined the room.

The slate foyer stretched into light-pine hardwood. The room was open and glossy, the warm wood streaming up the walls to the high ceiling. Light refracted off the roof, a sloped sheet of glass, and angled sharply down to metal runners on either side of the great room. In the center of the living area stood a woman stacking wood within a stone pit the size of a dining table.

"I see you got my messages," The woman said. You may leave your shoes on."

I didn't know if she referred to the leaves that spelled my name, the animal totems I'd witnessed, or both. Behind her, a teenager walked into the kitchen and took a covered plate of dinner from the granite counters. The stone looked as though it was cut from the escarpment I climbed to get here and polished. He left the room with the plate without acknowledging my presence, telling me his mother may have frequent visitors.

I paced around the length of a creamy leather sectional; its leather hides hand-stitched as if sourced from a farm in the valley of Mattawa.

"You may sit," the woman said as she piled the wood into a pyramid.

I sat opposite her on the corner of the sectional.

"My name is Ivy," she said and wiped her hands on her jeans. "Care to help with lighting the wood?"

I extended the Fire Charm from a palm, and flames licked the wood. A moment later, the tinder cracked and popped of its own volition.

Ivy walked to the eastern wall to a keypad along one of the metal tracks. She pushed a button, and the mechanism along the tracks groaned, the glass ceiling parting from the peak above and sliding down the wall. The light within the room no longer reflected down upon us but dissolved into the inky sky above. Smoke from the fire curled up, only to disperse into wisps among the wind and stars.

The stars appeared closer.

In the north, the absence of light pollution lets viewers see the stars in their uninhibited beauty, but these stars were too large, like they were below the stratosphere. It was as if Ivy, when she opened the roof to her home, had opened a gateway into the universe.

I stared up, and a hot mug of tea was pressed into my hands. "Thank you," I said.

Ivy sat down, and her eyes caught the light in a way that reminded me of Roman.

"Do you have werewolves in the family?" I asked.

She shook her head. "I was gifted the Earth and

Light Charm, but I also carry the magic of my ancestors. The dark matter, like gravity, or the pull of our planets, the opposite of the light of our universe. We call it the Nexus."

"But gravity and compression create explosions and light in space."

"Very good. You know your physics. Yes, the balance of light and dark are eternally linked; light cannot exist without the other existing first. The magic of my ancestors stems from our Earth Mother's core and the Creator's sky above us. Our power exists, Karolina, to enforce the balance."

The Creator.

"I've started to encounter more individuals with the magic you speak of, ever since I read a contract my mother, Ana Dalca, signed many years ago."

Ivy nodded. "I sent you a message on the wind after she died."

So, Ivy was responsible for the wind that cast my name on the ground with frozen leaves. The type of magic I was experiencing was the Nexus. "The agreement speaks about the Blood of the Creator, but I have no idea what the title refers to."

"The Blood of the Creator is what you wear around your neck."

I clutched the only tangible piece of my father I ever had. "But," I said, "this gem is from my father's side of the family."

"Yes, it is."

A heaviness gathered in my stomach, gripping my innards like it was falling with the earth beneath my feet, yet I sat still on the sofa. The images of my father's brutal rule, implanted in my memory from

Kazimir, flashed through my mind. I suspected Kazimir fabricated those memories as painful revenge before he died—but what if they were real? "Why would my father possess such an important indigenous artifact?"

"He was once betrothed to my great-great-grandaunt, and as a token of their promised union, she gave him her most sacred possession."

My stomach, still held in suspense, warned me that her story was about to get worse.

"She died before they could marry, and your father refused to return her necklace to her family. He claimed she gave it to him to protect him throughout his rule, but we knew she wanted the Blood of the Creator with her people, as she and your father had not yet produced any children who would have inherited the Mantle of the Blood."

I wanted to deny what she was saying, but I could not. Mama signed a contract for me to return the necklace to its *rightful owner*. Her spirit message at her grave even spoke to the estate documents I'd discovered. My necklace gifted me immunity from wolf magic and perhaps even immunity from the magic which Loukin was testing through our missions. If the power of the Nexus kept the balance between light and dark, did this mean the vacuous magic I experienced at this village was also the magic that protected me? How much power was within my ruby? I hadn't yet tested the extent of its abilities.

Yet, an undeniable truth was before me; my father's ruby belonged to the Anishinaabe. Mama had kept me ignorant, and my father kept what didn't belong to him. One's parents may have flaws, but one didn't have to inherit them.

I undid the clasp, and images of my father's rule barraged my mind. I handed the necklace to Ivy. Not because I felt guilty for my father's actions, and not because I thought Mama wanted me to. I gave Ivy the gem because I intrinsically knew it was just.

She took it, and when the metal touched her skin, her eyes glowed gold. Darkness shimmered around her body. She sighed, and a tremor traveled up her arms. Light erupted from the ruby, casting the room in a red hue.

The heavy feeling still pooled in my belly. Ivy's magic felt like the void I was now accustomed to, but I suddenly felt vulnerable. The hairs on my shoulders raised like I was haunted by an unseen spirit that crept up on me.

The ground rumbled.

Ivy's home shuddered, and with a deafening crack, the great room split down the middle. Glass shattered. The lights flickered off. The outer half of the house fell away, splintering on the rocks of a dark chasm. The faint light of the moon glistened along the stone as a deep boom resonated within the sinkhole.

Chapter Sixteen

I clutched the sofa, bracing and anticipating the remainder of the house to shift. I checked on Ivy, but she seemed mesmerized by the light of the gem, whispering words that added to the glow like gasoline on a flame.

Movement stirred within the trench.

Hands raced, rigid and disjointed, from the darkness meters below. A veil of writhing blackness followed, like oil cascading over rock. Moonlight streamed in a patch at the edge of the torn flooring, and as a body approached, Kazimir's face was illuminated. His eyes hollowed out, his ashen skin flakey, and his mouth pulled back in an unnatural expression like he was gleeful.

Gleeful he was free.

He crawled so fast I couldn't see his next move. He was at the edge of the house, then his hands were wrapped around my neck, and I was on my back against the floor. I released my fire, but his steely body stayed above me, untouched. His crushing grip searched my neck, then his head spun unnaturally to his back, his gaze pinned on Ivy. He pounced.

A golden wall materialized before I saw Kazimir land. It was the spirits of the Anishinaabe ancestors from outside. They linked arms, encasing Ivy in a circle. Kazimir slammed against one of the ancestors and crumpled. Then charged them, again, and again.

A strike against any inhabitant here is an act of war.

The sky stirred above us, a small cyclone forming into one of the fluttering clouds that stood outside. Bystanders gathered opposite of the sinkhole. A whistling rose through the air. The darkness from within the rock flowed over the jagged edge of the floor. Shadows, the vague outlines of human forms, crawled in a swarm, similar to the hive-like pattern of the Forged. Yet, Kaz's Forged were dead, and the act of Forging shredded their souls.

Yet, the writhing horde raced at me.

Holes were where their eyes and mouths once were; their screams tortured whispers, carried on the breeze like a rising storm. Their disjointed, strobe-like movement turned my stomach. The hairs on my arm raised like electricity was in the air as if the beings before me had forced their way into existence against the laws of nature.

A caw tore through the wind.

In a flutter of obsidian feathers, a body formed amidst the dark cyclone. A gigantic hawk claw punctured Kazimir's back and ribcage, folding him in half and crushing him into the floor.

The wave of tortured souls crested at my feet, and I released my fire. Twisted shadows broke through my flames like iron through a smelting fire. I summoned the Light Charm, but three of the flickering black masses crashed into the floor before me. Their impact sucked all magic inward, then the next instant, it was hammering out in a sonic boom.

The horde evaporated like mist in a hurricane.

I turned to Kazimir. Talons withdrew from his flesh, and Kazimir's body collapsed in on itself like sand pilling on the floor. The claws disappeared into the swarm of feathers, retreating to reveal the smooth, tan skin of a broad abdomen, then a neck and a jaw. Ben's face emerged, chiseled in the lowlight of the moon, his eyes blacked out like he possessed the Dark Charm. But the magic at work wasn't the Charm. It was the unseen force that held our planet together, held the universe together. The neutral birthplace of life.

The Nexus.

Onyx plumes, glittering in the light, dissipated, exposing the warriors at my feet. They walked toward Ben, creating a barrier around Ivy. I lit dual flames in my palms and followed, watching Ivy whisper her incantation. As I approached, the red light peaked, and I shielded my eyes. From beneath my arm, I watched the ruby melt, dribbling to the ground in bloody drops. When it touched the floor, the liquid hissed and unfurled into wispy red tendrils around Ivy.

She breathed in the scarlet vapor. The golden glow that once filled her eyes turned crimson. The floor vibrated, sending Kazimir's dusty remains drifting across the hardwood. A dark circle formed around Ivy at the feet of her ancestors. The vibration grew so strong its hum rang out into the room and over the chasm.

I leaped back just as a force field sprang from the ring. Ivy's chanting was clipped by the rise and fall of the wall of energy, and at her word, the longest note, the torrent of power ceased. My flames extinguished. The room pitched into blackness. Quiet fell over the remains of the house, save for the footsteps of Ivy's son in the doorway and the chatter of the crowd across the pit.

"Karolina," Ivy said. "Can you please light the fire?"

I obliged her, and the ruined house came back into view.

"Mom," Ivy's son said from the walkway outside, "get out of there before the rest of the house shifts."

I fought the urge to beat Ivy to the door, not wanting to find out how far the chasm plummeted. There was a rustling behind me, and the warriors and Ben dispersed like a murmuration of birds, dark tendrils unfurling in their wake.

As I approached the door, a thought seized me. Had I created this sinkhole? Succession spells held the moment of transfer in extreme importance. Kazimir had implanted the perfect memory in my mind, one that plagued me and one that surfaced when I gave up the single tangible piece of my father. Did I summon Kazimir's soul by thinking of him during the transfer of owners?

Once outside, I sighed and, on reflex, reached to where my necklace once hung. Chatter about Ivy's eyes and the Mantle of the Creator rocketed through the crowd. Ivy clutched her son, then turned to me. "Come with me."

The warriors parted a path through the throng and led the way to another building of similar style to Ivy's home but much larger. We approached the entrance. Stone doors stood the length of two men, carved into a row of birch trees. The sculpted doors were so realistic they looked like the tree bark was made of granite.

Two hawk warriors, in their flock form, opened the

doors to us. We stepped inside, and as Ben passed by me, I whispered, "Ina?"

"She's safe," he said. "She's actually a few houses over. I'll take you after you're done here."

Large slabs of granite towered up through the floor. The backbone of the structure spanned the length of the hall like being inside of a stone whale. Stars shone through the retractable glass roof in the western sky. Historically, the indigenous peoples of Canada didn't construct buildings from stone; water would invade the cracks and expand during our harsh winters. Wood was the material of choice, as it withstood the cold.

But these stones looked primordial, like they were worn smooth from glaciers and years of melt and arranged here against the laws of physics. The walls were drywall and wood, but looking down the belly of the structure, I could imagine how the exterior might have changed over the millennia. All the while, the heart of this place remained ancient and unmoving.

As Ivy walked the center path, the stones lit with the same red glow as her eyes, illuminating with the markings I'd seen on the footpath to her home. One by one, the stones set alight until she reached a central fire pit. She sat down on a stone chair behind the sunken ring. The markings above her head set ablaze, then like wildfire, the red glow spread to the remaining stones of the building's structure. The hall danced with light, ambers of the raw coursing inscriptions flexing and waning with the twinkle of stars.

Ben and another female warrior, the waitress from the restaurant in Algonquin, lit the timber in front of Ivy. Another warrior turned on the mechanism to retract the glass roof, and the stars, unnaturally close and as bright as lanterns, hovered just above us.

"Please join me at the fire," Ivy said.

I walked the center path. Though the paths snaked in and out of the middle, to the left and right of me, each had its own pull. *Power*. Like a whisper in my head, the left-hand path promised power; to the right, the desperate need to preserve, to protect, weighed on me.

My father's and my mother's vices.

I held to my course, but I stumbled as I approached the fire. The left-hand path branched around the fire, mirroring the right. Yet, it was power's path that called me—one step, then another. Before I involuntarily made my decision, I thrust my arms out and parted the flames. With the protection of my own fire, I walked the middle path.

When I reached the stone once more, Ivy no longer looked like a mother. She looked like a deity, to whom I felt compelled to kneel.

"You've held onto your soul, Karolina. Your mother would be proud. You must wonder why your uncle seeks to destroy yours."

"I would be ineligible for the ruby."

She nodded. "Also, so we would reject you."

"Why haven't you?"

"We don't turn away decent people. You kept your mother's promise, and despite the pain on your face, you gave back what you loved to its rightful owner." Ben stepped forward, but Ivy held up a hand. "For this, I will tell you how to kill them."

"Kill who?" I asked.

"Those who seek to destroy this world, those your uncle is unknowingly seeking immunity from," Ivy said. "I'll tell you how to kill a Diamond Eater."

Finally, acknowledgment and confirmation. My narrow escape from Agatha replayed in my head. "I didn't feel immune when I fought one."

Ivy smiled. "The fact you could even fight one shows the strength the Blood gave you. Tell me, did you feel greed? Did you feel your darkest desire consuming you within their gaze?"

"No."

"They use what you covet to destroy you. When they came to this planet in the fifteenth century, the extraction of mineral wealth forever changed our world. Humans formed the first bank in Italy, then exploration came, and soon mining. Societal development holds its benefits, but the poison of Diamond Eater greed tainted leaders. The Eaters' appetite for power and control was tapered for a time, but their recent alliance with the Dyad traitors is an act we cannot ignore. The Anishinaabe are mobilizing for war for the first time in decades. With the Mantle of the Blood restored, I have my full strength, which in turn restores our wind walkers to theirs. We are linked through the magic of our people."

Bronwyn was creating her own army of Dyads high on Diamond Eater blood.

Ben spoke with a ferocity that challenged every aspect of his nature I'd witnessed thus far. "If they tip the balance toward destroying this world, we will restore equilibrium with their annihilation. On my word as a wind walker."

"Did you send me the message of leaves to summon me here for this reason?" I asked Ivy.

Ben answered. "When your mother was murdered,

her bargain became active. We were no longer shielded from your senses."

So, it all came down to the gem and Loukin's quest for power. He wanted to uncover the plutocrats of the supernatural community, and he wanted resistance to their magic. My father was killed so Loukin could assume control as Tzar of the vampire underground in Russia. I was made an operative so he could receive the power of the ruby when I fell to the Dark Charm.

"How do I kill a Diamond Eater?" I asked.

"The same way you destroy a diamond," Ivy said. "You can crush them if you have the strength, which most don't, save for wind walkers and Diamond Eaters." She shook her head. "No, your option, Karolina, is heat."

"My Fire?"

"Not hot enough. You must combine the Light Charm and Fire Charm."

I tried combining my light and fire magic on the Dyad enforcers and had only managed to crack Arie's helmet. "Why would this combination affect Diamond Eaters more than Dyads?"

"Because Diamond Eaters do not have the Light Charm," Ivy said. "They don't have the Charm at all. They are not from our galaxy. Vampires, werewolves, and wind walkers, we are all of the earth. The Dyads, whichever moon they came from, shared our sun before they evacuated to our planet. We can all enjoy the gifts of our sun bestows on us, the most sacred being the Charm. Diamond Eaters can do no such thing."

Gerel said almost all of those with the Fire Charm were victims of genocide but hadn't said when the genocide occurred. Kazimir's implanted memories implied it was during my father's rule, but I didn't want to believe it was true. The fact remained, exterminating those with the Fire Charm—who could destroy a Diamond Eater—would be a powerful bartering tool.

Would committing genocide spark the Dark Charm? When did my father give the necklace to Mama? In life, Kazimir didn't want my necklace; he had hordes of Forged, which might suggest he possessed dark magic. Did he strike a deal with Diamond Eaters to support his war against Loukin for the throne of the Tzar? It would explain Kazimir's involvement with Bronwyn and why Loukin was losing the war until my assassination of Kazimir. It also explained why Loukin wanted the ruby's power and why he was gaining intelligence on the Diamond Eaters.

The fire sizzled and popped behind me. Ivy rose, and I turned to see what held her focus. A dark shape formed in the fire, which grew, expanding into a face that was all too similar to mine. Loukin starred at us from within the flames. Muddled by the blaze, his eyes bore shades of black and gray and his skin shades of amber, as one would see in an old photograph.

The warriors flew to Ivy's sides, but she held up a hand.

"Hello, Karolina," Loukin said, his voice as crisp as if he were standing in the room with us. "You've gone beyond a loose leash. Did you think I would give you warnings? Did you think I would tolerate insubordination?"

"The ruby is gone," I said.

Loukin's voice was low and as seething as the hot coals of the fire. "I'll enjoy hearing about Miruna's death."

He vanished.

I ran, sprinting down the trail of center stones, blindly calling every ounce of light magic within me. I burst through the heavy stone doors and out into the mild night air. I kept going until I sank my hands into the dirt. My fingers, on autopilot, quickly modeled the rough outline of a bird.

The Light Charm peaked within me, and I gritted my teeth with the strength it took to restrain it. I summoned the Earth Charm with an intensity that jolted me from the dirt. With both Charms present, I funneled them into the lump of earth in my hands.

"Run," I said. "Run, Miruna! Loukin is coming for you!"

Light pierced the night. A golden aurora, luminous and shining, exploded into the air from my hands. Like fifty fireflies merged, a bird, composed entirely of light, rocketed through the sky.

I watched the Charmed message until it disappeared from sight. My throat closed as I stared at the empty midnight sky. My eyes welled, but the adrenaline I felt kept the tears from falling.

"To the divinity of the universe," I whispered into the wind. "The matter that holds this planet together, the Charm that flows around me, please, please let Miruna get my message."

A nearby cricket chirped like a death knell. With the ruby necklace gone, Loukin no longer needed me. He would send more *Ispolniteli* to collect me and extract all I know. I was now as disposable as all his other operatives, if not more so.

Ina approached me while I was still on my knees.

"What happened?" She sank beside me onto the dewy grass.

"Well, in addition to our condo being broken into, Loukin knows I gave away the only thing that gave me value."

"Which was?" Ina asked.

"My necklace." I summarized all I had learned from Ivy and Andre. "I didn't expect his ability to spy on me through the fire." The memory of staring into the candle flame at the restaurant in Algonquin, wondering how Loukin tracked me there, came racing back.

Ivy approached us from behind. "The fire in our sacred hall is used for vision scrying, it is an open portal. No threat can physically invade, and no spies can channel it, but the bond of our family and ancestors lets us connect."

"Most wouldn't expect their family to want them dead," I said.

Still, there was a benefit here. I now knew Loukin could spy on me through an open flame. Wards protected me from any magic, but outside of them, any open fire was a potential threat. How much of our conversation did Loukin hear? Did he also know how to kill a Diamond Eater? If so, he required the Light Charm.

I had to plan my next strategy, and the dread for Miruna was building within me like a rising tide. I took short, rapid breaths. The sight of the waterfall beyond—its continuous rumble churning with my stomach—felt like a barrage of guilt. Enough guilt to sink me.

"Ina, are you okay staying here with Ben for a while?"

She smiled. "You might have to twist my arm."

I laughed, clipped and quiet. "Okay. I'm going to go for a little while. I'll mostly be at the safe place my emergency spell indicated."

"Mostly," she said, holding my gaze and clutching my hands.

"Mostly," I repeated.

"Be careful. Remember you are not the scariest thing out there. Hide your identity always, and if you need me, call me."

I wrapped my arms around her. "I will. I might need your help already with something, but I have to deal with some issues first." I wouldn't chance speaking my plans aloud, but I knew I needed her to help trace the accounts on Andre's list.

Ben crossed the lawn, with his upper half in human form and onyx flickering from his waist down. Before discovering if shifting out of his supernatural state left him nude, I rose to leave.

"Thank you for sharing the truth with me, Ivy. I'm sorry for my father's mistakes."

She nodded. "His faults are not yours. You gave it back."

****

The journey through the ether this time felt like coming home. The feeling was so painful, as never had I felt more unworthy in my life. I collided with Andre's warm, broad chest, the fabric of his shirt so soft it could be an embrace.

Andre gasped as my knee landed just between his legs. He was lying on the couch with coffee spilled over his arm and the floor.

I lowered my cheek to his chest, the rhythm of his heart beating like a siren's call, yet his soft touch held the overwhelming promise of security. The hyperarousal that sent my heart and breath into rapid succession came to a head at the thought of Miruna. The control I'd maintained dissipated. Tears streamed from my eyes, wetting Andre's shirt. I clutched the fabric and gave in to the release.

He clutched my face, pulling my eyes level with his. "What happened? You were gone for days."

Time must have slowed in the Anishinaabe village; what was hours for me was days for Andre. I wanted to answer him, but I couldn't stop panting.

"Karolina." His lips pressed into mine, slow and tender. "Breathe." He kissed me even slower, and in the smooth, soft motions, I found myself meeting him in kind. I drew a deep breath.

He paused. "Tell me, sweetheart."

Through my tears, I told him what I learned from Ivy about Kazimir's attack, what Loukin now knew, and Loukin's threat against Miruna. My last sentence sent me into another tailspin.

Andre clutched my jaw. "She's not there."

I looked up.

"On my way to Canada I stopped in to visit her. I told her Loukin had the Albesuc book of light magic, and he was blackmailing you. She has friends she can trust. She wasn't going to sit around and wait for Loukin to kill her. She went into hiding."

"Can Loukin find her?" I sat up on his stomach. "He can find her with a tracking spell," I thought aloud, "but maybe my warning will get to her first. Maybe she can take precautions." *She has a chance*. I breathed slow enough now to see Andre's appearance in detail. His hair had dried in wavy tendrils that hung down to his cut jawline. He'd managed to acquire a shirt, and the deep collar plunged, exposing the smooth muscles of his chest. My hand glided up his abdomen, taking in every ridge and valley.

Andre warned Miruna. He knew I loved her, so he protected her for me. I didn't risk challenging Loukin's threat; I was too fearful. Andre had done what I couldn't, and he did so undetected, as Loukin would make his wrath known. Andre worked for us, even after I abandoned him.

I met his gaze and held it as if I saw beyond his eyes. "You found a shirt."

"I did."

I traced the edge of the soft fabric on his stomach and lifted it above his head. My breasts rose and fell as I looked down at his naked lower torso, my breath now a steady rhythm of the crescendo between us. His shirt slid from my hand to the floor.

I stood and stripped.

Andre watched me, tracking my movement, each of my gestures elevating his heartbeat in waves. His undeterred silent attention, the softness of his face, and the intensity in his eyes all sent my pulse bounding with his.

When I slipped my panties off, a shiver slid down my legs, making my knees shake. I pulled Andre's pants down, and he wet his lips in anticipation. I stared at his mouth, yearning to taste his bottom lip. His fangs descended. I straddled him. His eyes burned into mine, and I slid, slowly, down the length of his shaft. With each tiny pump of my hips, I dampened where his smooth, delicate skin met mine. When our hips, at last, pressed together, I sighed at feeling him within the very depth of me. I rose abruptly, then dropped down, stifling a cry.

It was my turn to watch him. Each movement deepened the expression on his face. My thighs trembled with the height I had to achieve to slide down his full length. I gripped the spine of the couch, pumping up and down, watching him groan and squirm beneath me.

I felt like a hollow vessel being filled over and over, until a surge of heat built within me, and my hips rode the rush, elevating me higher. The nerve from my belly button trailed a line of fire to the center of my legs. I broke his hold on my gaze, unable to keep my eyes open any longer. My head tilted to the ceiling as I cried out, and fluid gushed from me.

He shifted to his knees, spinning my stomach into the backrest of the sofa. My buttock pressed against his hips, he slid into me. One hand glided into the back of my hair, and the other clutched my breast, holding me in place. Hot breath poured over my ear as he kissed my neck. "I love you," he whispered, each word punctuating a powerful thrust. Deep within me, a nerve I didn't even know I had ignited. My breath stalled. In the continuous barrage of pleasure, his words played within my mind until I wanted to shout them out.

The bond swelled between us, and I remained present this time. I took in every peak of his emotions—his fears, vulnerability, and love. I devoured his love, letting it fill me as I plunged my fangs into his forearm to fill me again as his bite pierced my shoulder, carnal and euphoric.

When the magic between us dissipated, we lay entwined on the sofa in the aftershock. We made plans to flee the country. We would find Miruna and follow the lead we had with the Diamond Eater artifact.

Chapter Seventeen

I rolled out of Andre's arms and flailed my hand at my cell phone. It fell to the ground, its ringtone echoing loudly over the metal heat vent. I buried my head deeper into my duvet.

"Sweetheart." Andre's voice was a cross between a groan and whisper. "Put it on silent."

I peeked at the clock on my bedside table. It was four o'clock in the afternoon. Not only had we stayed up all night practicing ways to make each other climax harder than the last, but we also slept the day away. It wasn't a bad way to pass the time in a safe house when trying to avoid being hunted and killed. My wards kept me from being traced, but Loukin could track me through open flames or magic once I left my apartment if my identity spell wasn't in place. I just hoped I'd enchanted my phone well enough to keep Loukin's operation from tracking me the old-fashioned way.

I leaned down to reach my cell and tumbled onto the floor. I laid there in the hot beam of sun escaping from the drapes, tempted to close my eyes once more.

"Karolina." Andre rolled over, covering the exposed side of his face with a pillow.

I flipped my cell phone screen open. Roman had called me thirty times over the six days I was gone. I had ignored my phone. Some calls were from his cell, others from his parents' home. I pulled up our text conversation.

—Please respond— he wrote last.

I clicked up to read a series of messages from new to old. *—Karo, are you okay? I can't find your scent anymore. When can I see you? We need to talk. Karo, please don't do this. Talk to me. We can sort this out. When?—*

I sank my phone to my chest and took a deep breath. I didn't intend to put Roman through the torture he went through. Yet, there was only a narrow part of me that felt guilty. He hurt me deeply. The role he attempted to box me into before we broke up was cruel, and I was appalled Roman couldn't see that. I cared for him my whole life, and he didn't see how much he was hurting me. He thought he could force me to submit to the future he devised, and it made my stomach roll.

Yet, hurting him still felt like hurting myself.

—I'm okay.— I responded. *—Work stuff, please don't worry when I don't respond. I can talk today.—* I contemplated where Roman would be most comfortable for closure. We met for drinks at the Laff long before we started dating, and though it was within the inner city, it was a reminder of our friendship before we went awry. I could also assess how many more operatives were roaming the city and whether Loukin had already put a bounty on my head.

—Meet me at the Laff at seven?— I typed.

****

Andre sat watching a movie as I readied to leave. It was an action movie where a bombshell kicked the asses of ten men per scene. He ate popcorn in the candlelight, and though he focused on the screen, I could see him noting any effort I put into my appearance.

My hair had air-dried in a thick mass of loose curls, and I wore shiny leggings and a tight, off-the-shoulder, chiffon, mint-green top. I was disguised as an unmemorable party girl with my perfume and black lipstick. I searched for suitable footwear, pacing from the front door back to my closet. The caramel riding boots Andre bought for me in Russia were hidden behind a trench coat. I pulled them out, noting they were the best dressy footwear I could run in.

I approached Andre from behind, wrapping my arms around him, just in time to catch the woman ripping her lover's heart from his chest. "Ouch," I said. "The betrayal in this scene gets me every time."

Andre kissed my wrist. "She's tough, she'll get over it." He turned, lifting a brow at me. "You're going out to see your ex in the boots I bought you?"

I smiled and kissed him. "Yes. You bought me practical and fashionable footwear." I pulled back before he could catch my lips again. "I should be back in an hour. Then we can pack."

"Hurry home." But instead of turning back to his movie, he leaned back, taking me in.

I twirled for him, letting his eyes linger. "When I get back," I said. "You can have the view of my outfit on the floor."

Andre grinned at me. "Then I'm very, very lucky."

"Thank you for thinking that," I said, biting the inside of my cheek to tame my expression. Growing up trying to subdue my monster impulses, I never felt worthy of the affection bestowed upon me. I smiled and averted my eyes, as not to be caught in the heat surging in his gaze. Then I passed through my wards and out the door.

My heart was still humming when I exited the stairwell and ventured into the snow. I sheltered my face with the hood of my coat. Rather than a fluffy first snowfall for the city, the flakes came fast and furious in the biting cold. The city would be buried by morning.

The first few blocks were quiet, muted in the whiteout, then the bustle of the city core increased. I summoned my vampiric senses, trying to see farther than three feet; the snow fell so densely it looked like a solid wall. I relied on my hearing. Heartbeats were scattered, fleeing the polar winds to their destinations. The music carried through the storm, and as I approached the bar, I noted the flyers on the windows indicating a guest DJ set tonight. I joined the thick line. The beat in the bar sounded like the acceleration of a train, pausing to let the twilight of the rhythm set in, then rocketing once more. Bodies gyrated across the glass, filling the space between tables.

Operatives would be out tonight, using the cover of the storm and the noise of the crowd to their advantage. I survey the line for *Ispolniteli*. A pair of men in the middle matched the appearance of those I'd encountered thus far, but their arms were covered.

The line moved up a foot, and I shuffled along. When I was close enough to the front, I caught a glimpse of the bouncer within a break in the flurries. It was Sébastien, Roman's lackey who drove his car.

I left the line, and I could feel my identity spell shifting with my intent as I approached him. He recognized me and lifted the velvet rope. As I passed, he stamped my hand.

A blast of heat whooshed down from a heater

above as I passed through the door. There was no ward, which meant the pub was still in neutral civilian territory. A stream of melting slush led to a mass of people waiting for coat check. I pushed by them and, in the cover of the hallway that led to the basement, searched the tables.

The DJ was set up along the back wall. Those not sitting occupied the floor space, dancing with drinks in their hands. In the center of the room, I spotted a man who looked like an *Ispolniteli* seated with a young woman. I closed my eyes, and the Charm whirled within me. I focused my energy on parsing out additional sources of the magic.

Three people with the Charm were a foot from me, opposite the wall. I gingerly probed my senses further, not wanting to bring attention to myself. The seething vibration of the Dark Charm confirmed the man in the center was indeed *Ispolniteli*, or at least a dark magic user, as was the woman beside him. I felt two light magic users at the far wall. Yet, their light magic was tinged with the same strange force I experienced with the *Custodes*.

When I opened my eyes, I caught a lone man staring at me, his gaze primal and still.

The more I scanned the moving crowd, the more I spotted those who were stationary. Though the rest didn't stare, their casual conversations didn't lessen the tension on their shoulders—coiled tension, as palpable as the intensity of the stalking wolves from the woods.

My scent and identity were hidden, but my presence was noted.

The first man turned to another, and a golden aura lit the irises of his eyes. The gesture spread through the crowd until, lastly, one man met Roman's eyes.

Roman's pack was here.

Like Roman was visible all along, he sat waiting at a booth to my far left. My senses felt dominated by his presence like his unseen energy was trying to command mine. He looked taller than before, his muscles thicker.

I felt Sébastien approach my side. I'd lingered for too long. When I decided to advance to Roman, I felt my spell shift for him. Rather than worry lines creasing his face, he smiled at me. Two cinnamon martinis sat upon the table, our old drink of choice for a night out, but Roman's was already half-finished.

"Hey, you," he said as I sat down.

I was so grateful he knew not to use my name that I let out a long breath. "Hey." I unzipped my coat and slipped it off my shoulders but kept it close. Roman's pack stayed where they were. The song transitioned, and the rising drumbeat, paired with the guttural exhale of the vocals, built a sinister ambiance. The crowd reflected it too, their dancing taking on an edge, laughter turning clipped. It was as if the predatory aura of the wolves was seeping into the air.

"You brought the whole gang," I said and nodded to the closest wolf.

"Well," he said, "*You* ghosted *me*." He sat back in his chair, forcing me to absorb his emphasis. "I thought you were detained, or worse. After you texted me, I didn't know if I would need reinforcements for whatever trouble might follow you."

I considered his explanation, but it didn't strike true. Bringing his pack into our intimate moment felt like a flippant act after everything we had experienced together. He knew I was capable of sneaking around, and he wasn't afraid. I couldn't tell if it was an act of defiance or an extension of his ever-growing ego. The way I left him was hurtful, but his posturing stung; it solidified my theory he would always want the upper hand.

I took a big sip of my drink. The flavor was syrupy sweet, a slight reminder of Roman's sugary *Ţuică*-tasting blood. I looked up, absorbing the profile of his face, the color of his big honey browns fringed with long chestnut lashes. "I'm really sorry for the way I left things with you." I looked to his gaze until he finally met mine, but his eyes didn't soften, so I took his hand. "You must see now, though, how much you tried to back me into a corner. You hurt me so badly, Ro."

He laughed, his voice harsh, poisoned by anger. "You still haven't taken off your naïve, rosy glasses."

"Don't," I said.

"If you cannot respect the position of power I am in now," his voice dropped to a whisper, but his eyes glowed like the beast within wanted to claw its way out, "if you cannot respect future I can offer us, then you do not respect *me*."

Roman was always stubborn, but the impasse we entered was dark and unnerving. I have never been on the receiving end of Roman's wrath, and I never thought he would disregard my perspective. It was like I didn't matter, as if he wanted a compliant shell of me and didn't want to consider the person at my core because that person had ideals that conflicted with his own.

Rather than responding, I downed my drink.

Roman showed his teeth in a wide grin like my reaction was what he wanted, like he had won.

"Well, I'm sorry things have ended this way, Roman. I hope maybe once we've had some time, we can be friends once more. I wish you the best with your expansion into Québec, and maybe we can touch base once work calms down for you."

I rose to leave, but the room wobbled.

Roman's expression finally met his eyes as his gaze stalked my progression around the table. There was a twinkle in his eye, like an exhilarated predator who had finally caught its prey. He approached while I stumbled back. The music swelled in my ears like a rising wave, my awareness swallowed. The lights strobed, disorientating me, and obscuring the path between figures and tables. I got lost in the sway of bodies, and each touch and graze sent my senses soaring. I lost control. The mass of heartbeats in the room thumped with the power of an orchestra, a rhythm edging me to violence or sex. My fangs descended. I reached for the closest person, looking for pleasure, for unison in the mass, mindless chaos.

Roman's hands found my hips and pulled me back. He rocked with me. One of his hands slid up my waist and pulled my hair aside. My head rolled, and his plush lips pressed into my ear. "It's all going to work out, Karo," he whispered. "You'll see."

My stomach swirled, the motion of the crowd now too strong, my vision too blurry. I felt sick, but I couldn't speak. My body felt like a wet rag. I upchucked into my mouth, then swallowed it down as the floor flew to my face. I curled into a ball, the coolness of leather pressing into my cheek. I heard the thunk of a car door closing. The space before me pitched and rolled like I was on a rollercoaster, yet I felt the heavy pull of gravity as I lay unmoving.

****

Cool, hard stone pressed against my face, but it was stationary. I basked in the stillness. Then the smell of death filled my nose. A putrid, bitter taste coated my tongue. The knell of beating hearts still rang out, and though I lay still, the motion of the bar raced back. I vomited on the floor. I retched on, and when I finally lay my head back against the hard stone, I opened my eyes.

I was in Roman's basement.

I looked up the stairs leading to the door with the newly equipped security system and wards, the one I paused at when I was last here. Rising, I looked through the slim window to the snowy shrubs outside. There was no moonlight tonight; the waning moon finished its cycle with the dark moon. I sought out its magnetism and sensed it low in the southern sky. It wasn't close to midnight, which meant Andre's blood helped me burn off the drugs Roman put in my drink within an hour. It was far quicker than Roman expected, or I would have awakened to him here.

A blanket was pulled over me, now bunched at my legs, and a bottle of water was placed on the floor near to where my head rested. My coat was gone. Farther back, a wooden bowl was filled with oily black blood, the source of the smell of death. A tremble rose up my spine. I sniffed the air. Sage, dirt, and weeks-old animal blood—the rot that filled the room mirrored the taste in my mouth. It was the darkest sort of magic. A binding spell, and though it was trivial, its cost would be a sliver of the practitioner's soul. Mrs. Lupei wouldn't take part in such an act; she'd weep if Roman had done this.

Where were Mr. and Mrs. Lupei? I resisted the urge to call to them and alert Roman.

The basement hallway had changed. The door to where Roman and I once had our movie nights had an electronic lock. Another keypad on the second door behind me made this entrance hall into a holding cell. The Lupeis's sports equipment that once hung on the wall was now piled in a mesh storage locker. The tattered red-and-white tape on the tip of Roman's lacrosse stick jutted out. *Roman's lacrosse stick.* The stick I'd found upstairs was Mr. Lupei's. I forgot the color of the tape on Roman's handle until now. Yet, the tracking spell I'd used led me to Roman and his family's land. Was Roman's father at the pack meeting? I doubted it, noting Roman was now obsessed with his image of power. His predecessor overseeing him run the pack seemed counterproductive to level of dominance he was trying to assume. Still, Mr. Lupei's stick brought me there.

I looked again at the bowl.

Urgency crept along my skin, spiking goosebumps. The tempos of the heart rhythms were incessant, a nagging feeling squirming in my stomach. I wanted to flee, but the implications of the volume of people behind the locked door doused me like cold water. I shivered. Who was behind the door, and why were they so quiet? I bit my wrist to test my ability to escape through the bond. My blood dripped onto the floor, the air placid around me. The binding spell indeed kept my soul stationary. My only way out was on foot.

I rose. I could electrocute either keypad. I could shimmy out through the rec room's culvert windows. I didn't have to enter the second door, where a potential threat could reside. *But why were they so quiet?*

I paced my hand on the keypad of the second door and loosened the Light Charm.

The lock let go. The wards encasing the door flared in white light and sizzled down the doorframe. Again, I wondered who crafted these wards as I pushed the door open, then halted.

The room was pitch black, save for the semicircle of light stretching from the open door. The scent of old blood sullied the air, which flowed from the heat vent on the far wall. The edge of a cage was exposed within the patch of light, and inside it was a dainty, bare foot. It moved out of sight.

I stepped inside, and the wards fell heavily over my shoulders. I closed the door behind me as not to give off my position straightaway if Roman came down. I just hoped I'd be able to leave as easily. There was rustling in the dark, but I didn't hear any footsteps walking toward me. My senses adjusted, and I pulled the drawstring of the light overhead.

Dog cages lined the length of the room, but women were inside. The closest one to me was pregnant, looking like she was halfway along. Duct tape encased her mouth, wrist, and ankles. The next cage was empty, except for tattered, bloody clothes. A slim woman lay in the next cage, curled into a ball with bloodstains down her legs as if she had miscarried.

My knees buckled. Paper crunched beneath me; it was the scrapbook paper Mrs. Lupei used for my photo album. I looked to the source of the spilled paper and saw Roman's toolbelt and razor blade on the workshop desk. I drifted to the wooden counter. Photos of Roman and me were scattered and clipped.

My stomach dropped to the floor.

I clutched the desk for stability, proceeding to the first cage to unlatch it, then stopped. Once one woman crawled through the windows in the rec room, Roman would be alerted by her escape. They all had to flee at once. I walked the length of the cages, assessing their bellies and their ability to fit through the culvert windows. None of them were too big. It seemed they weren't entering the later stages of pregnancy, which meant this horror scene before me had existed for months. But that didn't make sense. I first noticed the wards on the basement cellar door when I was here a few weeks ago. How long was I away since my last visit before that? These cages couldn't have been here for five months, which signified werewolf babies developed faster than human ones, and with a much higher rate of miscarriage.

Packmasters only want breeding stock.

Andre's words from when we first met weighed on my chest, constricting my breathing; Roman couldn't do this. An object clinked against my boot.

It was the lipstick I lost in Greenland, the one that rolled into the portal. Bronwyn attempted to portal me here. *No. No, no, no.* The pillow. The sparkly lip gloss on the pillow in the rec room matched the one I used to write the message to Lukas on the mirror. Bronwyn knew this room existed. She had been here. She'd sat in my and Roman's date spot. Why was her face low enough on the sofa to smear her lip-gloss? Why did the couch smell of flowers?

The room spun, and I realized I hadn't inhaled.

I opened the cages and ripped apart the duct tape.

"Everyone stay silent," I whispered. "I'm getting you out of here." I proceeded to the end as the women gathered behind me. The last woman was the furthest along and looked the most fragile. The vitality was drained from her face; she seemed as delicate as a glass bird. As I unlatched the cage, I noticed the dark bite marks on her forearms.

Coldness crept in from underneath the door.

The hairs on my body raised like the room temperature plummeted to glacial degrees, making my teeth chatter. Light flickered underneath the door, like movement stirred in the holding cell. A presence gathered opposite the door, menacing my senses, making them scream out in alarm. Not quite the Dark Charm, the gathering force felt far more primordial, profound, like the vacuum of the Nexus yet tainted. The lightbulbs popped. We were submerged in darkness, save for the light from the doorframe.

Tendrils of shadow reached out from under the door like claws.

The women scuttled to the back of the room.

The door opened, and a figure stood against the light like a brick wall, a wispy, black aura surging out with a consciousness of its own.

I lit the Light Charm in both palms. Sparks and white-hot light filled the room. Roman stood before me, but it was like he was made of shadow. His eyes smoldered like amber coals beneath a black flame. I rose, and the darkness that surrounded him pulled back like a widow's veil, like it was fleeing the touch of my light. His smooth skin returned, but there was nothing soft about his expression.

"Roman," I whispered, my voice tight, slipping

from my clenched throat. "Where are your parents?"

He walked toward me, and another set of eyes stalked the back of his head. Luminescent almond-shaped eyes hovered in the growing darkness, gathering like a storm cloud behind Roman, urging him forward. A low rumble trembled across the floor, sounding from the shadow wolf behind him, except the end of growl ended in Roman's mouth as if he were fighting possession.

Coldness crept out, and I retreated to avoid the biting sting. My boot kicked my lipstick back against the wall, but I kept my gaze locked with Roman's, not wanting my retreat to trigger his predatory instinct. I had given up enough ground that I now pressed against the women.

"Roman!" I commanded. "Where are your parents?"

The whites of Roman's eyes blacked out. "They're gone, Karo."

My spark, fueling the Light Charm, flickered. "No. Please, no." I pleaded. "Roman, no!"

"It's time." His face was a statue, smooth, hard, and empty of emotion. He was committed to his plans, plans that made him smile. His jaw elongated. The corners of his lips split to his ears. Fangs descended from the raw wounds, black blood dripping down his chin. He moved toward me, but the blackness behind him rose to the ceiling, morphing into the huge, gaping jaws of a wolf, and swallowed him whole.

I stumbled back. As the vapor cleared, a glistening black puddle rippled on the concrete, then went as still as glass. The women whimpered behind me. I hung in the quiet suspense, watching for any sign of Roman.

A low humming came from the puddle. At first, the water stirred, a subtle ripple, then waves splashed with the momentum of noise building to screams—screams that sounded distant and augmented, like white noise traveling between dimensions, entering our world.

They were the screams of the Forged.

Roman was Forging, which meant I was the last piece of his soul, and he'd committed to an act to destroy it.

A hand shot from the oily water. Roman's face emerged, coated in slime as he struggled to pull himself from the hole. "Karo, help me!" he cried.

I extinguished my light magic in one hand and reached out to him, but the decayed limbs of the Forged pulled him down. This wasn't how regular Charmed Forged.

The dark portal went still.

"Run," I said to the women.

Chapter Eighteen

The women dashed around the hole as I stooped to help the most fragile woman rise. A jolt tore through the room, and a woman pitched to the floor. Though the door was open, the ward stopped them from leaving. I pushed to the front of the group and searched the glistening weave filling the doorway. It was constructed identically to Kazimir's wards in Russia. *Bronwyn.* Even her light magic was poisoned like diluted darkness was creeping underneath the light, a subtle shadow. I dismantled the wards and hauled the woman in my hands up the stairs. One woman helped me, but the rest gathered in the hallway.

"To the great room!" I called up to them.

Once on the landing, I lowered the woman onto a rug. "To the doors, get out of the house! Run to the road!" I pulled the woman, dragging her across the hardwood to the glass sliders.

A howl cut through the noise of pattering feet.

The floorboards at the end of the stairs cracked, then exploded into the great room. A black mound barreled out so fast it met the hardwood with the force of a meteor. The glass shattered behind us.

"Run!" I screamed. Using my vampiric strength, I pulled the rug and the two closest women through the broken glass and out into the snow.

The ground shook with another howl, and hundreds

of yips and calls replied in kind.

"Stop!" I called to the fleeing women. "Come to me!"

I unleashed the Light Charm, letting it stream from my hands into the whipping snow above. I parted the energy into a dome as Andre had for us before. With a crack, lightning lit the snow like a forcefield sweeping out to the women while Roman's pack closed in at their heels, their eyes like flames in the furious night. One woman didn't make it. Her screams were pulled into the blackness, untouched by the circle's light, until she silenced. The surrounding forest was as pitch-black as the sky above, bleeding into one another in a sinister, whistling abyss—the smells of winter and death gusting through the air.

I turned to the house. The beast skulked out, and its murky shape, stark against the falling snow in the light, was now three times Roman's size. As if they were now one, Roman's honey eyes shone where the wolf's once were, glowing like amber moons.

"Karo." His voice was a whispered hiss that carried on the air like a storm of dead leaves. "Come to me, be my mate."

The pack howled, their calls rising with the whirling wind within the forest and the cascading snow, coiling together. When the crescendo reached its apex, Roman rushed forward, morphing onto disjointed hind legs. His broad chest formed in the parting shadows, smooth skin flowing up over his jaw to his full mouth— the seams where his cheeks split dark and raw. Smoky tendrils crowned him like antlers, and with his eyes luminous, he reminded me of a god, a dark spirit. The folklore varied; be it Pan or Cernunnos in Euro-Pagan culture, or Wendigo to the Anishinaabe, the undertone of intoxicating power in the air—poisonous want—urged all near him to the point of violence.

Darkness crept between his wolves, and they yipped and snapped at the air in frustration. The women within my protection grew agitated, and I could sense their heart rates spiking, the adrenaline souring their sweat.

"Roman, I know you're in there. Please, don't do this," I said, but my voice faltered; to hold a shield of this size was beyond my ability. "Fight it!"

He flickered to the dome, traveling as fast as Kazimir's spirit had, gazing at me through the electricity. "Why would I fight what is natural, Karo? Does my power scare you? I am no longer your lapdog." His pack erupted growls and yips. "I embraced my nature; you should do the same." His voice dropped to a whisper, like a caress made of words that touched me deep within my soul. "You and I are the same, Karo. We're both ugly on the inside."

I shivered. At times, I felt like I *was* hideous at my core. My whole life, I'd battled my nature to feed, and I'd berated myself into submission. All this time, Roman had fought the same war against his wolf, and though he'd never portrayed his strife, he'd lost. *Why now?* I wanted to blame Bronwyn, but the truth bore into me; I knew my rejection contributed to his madness. Andre gave me acceptance and security, and I gave Roman abandonment. I wasn't responsible for the decisions Roman made, but I missed the depth of his transition, caught up in my own dreadful circumstances. He succumbed to his ugliest nature and eliminated the loved ones who could stop him. *Except for me.*

"We don't have to be," I replied, my eyes pleading more than my words. "Please."

He placed a hand upon the shield. His veins swelled, and his fangs gritted; the dark wolf jolted from him for an instant, but he didn't drop his arm from the pulse of electricity. Instead, swirling shadow leaked into the orb, snaking its way down to me.

I buckled. Searing black veins streaked up my arms, numbing my senses. My shield shrank, and the women dove to remain within its fleeting safety. One woman screamed. She lay just outside the orb with two wolves tearing open the soft skin of her swollen belly. The noise, horrible and slick, made me screech. "Roman!" If he fathered that child, his face didn't show it.

Artur's tarot reading replayed in my mind. *It craves your future blood and absolute power.* He wanted my future babies, the strength I had, and the traits I would pass to our children. My vision spun. Roman's magic felt like poison, constricting my air and my grasp on the world. I clutched the Light Charm within my heart, holding onto it like oxygen, like warmth in the frigid darkness consuming me. In the fog, a speck of light hovered behind Roman. It looked like a small lantern, but it grew larger and larger until I recognized the glowing bird I'd constructed of earth and light magic. Yet, the bird was too large.

Miruna, dressed like a Dacian warrior, swooped from the sky on a blazing falcon and drove into Roman.

The chariot-sized bird carved a wake through the pack, forcing Roman across the lawn and deep into the frozen earth. She soared back around the garden and leaped from the bird, rolling onto the ground. A pulsing shield of light magic snapped around her. She spun to me. "Get them on the falcon!"

The bird pierced my shield and landed before the women, lighting the snow in a sparkling glow. With the effects of Roman's magic gone, I rushed to the women to help them aboard. If they had never seen magic before, they now were well adjusted to the concept after meeting Roman.

Miruna raised a hand and guided the falcon into the air above the Lupeis's acres of forest to the road. Roman charged at her, but her shield held, sending a cascade of sparks around him. The wolves rushed me, their eyes now black with a frosty-silver glow like they were possessed by the toxic magic spewing from Roman. I siphoned the Light Charm inward, my body tightly enclosed with magic, and forced a bolt into the wolves. A number went down, but the mass continued to swarm me. I struck out at those I could and blasted others, chiseling my way to Miruna, who circled her other hand over the ground.

The frozen earth shook.

Shards of icy clay speckled the yard. Hands reached out from gaps in the snow, and bodies rose from the ground, formed entirely of dirt. Light coated them and erupted into a burning aura of electricity. Miruna's warriors collided with the wolves. At last, a path cleared to Miruna.

Roman intercepted me, his size and cloak of darkness threatening to black out the scenes of battle.

I expanded my shield as his arms encased my shoulders, hurling him into his back. Roman howled— the tone of two voices cried out together, one deep in pitch, sounding like an electronic perversion of

Roman's cadence. "Bitch!" they screamed in unison. Roman writhed against the ground, both of his arms lopped off. Dark stubs protruded as he screamed and rolled.

I collapsed within Miruna's shield. My muscles shook with exhaustion, but I rolled to face her. "You got my message. How did you find me?"

She flowed with the movement of her warriors. The wrinkles of her face weren't strained from fatigue but rather peaked with exhilaration like she was reliving moments long lost. Her hair loosed from her tight bun as she slammed her fist into the air, and a warrior collided with a wolf that lunged at me opposite the shield.

"I got your message, child," she said, "Albesuc don't abandon our own. I can find my kin whenever I wish."

"I gave Loukin the book out of pity; it was so stupid. He used it to blackmail me and threated to kill you."

"Loukin is not our concern right now." She looked above me.

I turned and saw Roman ten times the size he was before. He placed his hands upon the curve of Miruna's shield, and blackness poured from him once more. "Did you come here to die, old woman?" Roman's voices asked in unison, and the wolves went wild like they could taste our blood already. One wolf outside of the dome howled like he was shifting, but his fur peeled back, exposing bone and rippling muscle. There was a *whoosh*, a guttural scream, and he turned inside out. The corpse hung midair for an instant like it was caught within the rift of two worlds. Rotting limbs punched outward from deep within its ribcage. Pieces of the dead rushed out, morphing into one arachnid-like shape. Another scream. Then another.

Roman's pack was Forging.

"Rise, Karolina. Find your strength," Miruna said.

The falling snow lit from the eastern woods in a wall of white. A shining disk hovered like a small sun just above the snowdrifts on the far side of Roman's lawn, Dyads dropping from the portal like sparkling tears. They would carry out their duty and execute all who Forged, including Roman. A massive electric dome fell over the Lupeis's acerage, just like the Dyad's shield from the pawn shop, concealing us from the outside world.

They advanced, and I felt a pull within my blood as they drew nearer. I yearned for the blue substance I experienced at their headquarters. I sensed its presence in them. Jealousy bit at me, and I knew these were Bronwyn's shard-filled enforcers. They drew their weapons and marched forward, the sheen of their swords and axes luminous in the snowfall.

A cyclone whirled from the portal; balls of light crackled within. Bronwyn hovered within its center, holding the Light Charm within her hands. A body stirred behind her, shielding itself from view.

"Surrender," Roman commanded, but Miruna's stream of light thickened upon meeting the darkness in the shield and shoved it down.

I rose, Roman's eerie eyes tracking me to the edge of Miruna's shield. "Can you save them?" I asked.

"Yes, I can save the pack," she said, keeping her gaze on her opponent. "But Roman is beyond my reach, Karolina, like his parents were." Miruna was alerted to

Mama's death through her connection to the spirit realm. Mama came to her in a dream. I didn't know how she knew about Roman's parents, but I didn't doubt her. She sent another blast into the shield, causing the dark wolf and Roman to cry out.

I used the distraction to rush from the shield. I summoned the Light Charm around me and cut through the wolves like a cannonball. Dyads formed a blockade behind the pack and lit in unison at my charge. At the moment of impact, I released the Fire Charm, channeling the weight of my emotions, the trauma of all I witnessed, into one blow.

Fire and electricity roared outward like a tidal wave. The ring of fire swept across the snow, eviscerating all in its wake. Wolves yelped behind me. Dyads flew back, and the pang of metal cracking rang out.

"Move!" Bronwyn screamed.

Water soaked the ground as my magic dissipated. I pushed forward through the fallen Dyads toward Bronwyn. *Agatha.* The old woman I'd battled at the Dyad headquarters scrambled back toward Bronwyn's ice shield. One of her legs, bright blue and turned backward, crumbled as she crawled. I'd injured the Diamond Eater.

"What did you do to him?" I screamed.

Agatha rose on her newly forming leg, and Bronwyn blocked her from my sight. "He did what they all do when they meet Agatha," Bronwyn said. "He was corrupted by what he wanted most—his greed for power, to secure his bloodline's position through his offspring."

Family. Roman valued loyalty and family.

Yet he had bastardized both. Worse still, his corruption made him vulnerable to the dark entity that now possessed him. In a strange type of Forging, he'd merged with the spirit. If I submitted to Roman, would I be consumed as well? What would have happened to the ruby if I too fell to the dark spirit? If I had, and Ivy didn't have the Blood, no one would be left to rival the Eaters.

"You manipulative witch!"

I unleashed a blast toward them, except Agatha launched out from behind Bronwyn. Her blue leg turned scaly; each scale shone like the diamonds she ate, sweeping up her body. Iridescent and speeding like a comet, she blew through the wolves and light warriors straight into Miruna.

Miruna's shield held but wavered at the impact. She tumbled headfirst and kept rolling, her body whipping at a violent angle. Bronwyn blocked my blast but was thrown from the force. I'd realized my mistake as the Dyads closed in with Bronwyn at my back. They'd baited me away from Miruna, and I'd charged headlong into the trap.

Miruna rose then crumpled, pinned between Roman's poisonous magic and Agatha. They weren't here for me. Miruna's power was triple my own and could save Roman's pack. If Miruna's magic could be absorbed after death, Bronwyn would have power that would rival few. Yet, all Miruna's power still couldn't save Roman. Why wasn't it enough?

Bronwyn and her troop unleashed torrents of electricity, the vibrating streams blinding even my vampiric sight and obscuring the darkness beyond. But I'd learned from my abduction at the pawnshop. Using my fire and white magic, I blasted the ground while holding my shield to keep from sinking. The roar of the electricity threatened to pop my eardrums. I crumpled from the weight of the magic restraining me. The explosive force of my fire ebbed away the longer I sustained my shield.

A hawk call tore through the din of battle.

The streams of lightning from the northwest ceased, then the west. I rolled, darting to my feet, and faced Bronwyn and her remaining soldiers. Their blasts stayed with me like chains of light.

Billows of rolling blackness gleamed like jewels in the radiance of the lightning, raining down from the sky. The dark clouds claimed the next set of Dyads, hawk talons piercing their shields and lifting them into the snowstorm.

Ben materialized before Bronwyn. She split her strike between Ben and me, but Ben held up a hand, stalling the blow mid-air. Invisible swirls stirred the falling snow, like the fabric of our reality distorted where the Nexus flowed. "You are not an apex predator here," Ben said, "and I will wipe you from this earth if you seek to poison it." His hand, lightning-fast and transforming into an ax-sized claw, flew to Bronwyn's breastplate. He penetrated her magical shield like it was absent.

Her metal armor crunched in. Blood spurted down her chest. Bronwyn's breath froze, her partial exhalation mist on her chapped lips. She clutched his claw. Frost swept across her elegant face, whiting out her eyes. Her blood froze in place. Ice sped from Bronwyn up Ben's arm, forming icicles on his eyelashes.

Ben swept his other forearm down, smashing his wrist into pieces at the claw. Free from his connection to Bronwyn, the rime dissipated. Onyx feathers fluttered, and his arm reformed. Like a frost demon incarnate, Bronwyn sent a wall of ice sailing toward Ben. I used the diversion as an opening to race back to Miruna.

More Forged came, erupting from the carcasses and engulfing Miruna's light warriors. Miruna, on the opposite side of the lawn, danced bloodied within her shrunken shield, firing barbs of magic into Roman and Agatha. Roman's size doubled, again, rivaling the size of a tank. Agatha, embedded in the earth from a blow, climbed free.

Three hawk warriors appeared at Agatha's back and lifted her into the air. Their talons punctured her skin, shards of glittering prismatic gems sheading from the tears in her flesh. With the force of three small hurricanes, the warriors pulled in opposing directions. The seams of her skin slowly split, sparkling into the whirling snowfall. She screamed, her call sounding like a summoning to which only her kind would answer. She glowed.

A bright light flared, whiting out the acres of the yard, followed by a high-pitched screech.

When I regained my vision, Agatha was gone.

The warriors tackled the Forged. Ivy charged from the western woods, surrounded by the magic of the Blood, the Charm, and her warriors. Roman's magic engulfed Miruna's shield save for a mere foot at the bottom. Miruna curled into a ball within the snow.

I kept sprinting toward Roman's back, unleashing a Light Charm bolt as thick as a missile. He howled and whirled around, shifting his sorcery into me. I rolled, the chilling touch of his magic caressing my hips. I ran, zig-zagging toward Ivy, creating distance between Miruna and Roman. I kept my shield hugged close to my body, dodging the expanding tendrils of Roman's magic. Icy, electric pain bit into my calf then engulfed me. I skidded across a patch of ice and scurried behind Ivy, letting her shield take the brunt of the assault.

She flew at Roman, her warriors swooping around her, her magic shining red, white, and gold. The colors streaked into a blast, colliding with Roman. He shot backward in a storming ball of shadow, sailing across acres of snow and ripping through the patio. Flagstone exploded into the timber home. More glass shattered.

Miruna halted her advance toward us and turned to face Roman.

He rose, absorbing the energy of Ivy's blast still snaking around him, and grew taller, rivaling the height of his family home.

Ivy reached Miruna's side in an instant. Bronwyn and her Dyads still battled the hawk warriors in front of the eastern woods. I approached Ivy from behind. As we three women aligned, my mind narrowed into a keyhole, where one singular image blazed. *The blanket from the trading post.* Myself, Ivy, then Miruna. The maiden, the mother, the crone.

"Together," I cried.

Roman thundered forward.

Chapter Nineteen

"As one," Ivy called.

Roman, swirling like the fiery tendrils of a black sun, rocketed through the battlefield, poised to consume us and all that stood before him.

"Do as I do, child!" Miruna shouted, shrinking her shield and gathering light magic between her hands. The pictographs from the rock shield of Mattawa flashed before me, coming to life as the three of us gathered the Light Charm within our hands. The three painted figures stood behind one spear.

"One bolt!" I screamed.

Ivy let loose her beam of light, the energy sizzling above the snow and bridging the narrowing gap between us and Roman's colossal form. Miruna and I released our blasts, angling the blows into Ivy's stream. The river of lightning struck him, forming a disk upon his front and slowing his ascent. The light engulfed him. Roman's home and acres of land lit like a bomb was detonated. Despite our remote location, were it not for the shield, we'd be seen for miles. How long the Dyad shield would hold was unknown, time was as fleeting as our strength.

Roman bucked and howled. The wolves and Forged alike went mad. The Dyads flipped their directions, all charging toward us. Why did they need Roman and this evil entity? Why did Bronwyn want the

Forged in our world?

"Karolina," Miruna called over the raucous hum of electricity, her voice strained. "You are the most connected to Roman. You must be the one to focus your Charm. Infiltrate his defenses."

Streams of Dyad attacks barraged us, and I fought to remain upright. I focused all of my Charms, feeling the icy barrier between my magic and Roman. Yet it was the Light Charm that slipped between a crack in his defenses like water flowing through a fissure within ice, warming it to the touch and widening the opening. Thoughts of Roman's broad grin on a summer day filled me. I held onto the feeling, my thoughts of Roman, and our attachment birthed in childhood.

"I'm in!" I called.

"End him now!" Ivy screamed.

"Through your love, you must take his life, Karolina," Miruna gasped, her collapse resounding with a thick crack on the ice below her. The Dyads focused on Miruna, and now that she was pinned down, they turned their attention to Ivy.

Clinging to the Roman of my memories, I imagined his heart within my hands. The tides of shadow thinned with a gentle squeeze, revealing Roman, gray-skinned and sickly, hunched over. He buckled into the snow. "Karo, don't!" He called, his voice void of emotion, merged with the spirit who claimed him. "I love you. Don't end what we could be. You haven't seen the power we could have yet."

Ivy fell.

Light burned my eyes, and liquid dribbled down my cheeks. Miruna's moans stopped me from releasing Roman's heart, but I could not bring myself to compress it any further. The snowstorm swelled, and Bronwyn soared across the land. She released a glowing blast.

In martial arts, the moment before the exertion of force was serene. The more time stretched, the calmer one became; thoughts could be searched, and when one struck, one was sure to strike true. Time lengthened now—Roman's beating heart in my hands, Bronwyn's blow descending, the Dyads shifting from Ivy, the magnetic pull of the dark moon at my back. *Energy never dies*. Death was a transfer of energy but so was a banishing spell.

I held onto the pull of the moon as Roman's heart faded from my fingers.

Bronwyn's blast knocked me onto my back.

The swirling shadows of the dark wolf, stark against the sheets of snow, vacuumed inward on itself with a thunderous clap.

Bronwyn lunged.

Lukas, falling from the sky, intercepted her mid-air. They rolled through the snow where Roman once stood, Lukas's ax swinging down and clipping her malformed breastplate. "When did you start battling wind walkers!" Lukas shouted. Bronwyn crumbled and rolled, but Lukas advanced. "When did you let the Forged multiply, and oppose those who fight to keep them at bay?"

Units of Dyads rained down from the black sky, gleaming like legions of Valkyrie, with *Drotten* Arie leading the charge. Their forms pierced the massive dome and smashed to the ground. Arie's troops, three to one, wrangled Bronwyn's enforcers into submission, while others reinforced the shield.

Arie collided with Bronwyn from behind, taking out her legs. She flew forward into Lukas's grasp, and within that instant of vulnerability, he bound her with hundreds of strings of light at once. She fell onto the snow.

"What were you feeding us?" Arie demanded. He approached Bronwyn, flicking out a thin blade and scoring a small cut into her neck. He sniffed her blood, no doubt feeling the siren's call of the Diamond Eater shards they consumed.

I was at Miruna's side, and as Ivy took over surveying her wounds, I walked to Lukas. With the power of the dark wolf gone, the wolves transformed back into their human forms, many laying injured and shivering amidst the storm.

"Diamond Eater blood," I said from a distance.

Lukas turned, and Arie's gaze rose to meet mine. "Diamond Eaters are a myth," Arie said.

I doubted Arie meant that. As the head of intelligence and operations, he, like Loukin, must have suspected a supernatural community was controlling our world.

Suddenly, Ben was at my side. "We slew one tonight, one that fought side-by-side with your prisoner. She used the Diamond Eater to corrupt the Packmaster of the Northern Ontario and Québec packs. The werewolves are a part of the sacred guardianship of the earth. To compromise one with dark magic, let alone a Pack Leader, she opened him to one of our world's darkest spirits.

Roman once said that werewolves were of the earth, so only the Light and Earth Charms worked against them. I didn't know that they were guardians *of* the earth, but it made sense. If the Eaters sought to expand their mines beyond the land's limit, they would want the wolves incapacitated. If diamonds were their fuel, and they planned to create an army of Dyads filled with Eater blood, they would have to increase their supply.

"The dark wolf," I replied.

Ben nodded and whispered in my ear. "If Roman had claimed you, you could not have returned the Mantle of the Blood to Ivy, and you would not know how to kill a Diamond Eater."

"But she was too late," I whispered.

I was also a loose end to Bronwyn, but she was much more to me. Revenge seemed such a dull word, duller than the ache in my chest, colder than the void left after Mama's death, and more numbing than the act I'd just committed against Roman. My fire flared, uncalled, and I could feel the residual dark energy that stained the land building beneath me, goading me to take her life. Black flames flickered at my feet as I stepped forward.

Ben's hand shot to my stomach, halting my step and breaking my trance.

Lukas's and Arie's attention rested on me once more, no doubt noting the dark flames I produced. "And you are?" Arie moved in closer, breathing in deeply as a gust of cool air swept across my back. *You smell really good*, Arie had said at the Dyad base. Had the slightest shift in my intent compromised my perfume scent when I was impaired?

"I'm a friend," I said, noting my identity spell might not last much longer.

Bronwyn laughed, her voice still melodic despite

her bloodstained mouth.

"Still, you say nothing?" Lukas knelt to her, his face incredulous, tears of anger, or hurt, welling as he searched her eyes for any sign of remorse or explanation. She looked back at him, like a sculpture of ice, dead and unfeeling, save for a slight upward curve forming at one side of her lips.

Ben stepped toward them. Arie produced an ancient-looking dagger glowing with white light. Ben and Arie said in unison, "In the name of the Nexus and the Charm, I hereby strip you of your—"

Bronwyn flicked her gaze to mine. "I'll be seeing you, Kay." A muddy-gray orb burst from her, ripping Lukas's bonds. The Dark Charm enveloped her, and she was gone.

"Search the grounds!" Arie ordered. "Get a trace on the spell!"

I moved to trace the spell on the ground where Bronwyn had laid, but Ivy clutched my shoulder. "I need you, it's Miruna."

Miruna lay still in the snow. I raced toward her and warmed her arms in a hug. She was cold and limp. "What's wrong?"

"She's beyond exhausted," Ivy said. "She expelled too much of her magic at once; her life spark is barely aflame. I can heal her, but she will need to stay with me for a few months."

"Miruna, can you hear us?" She groaned, and I kissed her cheek in reply. "Whatever you can do, Ivy, is much appreciated," I said.

The Dyads tended to the injured. Those within Roman's pack who were well enough shifted and ventured into the woods. Police cars and fire trucks, from the town across the miles of forest, passed by on the main road looking for the blasts visible before the shield sealed, but the Dyads' barrier held fast. After they had passed, Ivy agreed to lift an edge of the dome so I could escape before the Dyads found time to question me further. After I reported the women who escaped Roman's basement to the closest Dyad, I snuck inside the Lupeis's home.

My coat and purse were on Roman's bed. I called Andre, but my call wouldn't go through. Either he had no reception, or he turned his phone off. I pocketed my phone, but my feet remained planted. I ran my hand along Roman's soft cotton sheets, then succumbed to dropping onto the feather duvet. The fabric still smelled like him, the same scent that coated his sweater when I first fled Canada months ago. How had things unraveled so fast? With my eyes closed, breathing in his scent with each inhalation, I pretended he was next to me. But he wasn't.

I rose and looked out to the sky. Roman was banished to the dark side of the moon, a fate just a shade more merciful than death. If energy never died, I now knew that love didn't either; it could only be transformed. I collected my things and stepped into the night, leaving the Lupei home looming like a specter at my back.

****

I met Ivy at the northwestern corner of the property, where the walk to the road was a mere ten minutes. She collected her light magic and lifted an edge of the dome as promised.

"Ivy?" I asked as I stepped through the opening. "There is one thing I still don't understand. Why did meeting Agatha have such an extreme effect on Roman and not me? Even during the battle, tonight I felt the pull of Agatha's blood, but nothing more."

"The reason is one your father never knew. The Blood never leaves those who are worthy, it becomes a part of you. You will carry a resistance to Diamond Eaters your whole life, Karolina. Other species too."

****

I trudged a quarter of a mile in the snow. Every few steps, I tested my bond with Andre to no avail. With the bond wide open between us, if it were functional, he would have felt my distress and came to me. I was sure of it. Yet, I'd been gone too long not to raise his alarms. Had Roman's dark magic spell also blocked the bond on Andre's end? Andre might be searching the Ottawa streets for me. Older buildings in the city tended to block reception. We still had time to continue our plan. We could flee the country by morning, but first, I needed closure regarding Roman's parents.

Ahead, the original Lupei workshop stood dim and still. Snow enveloped it, curving up to the roof, making the old, sagging building look like a large snowbank. Not much business was conducted from the shop anymore, save for company vehicle repairs. My stomach turned as cold as the icicles hanging from the roofline. Roman would now be a missing person case, along with his parents. If I took one of the Lupeis's delivery trucks to get home, I would draw attention to my escape. Yet, if I found the Lupeis's remains, dumping the truck at the site for the police to find might allow them a proper Charmed burial. I could leave money and instructions with a member of our community, like Artur.

I doubled back and approached the rear parking lot. The second truck in line had its keys in the glove box. I drove down to the highway, then east across the river into Québec, to where Mr. Luepi's lacrosse stick led me before, the abandoned lumber mill.

The chain-link fence still gaped where I had smashed through, the metal wires now gleamed with ice in my headlights. I passed through the hole, the *Ne Pas Entrer* sign now overturned, as if the site now welcomed the discovery of the act that stained its grounds. The earth and trees felt scarred here in a way I couldn't identify before when the fear of a hundred wolves occupied my senses. The trees lurched in the wind, reaching out to me as I rounded the building, the truck's large tires hauling through the snowdrifts. When I reached the back field, where Roman's pack had gathered before, I got out.

My footsteps crunched through the upper crust of the undisturbed snow. I reached the middle of the clearing, then pulled the Earth Charm up through my feet. "I call out to the soul of Robert Lupei, if you are here, please show yourself." I release the Charm into the squall, watching the golden flecks scatter among the flakes, then disappear into the night.

The air was quiet, save for the rustle of branches and gusts of wind in my ears, but in the distance, what looked like the delicate flame of a candle sprang up in the dark. It grew, hovering closer through the layers of falling snow. Except it wasn't a flame at all. It was a small orb of golden light, like the flecks I'd cast away united and swiftly approached. The orb shifted into the form of a man who bought me to my knees.

"Mr. Lupei," I cried. "I'm so sorry."

Rather than standing above me, his spirit dropped to his knees to meet my face. "Don't cry, Karolina. Save your strength. Roman has lost himself, and I fear you may be the only one to reach him."

My breath hitched. If I had slain Roman, his father's spirit would have known. But I hadn't killed Roman. I braced for the pain that would ensue. "Roman is beyond my and Miruna's reach. His spirit's gaze seized mine like it was the sole connection that tethered him to this world, as if any sudden movement would dissolve him in the wind. "He Forged," I continued, "Not a regular Forging, but with a dark spirit."

"The dark wolf," he whispered. "I saw it once in the woods after my succession of power. I thought it was a trick of the mind since I never saw it again. I was such a fool. The signs that Roman was changing were there, like a subtle whisper in my thoughts, but I didn't want to believe it. I couldn't."

"I didn't have the strength to kill him." I shook my head like my body was still denying what I had done. "I banished him."

"Where?" his hands balled into fists at his side.

"The dark side of the moon."

At this revelation, his image faded, like the thoughts of his son, desolate and alone, could dismantle his soul.

"Where is Mrs. Lupei?" I rushed the words out before he could leave me.

His eyes were barren when he answered me. "I was at my last pack meeting, watching Roman conduct our business when he shifted. Within his shift, there was a flicker of darkness, and all I wanted to deny – his strength, his massive wolf form – could no longer be ignored, because if our son possessed such power, my beautiful Silviea no longer held our family power in check. It meant she was dead, and that he killed her after I kissed her goodbye that morning. I ran at him in an instant." Golden tears flowed down his face. "That was where I failed him, lost in my grief. Once the succession of power occurred between us, my power was inferior to his. I knew this, yet I wasn't thinking of it. I was only thinking of my wife and what our son had done. He murdered me before his pack, committing himself to his dark path even further." I reached out to him on instinct, and my hand went through his knee into the cold snow. "If I had had a different reaction," he continued, "maybe I could have stopped him."

"I'm so sorry," I said, struggling to conjure any response that would console the inconsolable.

He broke the blank stare he maintained during his recollection. "You may save him yet, Karolina. He's not dead. He is lost, but he still exists. Promise me you'll save him."

To deny him this felt like torture, rebelling against all parts of myself I hoped were still kind. "I can promise you I'll try."

He nodded, a weak smile gathering as his form disintegrated. "You'll try."

Chapter Twenty

Wind licked at the wet streaks on my face, a biting cold compared to the numbness in my fingers. I shivered. Flurries soaked my hair and leggings. I slogged back to the truck and wiped down my prints. The snow would cover my tracks; now, I had to put distance between myself and the mill.

I felt for the moon in the sky, trying not to think of Roman with its presence. It was well past midnight, and morning was just hours away. I headed into the white abyss once more on foot, hoping every twinkle of light I saw might be a driver approaching who would take sympathy on me. I tried my bond with Andre with no success. Panic crept from my belly into my throat, but I swallowed it down. *Hope. Trust.* Part of the personal change I'd committed to was dependent on both. I shifted my thoughts.

Calling a cab was an option, but I counted on the transit surrounding the mill being reviewed during the investigation later. I knew too well what it was like to be a person of interest for Mama's murder, and being one for the Lupeis, even while I planned on leaving the country, was beyond my emotional capacity. Plus, there was another type of transit I had to consider.

I pulled out my phone and texted Ina. *—I'm stranded. Is there any chance Ben could give me a ride?—*

She responded right away. —*A ride in a car, ride? Or poof feathers ride?*—

—*Poof feathers would be ideal. Is that possible?*—

My phone vibrated in my hands. —*Yes.*—

—*Can we meet too? At our safe place. I need to make some arrangements that I need your help with.*—

I walked a few more paces, and she responded again. —*Yes. Ben will drop you off, but I just got out of the shower. I'll come when I'm ready. All good?*—

I wanted to ask about Miruna, but since this phone was supplied by Loukin's operations, data blocker and all, I didn't trust it was secure.

—*Totally, you need more time to get ready than the rest of us.*—

—*Careful, I'll cancel your ride.*—

Before pocketing my phone again, I replied, —*Thank you, Ina.*—

****

Ben arrived in a whirl of ebony feathers skirting the shadows of the woods along the highway. After some instructions from Ben, the world dismantled around us, and we entered the ether of astral travel. The sensation wasn't like my bond with Andre, but more of a warm fuzzy feeling lining where my body should be, like an outline of myself. My directions brought us just outside my building. We materialized in the bitter cold, and the wind slapped stands of hair against my cheeks. Snow packed against the back door, glowing a hazy shade of gray. Dim light escaped from the ice layered on the fixture above the back door.

I thanked Ben and dug out the door. As I left the stairwell and stepped onto my floor, I could feel the tingle of my identity spell lifting. I knocked on my door in short rapid succession, hoping Andre was close by to open it for me faster than I could find my keys. He didn't.

My keys were in the last pocket I checked, zippered deep within my coat. I fumbled the key into the lock with shivering hands and stepped inside—the room was dark. With a sweep of my magic, the candles around the room bloomed in flame. Andre had tidied up after his movie and snacks. My china was organized on the shelves, and the floor was swept. Even my cushions were fluffed, looking fuller than when I left.

"Andre?" I called as I slipped off my coat and boots, then hovered my hands over the candles for a moment. Silence hung in the air, louder than any crisis alarm. "Andre?" I checked the bedroom, expecting to see a large mound of a body underneath the duvet, but the bed was made. "Andre?" I swept through the remaining rooms, my chest rising and falling with each bout of trepidation. He wasn't here. I delved into my subconscious, searching for him through the bond. Our connection stretched into infinity, but any beacon or warmth was null.

I went to the bookshelf, pulling off several volumes and letting them fall to the floor until I found the right one. I dropped to the hardwood, flicking through a book of dark magic I'd purchased from Artur's shop. Midway through the tome, I found the spell Roman had performed—it should have worn off within hours. I clutched the book and dialed Andre. I hung up and dialed him again. Each time the electronic message clicked over, another invisible blow winded me. Panic swallowed me like a wave; images of clutching Andre in the Black Sea smothered me, except this time, I was grasping at air.

Andre wasn't here.

I folded over into the floor. "Breathe," I said, "breathe." *Hope and trust.* One may call it naïve to hang onto both, but giving in to despair was far easier. Hanging onto the former two took more strength, more sinew.

I rose, pacing the length of the living room. With a strip of Andre's dress shirt, I tried every locating spell possible. Not only was our bond blocked, but all magical access to him was also cut off. A greater spell was at work, one not cast by Roman.

If Andre were out searching the city, he would come back to the apartment periodically to check if I had come home. The clock read *4:00 AM.* I could afford a twenty-minute wait. I reorganized my books, washed, selected warm clothing, and refreshed my lipstick and perfume. Then I sat, watching the clock click over to *4:18 AM.* With two more tormenting clicks, I hit the streets once more.

Andre would have checked my last whereabouts first, perhaps cycling back to it, if he assumed I wasn't detained. If he believed I was incapacitated, Roman would have been his first suspect, but Andre hadn't shown up at Roman's property, which brought me to the fear still roiling in my gut. Andre was captured, and I couldn't use magic to find him.

Except for the hollow lines the foot traffic had carved along the sidewalks, the city was buried, the snow now reaching my upper thighs. Heartbeats were sparse, even within the city core. Partiers had deserted the Laff. Music played lightly opposite the windows as staff hurried through their cleanup. Yet, a suspicious number of stragglers remained at the tables within, finishing their drinks two hours well after closing time.

I passed through the wall of heat at the door once more and was intercepted by a server, her lips stained red by her end-of-shift drink. I showed her my stamped hand before she could speak, the bingo-dotter dye weathering on despite battle and shower. "I left my purse inside," I lied.

"Be quick," she said and walked to the bar.

I scanned the room.

The operatives present during my earlier visit had left, but I sensed the Charm in the room. Probing my senses further, I mocked a search for the missing purse. The Dark Charm was in abundance. Two thickly muscled men sat with vodka on the rocks, watching me, but I appeared their blatant diversion, their senses likely focused on the pair of women in the shadow of the bar. I recognized the women from my narrow escape at my condo. *Custodes*. Before I abandoned my plan, I remembered their issue with my presence was circumstantial to my condo. They could only detect the Charm and sense my identity was masked.

I rounded a table and feigned looking underneath. The remaining four customers sat together. A Team Italy logo on one man's duffel bag hovered at my sight line. All of the men and women within the group possessed the Dark Charm, but with another Charm in use; its tingle was almost familiar. I focused on the person it emanated from but couldn't look at the individual directly. An identity spell was at work, one crafted with earth magic. They spoke quietly to another, drifting between Italian and English.

I weighed my options and considered the repeating

origins of the operatives I continued to encounter. Loukin's *Ispolniteli* were a consistent threat, but the Italian vampires at the House of Commons were a surprise. The *Custodes* scared the shit out of me, and Diamond Eaters were beyond rare, with their influence within arm's reach. But who would have the ability to incapacitate Andre? Thoughts of Andre's near demise at the hands of the *Custodes*, unbidden, came surging back. His tears.

I braced against the table to stand, then strode past the *Custodes* before thoughts of loss or fear could cripple me. "Meet me out back in five," I whispered a decibel above silent. Then I was submerged back into the cold night. The flakes waned in between buildings. I walked into the alley where Andre and I had materialized before. I was trapped, but an assault would come from one direction. Leaning into the shadow of the wall, I pushed my identity spell into my surroundings, blending my body into the building. I gathered the Light Charm and watched for the *Custodes'* approach.

Eyes glowing like blue stars, they rounded the corner.

I released my spell as I spoke, "I want to trade information." My voice bounced off the walls in echoes, its direction indistinguishable.

They stopped just inside. The tallest one called out into the dark, "What could you have that we'd want?"

"The name of the Diamond Eater who died tonight."

Agatha's death would eventually be known amongst her kind, her disappearance, and her presumed demise. But information was currency, and I imagined access to the most current intel was of the highest priority to the different factions of the supernatural community.

"Diamond Eaters are a myth," the other woman said.

"Yet, the name of the Eater who was killed tonight is circulating the channels," I bluffed, my voice ringing like a dropped coin back and forth between the walls.

The sound of a blade I'd not seen being sheathed filled the pause.

"What do you want in return?"

I phrased my words with caution, plucking one of the preconstructed lies in my head. "There's a bounty on a vampire my community is looking to collect." I paused, letting that sink in, letting them think I was working for an emissary. "He's an *Ispolniteli* operative." Knowing these women were at my condo, I didn't dare say Andre's name. My presence at the time alerted their suspicion and led them to my residence, but they were already investigating my building, which suggested that they'd been tipped off. Either their goal was the missing letter I'd stolen from the House of Commons, which signified they had a mole inside Base Franklin, or I was their objective. The latter was critical because it would mean the *Custodes* weren't just notified of our escape route from the base, but my or Andre's identities were discovered.

"If House *Custode* detained your target, consider them gone."

"That's not an answer," I said. "Did the *Custodes* detain any *Ispolniteli* operatives tonight? One with both the Light and Dark Charm? If you want the Diamond Eater's name, you'll comply."

"From what we know," the tallest woman said, "two. One with both the Light and the Dark Charm, as you say."

A wave rippled through me, one of shock and grief. Reaching into our empty bond, unable to feel Andre, left me to worry blindly and to ruminate over Andre's near-death experience with the *Custodes.* Fear churned in my stomach. I was ill-prepared for the influx of emotion, grateful for the camouflage that concealed me. Yet, I hadn't felt the same bone-chilling loss that seized me in Russia when I experienced the severance of the bond through death. Andre was alive. I hung onto that thought, which kept my breath steady.

"Agatha," I said.

The short one unsheathed her blade in a furry. "Who told you this!"

Her partner hauled her back with the speed of a full vampire. Blue-tinted magic whirled from within her as she restrained her partner, and they disappeared in a vacuum of light. The alleyway was still once more.

I waited in the quiet to collect myself, listening for sounds of life to ensure my departure would go unseen. With my vampiric senses alight, I fought my way back into the falling snow. The Charm vibrated within me. I honed my power into detecting other sources of magic at long range. My breath came out in puffs of steam beneath the streetlights.

There was still a chance Andre wasn't detained. Andre's likelihood of being the apprehended *Ispolniteli* with both the Light and Dark Charm was high, but I couldn't accept it as confirmation. Not yet.

Instead, I prowled every location in Ottawa's entertainment district, then the dungeon clubs in the belly of the city's underground tunnels. Lumpy stone jutted into my back as I braced against the corner wall. I lingered just opposite the door of the last establishment on my prospective list, one I would never have dared to visit prior to my blackmail. The dampness of a leaking, half-frozen pipe worsened the chill in the air. The hard drums of the music—a haunting overlapping beat, perhaps a cello, mimicking the cry of a woman—made any conversations inside inaudible. The streets would remain silent above, despite the volume below, deep within the underground passageways of Ottawa. Clubs could break curfew here; they could make their own rules.

Even still, morning was an hour away. Any moment, the clock would roll over to five o'clock, and the music would die down to clear the guests out. I'd almost missed my window to scan the room under the cover of the club's din, the ambiance and dancing providing a distraction. I entered through a rough black door. The ward I walked through felt like a spider's web, clinging to me as I pulled away from the threshold. Sweat, blood, and patchouli filled my nose. My fangs descended. The Light Charm ignited within me like it was reeling from the threshold spell it just encountered. It took all the control I had to remain poised.

The room was saturated with the Dark Charm, so much so that the air felt thick with it. Vampires fed openly on humans in shadowed booths. *Ispolniteli* indulged, danced, and drank, their insignias on full display. Others bore oath marks of embassies unknown to me. Emblems of horses, swords, and flowers. I skirted the wall, keeping full view of the room and its goings-on. Of all the strategies I considered on my search, there was one that would ensure a response from any potential leads.

"Agent Smoke?" I whispered at a human level.

Countless eyes fixed on me, and not all had an *Ispolniteli* mark.

As if disinterest could appear as fast as their attention, they diverted their gaze, but within the flow of the rhythm, those whose attention I captured glided closer.

I kept my heart rate low, preventing a spike despite the anticipation I felt. I walked to the edge of the bar, holding the club within my sight line, but the reek of blood battled for my attention. Empty liquor glasses littered the bar, some of them coated in scarlet. A bartender turned a brass tap and a thick stream of crimson pooled into a glass—human blood.

I'd taken my eyes off those surrounding me.

Unable to predict the location of an attack, I retreated the way I came, brushing by those who stepped into my path to catch my scent or study my anonymity. "Do you know Agent Smoke?" I asked a wall of a man who refused to move, his jaw the size of a bear's.

He smiled down at me. "You're new." He wasn't *Ispolniteli* and spoke like a Canadian. My naïveté of my own country's underground was showing. I steeled myself. Naïveté only lasts so long.

"I'm new to you," I replied.

He cocked his head and inhaled deeply, his fingertips grazing my hips. "For how long?" He smiled.

I flicked my palm up, releasing the pent-up energy of the Light Charm in a small, coursing spark. "For as long as your heart withstands before it gives out."

He clicked his tongue. "My stamina might surprise you." Yet, he stepped aside, tracking me as I left, his eyes burning into my back.

A brunet across the crowd moved in step with me to the door. My bait lured at least one source to follow me, it seemed. I stepped through the sticky threshold, readying for his exit behind me, but the door remained in place. Drums cut short. The inner chaos of the club halted. I selected a tunnel and disappeared up it before the masses gathered outside the entrance. Pacing myself, I gave my brief stalker the chance to trail me.

Bare bulbs ran along a track on the tunnel's ceiling, lighting the way to street level, discouraging its occupants from the neglected branches, dark and deserted. I chose the dark path. Cool air lifted my hair from my shoulders, indicating I could still emerge aboveground on this route. Water dripped into unseen puddles until my eyesight shifted, my vampiric senses focusing within the darkness with clear-cut precision.

During the period in which I second-guessed my decisions, my footsteps picked up a second echo. I meandered a little longer, then spun.

White magic lit the tunnel, crackling into balls within my hands. "I'm looking to trade information," I said to the man.

But it wasn't just the lone man who had tracked me; he had two others with him.

Chapter Twenty-One

These men did not bear *Ispolniteli* oath marks. My
brunet stalker from the club flew toward me, the collar
of his shirt blowing back to reveal an emblem of a
thistle entwined with a banner dripping blood, almost
like the symbol for a Canadian mercenary company,
one riddled with bad press for their international affairs.

A glittering bout of dark magic collided with my
balls of light, fireworks ricocheting off the stone walls,
neon sizzling with blacklight. He paused to avoid the
spitfire, but his two companions rushed my flank in my
peripheral vision.

I produced a wall of electricity as a shield,
blocking the shadowy, cannon ball-sized fists hurtling
toward my ribs. The thistle emblem poked out from
underneath the cuff of the flirty man's shirt, and I
assumed the third man also bore the same mark.

The stalker seized his opening while I was
distracted, a poisonous cloud sweeping up the stone.
Enough. My time and patience were vanishing with the
dwindling night.

I called my fire.

A torrent of flames barreled down the tunnel.
Quick as the dark magic and moving with vampiric
speed, the trio retreated. Understanding flashed across
the vampires' faces. They braced in fighter stance but
held their attacks. My flames retracted to my skin, then

became a small flame within my palm.

"Who are you?" Stalker asked. His hair was a deep mocha, matching his eyes. I could see him studying my identity spell, no doubt questioning where my Fire Charm originated from, what my origins were.

"I'm willing to trade information with you," I said, "but it won't be regarding me."

"You want to know about Smoke," he countered; he had about two feet on his companions, skinny as a whip.

"Correct," I said.

"What are you looking to trade?" asked the last vampire.

The easiest way to flush out more Diamond Eaters was to pump the supernatural communities for information on them. Not information Andre and I valued, like the artifact or the Eaters' connection to the Medici Bank in Florence, but details that would piss the Eaters off—the death of their own. A society that held superiority and secrecy in the highest regard would despise Agatha's death circulating the rumor mill; they might even come searching for the source of the scandal.

"I'll trade the name of a Diamond Eater who was killed tonight."

The trio didn't contest Diamond Eaters' existence. They calculated my words, no doubt pondering my role in relation to my inquiry about Smoke. At that moment, I realized two things; one, these men knew about Diamond Eaters, and two, how desperate my actions appeared. I'd practically shouted Andre's code name in a den of operatives.

The flirty man from the club spoke first, "We can

tell this is personal for you. Whether he broke your heart or screwed you over, we'll tell you what we know. But," his expression turned hard and humorous at once, like a killer who'd see the satire in the funny position his victims died in, "if you see him, you tell him he owes us payment."

"Smoke was making a trade with us," Stalker said, "similar to what you're doing now, but his price was an escorted passage for two out of Canada. He was supposed to meet us at The Mole's House hours ago."

The Mole's House. It was the name of the dungeon club. "What was the exact time of your rendezvous?"

"Nine o'clock," Stalker said.

I held my chin high so as not to flinch, but my chest swelled and fell. Eight hours had passed since Andre was potentially taken, and with each passing hour, he'd be farther from my reach. Andre's meeting was scheduled two hours after I met with Roman. His movie and a popcorn routine put me so at ease that I didn't suspect Andre had any meetings tonight.

"Thank you," my voice was clipped despite every emotional tactic I could employ to control myself.

"The name?" Stalker asked.

I nodded behind them. "Back up to the edge of the tunnel, into the light, when you reach the line, I'll tell you."

They kept facing me, and while they walked as instructed, I gathered my magic into the spell I'd used for my voice with the *Custodes*, then waited. Once they touched the light, I released my spell. "Agatha," I said, my voice refracting throughout the tunnel.

Then, I bounded up one of the tunnel's curves toward fresh air with all my strength.

****

I emerged from the pitch-black into the dimly lit woods; the lights of Parliament glimmered across Rideau Channel, patches of ice forming along the dark water. The wind whipped through the trees, and a choir of cracks scattered in the woods. I was at Major's Hill Park once more. Fitting, since my last stop—and highest risk for exposure—was right next door, but Andre could be there, injured or detained.

The historical Château was lit in its gothic glory; snow cloaked its steeples, and flurries drifted by the iron windows and twinkling lights. The six o'clock hour approached, and the grounds were deserted like a fairy tale castle under a curse. I was terrified that there would be no prince inside.

I stepped into the light and walked under the stone veranda, the hotel's golden doors gleaming. With the doorman long gone, I opened the door and stepped inside. The lobby smelled of coffee and pastries, and as comforting as the scents were, I steeled myself and walked to the elevator. Andre's hotel room was rigged for self-destruction under the right circumstance.

"Excuse me," a woman called.

I was halfway across the cream-colored marble floor when I turned.

"Approach the desk, please." When I was directly in front of her, she whispered, "I have a letter for you. I'm under orders from the Prince of Monaco to deliver it with the utmost discretion." Her voice had a lifeless quality, slightly robotic like the tone I had taken when Andre used his mind powers on me when we first met. "He was very particular about how we treat his wife."

Wife. My first reaction to Andre's sense of humor

made me want to pinch the woman out of her compulsion, but the bond was considered a marriage. I remembered my conversation with Ina in Russia when I'd first discovered the implications of the bond. Ina had called it mating for life. Her words replayed in my mind, *A sexy marriage, but with no guests and a lot more blood.* I had just begun acclimating to the intimacy of our bond; admitting that I was Andre's wife was an entirely separate task. Yet, I didn't want to deny it. I looked down at the desk clerk's nametag and read, *Sara.* I nodded in acknowledgment.

"Follow me," Sara said and led me down a hall into a private room. The room was warded, and the touch of magic felt familiar like I could sense Andre in its essence. She pulled out a chair for me to sit at an antique writing desk positioned by an arched iron window that stretched from the floor to ceiling. Dawn broke over the canopy outside, illuminating the view of the choppy channel and snow-covered trees.

I sat down, and Sara laid a letter upon the polished wood before me. The words, *My Wife*, were handwritten upon it.

"I'll have breakfast brought in," she said and closed the wood-paneled doors behind her.

The area around the letter thrummed with the Charm, and for once, it wasn't the dark magic Andre usually employed. If the letter was enchanted for me, I had nothing to fear, but I couldn't bring myself to open it yet. Its presence seemed an ominous conclusion to my search for Andre. I stared into the darkness of the rolling water, vowing to reject any resolution that didn't deliver him into my arms.

Coffee arrived on a tray with an array of fresh fruit,

cheeses, and sweet delights. I had an appetite only for coffee, holding the hot cup to the tense muscles of my jaw. Only when I'd stopped clenching and drank half a cup did I touch the letter.

The magic surrounding the envelope coated my skin. It didn't tingle as I expected but felt warm, rather like submerging my hands into a bathtub. There were no traps or surprises as I tore into it, except as I unfolded the paper, a pressed heather thistle fell out into the desk. The letter read:

Karolina,

If you are reading this letter, I didn't make it back in time. I'm just as stubborn as you and met with a museum curator regarding a symbol I saw on the artifact. It looked like a Dyad symbol. I know, I shouldn't have risked it, but soon we'd be a continent away, and it was a smaller risk than heading to the base in Greenland, which you thoroughly discouraged. Don't go looking for the curator.

The Custodes are prowling Ottawa in force, and I believe it's linked to our interception of Mullins. Do not tell another soul about the account transfer or letter. I mean it, Karolina. Don't speak it aloud, ever. The Medici Bank funds House Custode. If Diamond Eaters are paying off the House, they control the Custodes. We have proof that not only do they exist but have policed the other supernaturals undetected for centuries. They are no longer a rumor.

On a more productive note, I've bartered for our escape, or now, since you are reading this letter, your escape. When you are ready, speak 'sinubhal' aloud while holding the thistle. Those you encounter will escort you from the country. You will need this, now *that we are without Loukin's connivances, but these mercenaries will require payment. You may give them the date May 21*st*, 1672. Nothing more is required.*

Lastly, I like to think that, over the years, I've developed a way with a pen. I've written many a letter, Karolina, but none as important, as weighty, as the one I write to you now. I'm going to jump right in as my indulgent, poetic self.

When I first met you, you ignited the piece of me I'd numbed. I was a ghost in my life, drifting from one scheme to another. When I met you–dirty, demanding, and on the run—I snapped back into the present, like I had awoken from years of sleepwalking. Yes, I wanted you from the moment I met you. You were tantalizingly perfect for me in every way. You know my dishonorable choices, but please know I cannot and will not regret being with you.

I could wait for eternity if it meant you would know me; if it meant the pull I know we both feel could grow. But I don't need eternity to know I love you, Karolina. I was biding my time to hear those words from your lips. So please know, if you feel my death through the bond, I'm imagining our future and hearing you say those words over and over and over.

Dastardly yours,

Andre

I clutched my mug, warming my ice-cold hands. At reading what could have been Andre's last words to me, I felt chilled all over, as frigid as the churning water beyond. But the spark of hope I held onto was fanned to a flame. Andre was alive. I smiled like a maniac into my hands, brushing back my hair. I hadn't felt his death through the bond, and Andre seemed sure I would feel the force of the bond breaking. Perhaps the bond could be blocked, but its destruction was a magical phenomenon much greater than any spell one could cast.

I finished my coffee and dove into the platter of food, feasting while I strategized. Andre's last whereabouts, the curator, seemed the most logical to discover the relevance of the symbol he was researching. It was difficult to deny that the *Custodes* were behind Andre's abduction.

If they intercepted him prior to nine o'clock, it was likely around the time he met with the curator, which meant that the *Custodes* were watching the curator, or perhaps they had their own set of trigger traps. This plan disregarded Andre's warning, but his letter implied his intent. Andre didn't want me looking for him. He didn't give me a list of locations to search; he said goodbye and gave me instructions on how to proceed on my own.

But I wouldn't desert him, not while he was alive.

Energy tingled within the thistle as I tucked it back inside the letter and slipped them both into my inner coat pocket. I went to the wood-paneled door and paused, listening for the stirring of life outside. After a moment of calmness, I walked back down the hall and exited the hotel.

The walk back to my safe house was crisp and clear. The clouds had parted as if to let the city's residents witness the colossal dumping of snow. Mother Nature's force was unpredictable and swift, much like fate. I waded my way up the lonely street, the rising sun lighting an orange-hued path on the unbroken snow before me, a taunting reminder of sunrise on the Black

Sea. I dug out the back door of my building again.

Ina hadn't arrived yet with Ben, which gave me time to change and collect myself. I selected the woolliest socks I could find and my thickest sweater, which hung mid-thigh like a dress. The result of my attire was the false feeling of a much-needed hug.

The kitchen was cold, not yet warmed by my candles. I prepared coffee in my French press. Steam filled the air as I readied my pink china teacup and saucer from the stacks Andre had organized. When I sat down at the table, I noticed my blue paperweight sitting on a small sketch. Andre had left me the imprint of the artifact. I looked at his drawing, the shading on the symbol done with the skill of a still-life artist. I wondered how fantastic his sketches might be if he had a more engaging subject. *I could wait you out for eternity if it meant you would know me.*

I shoved the thought away before it could weaken my focus.

Turning my concentration back to the symbol, I realized I'd seen this ancient symbol before on the rock entrance of Dyad central. The encircled double arrowhead pattern—one inverted and one upright—was placed up high like it was plummeting down to the markings along the footing of the building.

Air stirred in my living room. A gale blew my hair back before a black patch of glittering feathers materialized, expanding into two human forms.

"About time," I said to Ina, but my tone was one of affection. Time in the Anishinaabe hidden city was still jarring. Twenty minutes of Ina's time was an evening of mine, which implied there was no predictable pattern to how much time one would lose when visiting the city. I collected two more cups and arranged them on the table.

"Well," Ina said with a laugh, "if I knew you stashed your clean freak alter ego at our safe house, I would have been here a lot sooner." Ina and Ben sat down.

"It was Andre."

"That makes more sense." Ina spooned some sugar into her cup as I served Ben.

"He's been abducted," I added, "and Roman is banished to the dark side of the moon."

Ina paused, her eyes trailing up to meet the hurt in mine. "Ben told me about Roman."

"I'm going to find Andre," I said, my words sounding like an oath I was ready to kill for. "I just need your help."

"With what?" Ina asked.

"Well," I got up and walked over to one of my antique living chairs, "this." I pulled up the cushion top to reveal the stacks of cash within. "Most of our furniture is filled like this one. I need a lot of this cash put into an untraceable account I can use, one accessible around the world."

"You're putting the paperclip I earned to use."

I inhaled deeply. Ina knew that, with this action, there was a risk of her activities being flagged by Loukin's operatives but I was counting on her skills being superior to all others. She held her position in Russia on her own merit. "Can you do it without getting caught?"

"I absolutely can," she said, sitting taller under Ben's silent appraisal. "How much are your stashes?"

"Eight figures." Ina's eyebrows went up. "I figured

we'd split it."

"Sixty-forty," she said with a smile and sipped her coffee.

"You're fleecing me," I said, but my tone was pure amusement. Twenty percent was more than I needed. "Deal, with the condition I can leave the country within forty-eight hours."

Chapter Twenty-Two

Ben evaporated and reappeared in ebony clouds, now carrying a stack of suitcases that wobbled while he walked. He dumped the haul in Ina's bedroom, and to my horror, he disappeared to repeat the same task yet again.

"How much did you retrieve from our condo?" I asked as I topped up her coffee.

Ina's fingers stormed across her keyboard, her attention fixated on the screen, but a smile tugged at her lips. "All of it. He, what did you call it, *poofed* over hours after we received your warning, and since it was vacant, he cleared out my room."

"Smug, are we?"

She sipped her coffee, one hand still typing. "You'll find Andre, Karo."

In the time since Ina had committed to her task, she'd forged an identity for me under the name Anne Smith, the name I'd also provided to my landlord. After Ina filled me in on Miruna's improving condition, Anne was equipped with a Canadian bank account and passport. A foreign account, Ina's most significant challenge, was now in the works, and she'd been working on it for hours.

I bent down to look at the endless streams of code running along the screen. "Why don't you take a break?" Ina hadn't moved from the kitchen while Ben carried out his duties as a saintly boyfriend.

She rose and rounded the hall into the first room on her left. "It's blue!" Ina called from her bedroom. "I love the bed. Where did you find all the furniture?"

"The store across the street. Your room is the only one with comfortable furniture left."

"That's a lot of money." Ina reappeared. "A sliver of it would be all my family needs. You've made me a rich woman."

I smiled. "Let alone sixty percent. You should let it go straight to your head."

"I'll miss your prickly warmth, but I'll have a sports car." She hip-checked me on her way back to her computer.

"We'll be in touch," I said and popped a cookie into my mouth. "There's a spell we can use, its like a magical video call."

Ben materialized. "This is the last of it." He disappeared into Ina's room, looking desperate to finish the task he'd signed up for and then joined us at the table.

"Well, that's my cue to let you love birds settle in."

"Where are you going?" Ina asked.

I pulled on my coat, and with my ritualistic application of lipstick and perfume, I was out the door. "I have a date with a curator."

****

Finding Andre's curator was easier than expected. Of Ottawa's seven museums, only one had an archeology department. The Canadian Museum of History had two curators on staff, and one was on vacation. Located just across the Ottawa River, on the Québec side, I opted to walk the twenty-minute distance. My stroll allowed me to scope out the building prior to my approach. The streets were quiet, almost empty of life.

Ice hung from Alexandra Bridge's skeletal structure, just like the bony, lifeless trees beyond. I had to round the corner of the trans Canadian trail to gain the cover of some fluffy pines. From my position, I could see across a skate park to the museum. I watched the building's traffic, taking note of any suspicious persons who might be circulating. The snow had discouraged most visitors today. When confident, I approached the building.

The curving, sand-colored structure would resemble a rock escarpment if it weren't for the streams of floor-to-ceiling windows. I passed through the entrance and felt a surge of energy from all directions. Museums held ancient knowledge and artifacts from all cultures, and these magics only strengthened with time. My boots squeaked against the polished granite floor that stretched out to the far wall. Totem poles towered into the air, their faces carrying a mien of the fates one could embrace in life, vibrating with the blessings or curses they could unleash. I walked to the elevator and looked up the curator's office. *Room 444.*

The elevator doors opened with a ding, and I stepped onto the fourth floor. Gooseflesh crept up my arms like a phantom's embrace. A heavy pull of magic, like an enchanted call, beckoned me down the hall. Relics were abundant behind the doors I passed, but the steady, enthralling draw ahead was far superior. I counted the rooms as I approached. *Room 443. Room 445.* I stopped, doubling back. An entrance materialized in the wide gap between both doors as if it had risen from the sludge of the chestnut-colored wall. The magnetism of energy emanated from behind the door. I tried the knob, and it opened.

I gasped. The aroma of blood gripped my stomach, stilling my step. My fangs shot from the roof of my mouth. The door swung open, and with its swing, I was sucked into the room. There was a thud and the turning of a lock behind me, but before me, thousands of blood droplets rained upward from the glossy scarlet floor. A woman lay in the center of the room. Her gray hair splayed out into the red rippling pool. The dual seams of an open wound, raw and angry, ran from her throat to her sternum. The sickly-sweet scent of her blood hung toxic in the air, laboring my breathing.

I moved, and droplets pattered against my coat. My shift sent out a ripple into the center of the room, and the woman's body shuddered as she sat upright. Her eyes were milky, and as she cocked her head, her mouth gaped and hung unnaturally wide, wagging like she was coaxing her last meal. Her voice, scarcely a whisper at first, soon resonated with the sound of a hundred, "What you seek is gone. Be gone."

She exploded.

Viscera and gore splattered my face. Then the blood, which collected on the ceiling, drenched me, falling to the floor with the death of the spell. I kept my eyes closed and searched the walls for anything to wipe myself clean. On the seat of a chair tucked under a desk, I felt a soft fabric. I wiped my face and looked down at the remains of the curator's blood-soaked sweater.

If Roman's blood spell could make his ancestors sob, this blood magic was an abomination. In all my reading, I hadn't come upon a curse this sinister. She was more than just murdered; necromancy defiled her corpse. When Mullins spoke post-mortem, a message was sent through his vessel. Looking back, the source of magic was likely *Custode*. Dark forces, terrible and wrong, had reanimated this woman's corpse, occupied her. I couldn't dispel the feeling any of the voices within her would take possession of another living body if they could.

I looked down at the corpse. Judging by her peachy-gray skin, she'd only been dead for an hour. Her murderer eliminated her as a possible lead, but it was well after Andre's meeting yesterday, which meant her killer wasn't involved in Andre's abduction. It took all my nerve to remain and search the room.

Computers, notebooks, and papers cluttered the desk. I sifted through the appraisals and contracts until only the locked filing cabinet was left. I put my fist through the lock, and inside I found an agenda. I flipped to yesterday's meetings. The page was torn out. Either the last intruders in this office opened the lock with far more finesse, or the curator had destroyed the page.

Attempting a recovery spell in a room already stained with blood magic was risky, but the temptation brought my hand to the page. I said the incantation and focused my will. The Earth Charm's golden glow reconstructed the page.

Andre's meeting was scheduled under *Smoke* for seven-thirty, but she had marked him down as a no show. She had written a small note to herself: *Filed the prepared documents for a reschedule*. I checked the file folders, which contained nothing about the symbol. I tried another recovery spell, which didn't yield any records. I looked back to the curator's agenda. Andre would have tidied and left shortly after me, and along the short walk here or within the building, he was detained. Today's meetings were all clear. The curator's murderer was a surprise visit or one she didn't want to record.

I disbanded my spell and headed to the door, but as I crossed the room, I noticed scorch marks on the wall next to the desk. Ashy remains of paper dusted the wall where the pool of blood covered the floor. The burn marks didn't fan up the wall like the flames of a fire but burst out from the center like a small lightning bolt. I hovered my hands over the marks, feeling for any remaining essence of the Charm. Whoever destroyed documents in this room had used the Light Charm. I searched the blood pool with my boot, but there were no other clues left for me to find.

The door pulsed with energy. I felt for traps, but all I could feel was the taint of the spell. I braced and touched the handle. The door opened, and I stepped back out into the hall unhindered.

Now drenched, I hoped my identity spell would shield my appearance, but a vampire would smell the blood. My spell protected all that was me—my scent, my magic, my possessions—but it would not shield the curator. A trail of my bloody footprints followed me out the side door.

I cleaned my boots in the icy river below the bridge and hurried home. The streets became more active the more snow the city workers cleared. Three blocks from my building, a pedestrian looked my way as the wind bustled at my back. I slipped into a back alley and looped around downwind. Tracking their heartbeat, I crept into my building before they picked up my scent again.

When I stepped inside my apartment, I flicked the candle wicks aflame. I was alone, but Ina and Ben had left a few cookies out on a plate, so the Andre tidiness didn't have the haunting effect it had the last time I arrived. Still, Andre wasn't here. I closed the distance between myself and the bathroom and stripped down. Instead of trying to salvage my clothes, I threw them into the garbage along with my winter boots. Then I scrubbed every drop of the curator from my skin, rubbing myself raw with my bath sponge.

When it came to blood magic, I was understudied. I hated feeling inexperienced, yet I hated feeling disadvantaged even more. Unlike vampirism, where one's life force is sampled, blood magic is the offering of one's blood in exchange for access to dark forces. The more blood offered, the more a practitioner could gain. A droplet of blood was equivalent to a sliver of one's spirit. A body drained dry was an offering of a soul.

The practitioner gained access to the flow of negative energy in the universe. The Dark Charm came from this well, along with any insidious thought, feeling, or action any living creature ever had. It was where spirits, tortured even in death, chose to reside, to revel in their malcontent. It was the Charmed version of Hell. I never understood why one would want to connect to such a thing, save for power or pain.

Connection.

Andre had the Dark Charm.

I ripped a towel from the hanger and skidded along the tile into the hall. I searched my bookshelf for the dark magic book that detailed Roman's spell. I sat down and whipped through the pages until I found the spell I was looking for and then flicked to the pages beyond. More blood magic spells were listed in detail, but none for my purpose.

I would have to make my own.

I walked to the kitchen on autopilot, filling each moment with action so I couldn't second-guess my decision. I dropped to my knees and sifted through the cupboards until I found a wooden salad bowl. Then I collected herbs I could use to reach Andre—herbs of love, like rose and lavender. The scrap of his shirt was where I had left it on a side table next to the bookshelf. I'd forgotten a knife. Knives were ritualistic, and I didn't want to taint the spell with the euphoria of my fangs. Lastly, I collected the contract Mama signed. Any sentimental objects that could ground me from being lost within my spell had perished in our house fire. Mama's signature, though not ideal, was adequate.

Pacing a circle on the hardwood, I formed a ring of earth magic before sitting back down. I didn't have the Dark Charm, so the Earth Charm would have to do. Within the circle, I set the objects before me. When I built the energy inside me to a climax, I slit my palm above the bowl. Blood trickled over the herbs and cloth within the basin until completely submerged. Then I bandaged my hand, not wanting to give more of my essence than necessary.

The crimson liquid reflected my face up at me. As I studied the images in the reflection, I focused on Andre, on his Dark Charm. I reached out for him in my mind and let my power loose.

My consciousness was pulled into the bowl.

Scarlet and shadow whirled around me like I was traveling through the astral channel of the bond, but this was a realm that belonged to blood and darkness. The tunnel through which I hurtled soon narrowed. Warm, sticky walls clung to my skin. My vision squeezed to the size of my face. Claustrophobia threatened to set in, but I felt Andre's presence approaching.

Andre, bound at the wrists and ankles by a dark, seething substance, appeared within a spotlight in the abyss like our connection through the bond. I wanted to drop down next to him, but I couldn't escape the wormhole I had traveled through. I thrashed, each clawing and grasping movement bringing me closer. "Andre!" I called.

He looked up, searching the air; if he heard my call, it was a whisper in his reality. He appeared exhausted, on the brink of a hopelessness I thought he'd never succumb to.

I pushed forward with all my power and managed to crest the ring of light around him. "I'm coming!" I screamed, straining my vocal cords. "Where are you?"

"Karolina," he said, his gaze exploring the air but blindly like he couldn't see me standing before him.

"Where are you?" I screamed.

"Don't come, Karolina. Please don't."

Whispers ricocheted around me like the hissing of a snake, "*Blood,*" the word grazed my ear, "*give us more.*" A malevolent choir of voices, too similar to what had possessed the curator, rose like a wave at my back. "*The Blood of the Creator in your essence tastes so sweet.*" All thrill of seeing Andre vanished. I shook with gooseflesh as terror enveloped me.

"*Give us more!*" The voices screeched, "*Give us*

more! Give us more!"

I ran. Clawing through the pull of the substance enclosing me, I reached out and clasped Andre's arm Visions of Andre, of torture, flooded me—images of beautiful marble stonework, blood and silver chains, a statue of the Virgin Mary, plaques written in a romantic language, stone doors crested with crowned lions.

"Karolina!" Andre cried, breaking the illusions.

"I'm coming!" My hand seized. Andre's face shadowed, his eyes and mouth grew dark like black pits. Darkness rose up from him and drove into me, traveling through the connection of skin on skin. The Dark Charm tore through my flesh. The warmth in my chest where the Light Charm resided cleaved. I plunged into blackness.

"No! She's ours! Ours, ours, ours!" The voices hissed, bounding around the collapsed tunnel.

Unable to move or see, I focused my thoughts on the piece of paper with Mama's signature, her love for me, and what our family name represented.

With a massive thrum of air, I dropped back into my body. My head cracked against the floor. The bowl of blood and objects were knocked over with the kick of my leg. I rose to a sitting position, shivering, shaking so hard I could not steady myself. The pain in my chest burrowed into my stomach. I upchucked. Head spinning, I stumbled to the bathroom. After twenty minutes of piping-hot water on my back, I still couldn't warm. I lowered myself to the floor within the shower. Palm up, I dispelled the sorcery coiling within my torso like a seething worm. Dark energy crackled in my hand.

I'd connected to Andre through his Dark Charm, but through our connection, I'd absorbed it into myself.

I'd sparked the Dark Charm.

Chapter Twenty-Three

Hours passed, and I still hadn't adjusted to the insidious magic writhing within me. When I stopped shaking, I changed back into my cozy sweater and scrubbed my blood off the floor. All traces of my spell were tidied away or disposed of. I sat at the kitchen table with stacks of dark-magic books before me. I'd abandoned reading about my stupidity and shifted back to researching the Dyad symbol. Despite the risk I'd taken, I now knew where Andre was held.

The crowned-lion emblem I saw in my vision was detailed and vivid. The picture stood out in my mind from my history of economics elective in my first year at university. It was a short while before I confirmed it as the medieval crest for the Medici Bank in the fifteenth century. The language on the plaques was Italian. Andre was in Florence. As awful as I felt, my heart rate galloped at the thought of breaking down doors and yanking him into my arms.

A wind stirred in the living room. Ben and Ina *poofed* into existence.

"Hey," Ina said.

I greeted the two of them and closed the books on the table before Ina could read the spells exposed. Ben's gaze clung to me like he saw the Dark Charm worming in my stomach. I stayed quiet, and so did he. Relief washed the added tension away. I wasn't ready to tell Ina of my mistake.

"So," Ina looked between Ben and me, "You have a Swiss account, which you can use anywhere in the world, but you'll have to go there to finish its activation."

I raised a brow. "Really? I thought the purpose of a Swiss account was access and anonymity."

"Swiss accounts can be used by civilians in a list of countries, but for international withdrawals that are privacy protected—protected even from government surveillance—you have to be on the bank's supernatural list."

I took a deep breath. Travel came with its risks of detection, but it was necessary. If I used my free escort from Canada and had no access to funds beyond what I could carry, I could be left without shelter. Having a functional safe house was essential to my survival.

Ina could see me strategizing. "Keeping your identity hidden is essential; many travel with identity spells in place. You just need the appropriate documentation." Ina held up a black passport with a set of golden fangs outlined on the front.

I blurted out a laugh. "You've got to be kidding me."

"No," Ina countered, "For once, I'm not. If underground officials from a foreign country check you out, you may be asked to drop your spell, so just adjust your spell enough to show the face of Anne Smith."

"They will still sense a spell is in place."

"Yes, but most international vampires do have spells in place, many unrelated to their identity. As long as your spell shifts to almost non-existence, you'll be fine. Or have a second spell in place. Plus, Switzerland is one of the few countries where the government has embraced supernaturals. They have a zero-tolerance policy for violence, so many supernaturals conduct business there."

I sat back. "I really, really wish I'd had this information in Greenland." Ina was a wealth of knowledge, but I had to weigh the risk of her involvement against how much I told her. I didn't help my friend leave Russia to be with her family to endanger her life, at least endanger her life more than Loukin's operation already had.

"Do I even want to know what happened?" Ina asked.

I stood up to hug her. "I had a picnic." I felt her smile on my shoulder. "Thank you for everything, Ina. I'm going to miss you so much."

She held me back to look at me. "It's what friends do, Karo. You helped me, it was my turn to help you."

"Well," Ben said. "Before you two start crying, maybe we should have a drink and some dinner." He leaned back against the counter. "You said within forty-eight hours, so you still have some time on your clock."

"Wood fired-pizza?" Ina asked.

"Deal," I said. "And wine."

****

Hours into the evening, empty wine bottles glistened in the candlelight like celebration lanterns. A nineties-era dance music playlist repeated for the third time. Each time the playlist restarted, more wine was poured, and we found new aspects of the beat that were pure genius.

"Do it again!" Ina cried, buckling in a fit of laughter and knocking over a bottle.

I wrapped my arm around her to haul her up, but I lost my balance while I was swigging wine. I slipped down beside her with a thud, shoulder dancing to the music. Ben used his magic to make the empty pizza boxes talk to one another while using a silly voice. Ina lost herself like it was the greatest comedic skit of the century, which, in turn, made me lose my breath with her contagious cackle. Ben stopped his show for a bite of the last piece of pizza.

I laid back to stare at the ceiling. "I'm drunk," I announced. "Like, really drunk."

Ina giggled. "Stop it, Karo."

"Stop what?"

Ben sat down and swatted my foot, but it was a light gesture that told me to look Ina's way. I turned and saw a book hovering above her, which she whacked away. The book rebounded and continued its course. Ina hit it harder this time.

I rolled to my knees and crawled over to the book. It glided to my outstretched hand and flicked open when I touched it. It was a blood spell to summon a spirit. The Dark Charm prickled my ribcage, swelling up into my throat. I dropped the book.

I didn't call my dark magic. It bucked again, breaking down the door of my subconscious. I bent over, trying to suppress it, but my inhibitions were beyond low.

"I'm not feeling well," I said. "I think I'm going to get a few hours' sleep before I head out."

"Quitter," Ina said as she rose and threw her arms around me. "Love you lots, Karo."

"Love you too." I rose, sliding out of her grasp. "You two I have fun," I said to Ben. "Thanks for all your help."

My bed was lonely and cold when nestled into it. I curled my knees to my chest under the duvet, imagining the warmth my sheets had when Andre was within them. I turned, then turned again, like my body was searching for what couldn't be found. The Dark Charm zapped in burning streaks within my ribcage, pushing for its release and not caring for my comfort. To spite it, I summoned my earth magic. A tingling warmth spread through me, overpowering the discomfort. I had a lead to Andre's whereabouts, and I was going to free him. With that thought, as restless as I was, sleep found me.

****

Beeping blared out from the floor beneath my bed. I searched the ground with one eye open, my head throbbing with each high-pitched tone. I'd never drank so much as I did last night. My cell phone was knocked in deep underneath the bedframe. I rolled out onto the floor and stretched to snatch it. The screen read *3:00 AM*. It was the last time I would use Loukin's phone.

I had packed my rucksack yesterday before dinner, after depositing massive amounts of cash into my alias account. Only one of my bedroom chairs remained filled. My backpack was lined with more cash, then stuffed with clothes and my witchy essentials. My preparation gave me just enough time for personal hygiene, a blood breakfast, and coffee. I gorged on three bags of blood within five minutes—a new record. My strength would have to be at its peak should an altercation arise. My new phone sat on the table, equipped with a frequency buster Ina fashioned. Coffee was a slow task, as I knew when I finished, I would leave the first home I had created for myself since Mama's death and the fire. I would also finish my goodbye letter to Ina. So far, it was simple:

Dear Ina,

Thank you for your friendship. You are exceptional. Anytime you want to chat like we're having a movie night, just shake the jar and say 'vorbi.' I'm still here for you, always.

Karolina

A little jam jar sat on the table next to my note. A picture of Ina and me was within it, along with some herbs and the Earth Charm. I had a matching jar packed away in my bag. When I accepted I wasn't going to turn into a wordsmith over the new few minutes, I downed my coffee and passed through my apartment wards.

****

My cab pulled up to the salty curb, splashing slush onto the gray slab walkway. I stepped carefully to not dirty the boots Andre had bought me. The Ottawa train station was a modern mix of iron scaffolding and glass walls, hinting at the industrialization that came with the railway. I paid and stepped out, my spells ensuring my anonymity was intact. I kept the Earth Charm summoned, not wanting to attract the attention of other spies with the Dark Charm. My dark magic still attempted to surface when my guard was low.

I entered the building and was the lone occupant until I spotted the ticket counter. The skeleton service was in effect at this hour, but there were still two cashiers. Andre was in Florence, within the *Custode* central base, but the closest Diamond Eater was in Québec. I'd triple-checked the reconstructed artifact to confirm the location yesterday. If I was going to enter the base in Florence *and* leave with Andre, I needed collateral.

"Ticket for one to Montréal, one way," I said.

"Economy?" the cashier asked.

"No," I said with a smile as I thought of the fashion in which Andre traveled. "I'll take the best seat you have."

As I handed over the cash for my ticket, I had déjà vu, which brought me back to the moment I handed the ruby necklace to Ivy. I didn't know then that my choice would unbind me from Loukin's extortion. Miruna was safe. Ina had her immunity. Andre was out of Loukin's reach. Roman was cursed to live out the remainder of his life on the dark side of the moon for what he'd done to those innocent women, and I had no plans of rescuing him any time soon. Not until I understood more about his involvement with Bronwyn and the dark force possessing him. I purchased a ticket for one, but I didn't feel lonely. I felt free. Loukin lost his power over me, and my loved ones were out of his reach.

I would use all I learned from my missions surrounding Diamond Eaters to my advantage. I would collect what I needed in Montréal and use the thistle to travel to Switzerland. When I had a functional worldwide bank account, I would free Andre, no matter how many *Custodes* I had to kill.

The Dark Charm flared inside of me, and I almost buckled from holding it back. I focused on both the Light and Earth Charm and shoved it down. Once calmed, I proceeded to the boarding area. The room was decorated in blocks of beige and gray; plush leather seats were clustered together, alternating the two colors like shades of rock. I selected a seat that kept my back from the doors and maintained a surveillance point. A few civilians without the touch of magic trickled in.

A speaker overhead chimed, "Boarding to Montréal. Platform three."

Shivering within the short line, I kept my senses on full alert. We stepped around the shovled slush from one spotlight into the other, which beamed down from the iron latticework above. I didn't think to check above me for movement, but it was too late; I stood before the boarding car.

I sat down in the middle of my car, facing the forward movement of the train. As tempted as I was to take a window seat, I took a seat on the aisle, not wanting to get boxed in during a fight. Since I was the only occupant of my car, I tucked my rucksack underneath the polished wooden table at the center of the cushy seat cluster where a complimentary basket of toiletries sat waiting for me. The metallic box of a cream gleaming like a diamond in the low light.

The whistle sounded. It was mere minutes before the billboards outside flashed in French, lit up in the dead of night. Whether the advertisements were for cars, alcohol, or perfume, they all held the promise of belonging, of acceptance through love. The subliminal messaging stung, but in the pain, I found solace. I'd learned to love myself, to embrace my emotions rather than suppressing them—and this was integral—because now I had only myself to depend on. I didn't need the ruby. Or Loukin's operative resources. I had gained my autonomy.

At my glowing thoughts, I took a deep breath, and chanced sending a quick message to Andre. I would not let him lose hope. With my eyes closed, I bit the inside of my mouth, letting the blood pool. Rather than entering the blood realm as I had before, I summoned the Dark Charm and released my magic into the channel while drawing on Andre. *I love you*, I thought and felt the message leave me with my spell.

A moment later, as clear as if Andre had spoken in person, I heard his voice in my head, *You granted my wish. I love you too*.

I repeated the same enchantment. *You said over and over, so it's not granted yet. I'm coming*. Whispers rose in my ears, unbidden and unfamiliar. Before the insidious spirits could take hold of me like during our last encounter, I swallowed the blood. The spell broke, and I heard the car doors open and close.

When I opened my eyes, three men had joined me in my car. No emblems or oath marks were visible, but with my earth and light magic still in effect, I could sense the touch of magic within them. They all had the Dark Charm and, judging by the strength of magic emanating from them, they were primed for an attack. I hoped drawing on dark magic would be safe since I was alone, but I feared the magic was detected.

I remained calm as they scattered throughout the car. For all they knew, the individual with the Dark Charm just left, but moments turned into an hour, and the mystery men remained. The car door opened, the first movement in thirty minutes. A rickety cart rattled down the aisle followed by an attendant—the room filled with the smell of coffee. The man closest to the door ordered a cup, and since the car was so quiet, I could hear the clinking of the coin he paid with.

Light burst from the seams of my rucksack into a kaleidoscope of colors dancing in patterns below my seat. I shifted my bag, concealing the light show in part. "I'll have a coffee and a fruit-and-cheese plate," I said. Taking off my jacket, careful not to show my alarm, I slipped it onto my lap. A moment later, I let it slide down my legs on top of my bag.

The attendant with the cart arrived. "Here you are," she said.

I paid and sipped my coffee. My adrenaline was pumping so hard, my hands were shaking. The artifact could not be active without the flow of magic or a trigger source. I exerted all my control to slow my breathing. My grapes and brie were the least interesting thing on the train, but the remaining hour would be grueling if I couldn't handle maintaining my cover. I mulled them over, ate a few bites, and plucked a magazine from the side rack.

But the nagging pull of magic wouldn't let my attention rest.

The car doors opened, and a woman entered. The entrancing magic was emanating from her, and I knew the instant she arrived where I felt this power before. It throbbed within my veins still, wanting more. *Greenland. Roman's house. Agatha.*

The ageless redheaded Diamond Eater sat down directly across from me, my rucksack below her.

"Allow me," I said and slid my bag underneath my chair with my feet.

The doors bustled again, and a stream of women entered, as powerful as the first. As five Diamond Eaters surrounded me, I watched Loukin step through the door.

I looked out the window at the slim crescent moon. I knew what Roman was willing to do for what he thought was love and how it destroyed him. I shook my head as I stared up at the moon, imagining what he was doing right now, imagining what the realm he dwelled in looked like. After what I had been through, I didn't know if my choices would be just as terrible as his in the end.

I'd told Andre I was coming, so no matter who sat before me—I was coming.

A word about the author…

M. R. Noble has played a tug of war between science and art her whole life, but the rope broke when she wrote the first line of The Dark Eyes Series. Immersed up to her keyboard in paranormal romance and urban fantasy, she enjoys blending the real with the surreal. The only drawback is she misplaces her mug while dreaming up her next scene, and soon finds herself six cups overpoured.

Keeping to her Lake Simcoe roots, she is a member of the Writers Community of York Region (WCYR), where her muse is made not found . . . over a hefty cup of coffee.

Follow M. R. Noble on social media!
Twitter: @M_R_Noble
Instagram: m.r.noblefiction
Facebook: M. R. Noble
Bookbub: @mrnoblefiction
Goodreads: M. R. Noble
www.mrnoblefiction.com

Thank you for purchasing
this publication of The Wild Rose Press, Inc.

For questions or more information
contact us at
info@thewildrosepress.com.

The Wild Rose Press, Inc.
www.thewildrosepress.com